MADONNA
OF THE
EUCALYPTS

KAREN SPARNON

Praise for *Madonna of the Eucalypts*

Simply brilliant. *Madonna of the Eucalypts* is an important addition to our literature.

Alex Miller, author of *Journey to the Stone Country* and *Lovesong*

Karen Sparnon writes a lyrical, haunting prose that depicts the contrasting landscapes of Mediterranean Salina and their [sic] hypnotic Australian desert, where some found it difficult to transport their hearts as well as their homes.

The story of Delfina's journey to her outback shrine is one that will stay with you long after the final page.

Sue Wallace, *Border Mail*

Karen Sparnon's *Madonna of the Eucalypts* is a fresh piece of writing with a lively spirit and the verve of all good first novels...it is a kind book: my favourite sort.

Salley Vickers, *Weekend Australian* and author of the best-selling *Miss Garnet's Angel*

It's a real treat as a reader to come across a book that you just can't put down, and *Madonna of the Eucalypts* is one such book.

Diane Stubbings, *The Canberra Times*

Madonna of the Eucalypts is a beautiful multilayered story: a story of faith, cultures, families, and a fascinating glimpse into the lives of Australia's migrants in the early decades of the last century.

Reg Anderson, *Courier Mail Brisbane*

Madonna of the Eucalypts is a compelling debut, a powerful story of migration and the conflicting ties of family, faith and friends.

Text Publishing

Published in Australia by
Sanctuary Publishing
PO Box 337W, Ballarat West, VIC, 3350, Australia
Website: www.karensparnon.com

First published by the Text Publishing Company in 2006,
reprinted 2007 (twice)

This edition published by Sanctuary Publishing in 2018.

 A catalogue record for this
book is available from the
National Library of Australia

NATIONAL
LIBRARY
OF AUSTRALIA

ISBN: 978-0-6483108-0-8 (paperback)
ISBN: 978-0-6483108-1-5 (epub)

Page design by Elizabeth Glickfeld
Typeset in 11/15 Granjon by ipublicidades.com

Printed by Ingram Spark

This project was assisted by the Commonwealth Government through the
Australia Council, its art funding and advisory body.

To the memory of
Jean Sparnon nèe Giovanna Miranda
who remembered her field of red poppies.

And to all who make great journeys.

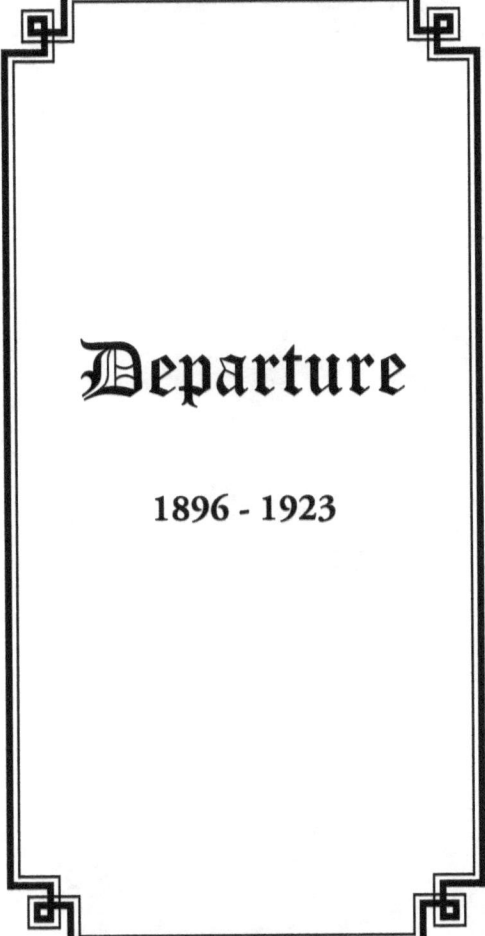

Departure

1896 - 1923

1

On a March morning in 1896 Aluaro Minieri stood at the window overlooking the shell-shaped bay of the Conca d'Oro. Below him orange trees radiated into the distance, vibrant against the blue of the Sicilian sky.

Aluaro Minieri had accumulated his land and prestige by taking advantage of what he liked to call opportunities. At the age of fifty-six he had two sons, three daughters and a wife who spent her days imitating aristocratic manners. He had yet to master the art of keeping his waistcoat clean and, as he drank from his bowl, splashes of coffee leaked into the silken fabric, leaving a chain of rings.

Aluaro moved away from the window to a map on the wall. With his finger he traced a line the full length of his holdings. These began in the orange groves spread out before him, extended to the west near the deserted Greek ruins of Segesta, and to the north-east in a small holding on the island of Salina. As he crossed the Tyrrhenian Sea, he frowned and jabbed at the seven Aeolian Islands with a fat forefinger, listing them under his breath.

'Vulcano, Lipari, Salina.' Aluaro stopped. 'To make sure those tenants are looking after my land, I must visit you again.' He raised his voice. 'But the rent they pay is hardly worth my trouble. By the time I get there, give instructions and…'

He trailed off and eased himself into one of the two leather chairs flanking his large desk.

The room was cool and dim. He sat back and folded his arms over his belly. Still for the first time since entering his office, he looked around quickly. He had not noticed Ludevina enter the room, slip to the far corner and lean against the wall.

She moved towards him and placed her hands on his shoulders. 'Why don't you sell the holding, Papa?'

Aluaro gazed fondly at his daughter. She was his youngest and favourite child. At eighteen she was fair-haired and blue-eyed, but these features, instead of producing a smooth creaminess, were stretched over high Sicilian cheekbones that formed shadows under her eyes and over her mouth. The result was a sharpness, a hint of cruelty that would deepen with age.

'Perhaps, my dear, perhaps. But we must always remember that a man is made by what he has conquered, what he owns.' Aluaro heaved himself out of the chair and walked back to the map on the wall. 'All this comes with its burdens and obligations.'

He sighed and fondled the tips of his moustache. Aluaro liked to see his life as a battle plan. 'I have to visit the island soon. You never know what tenants get up to in your absence or how much you can trust people.' He moved close to Ludevina and lifted her chin with his hand. They were not dissimilar, this sharp-boned father and daughter. 'Would you like to come?'

Ludevina was thrilled. Her first thought was the impact her clothes and her jewels would have on these islanders. Papa was sure to be consumed by business, and she would be free to display her worldliness and be graciously condescending. Her second thought was her mother, who had been known to suffer cruelly from much lesser events than her daughter's absence.

Ludevina, however, had learnt what to say, and in what order. 'What about Mamma?'

'Your mamma will worry, lie down, take a draught and sleep. When she wakes we will have returned, your dress will not be torn, you will not have been abducted and I will have had the pleasure of your company.'

Ludevina inclined her head and glided towards the door. Halfway across the room she paused to stare out the window. The sun emerged from behind its thin covering of winter clouds. Below her the oranges glowed like small golden coins.

Ludevina leaned over the rails of the ferry and let a winter wave spray her gown before hurrying back to the safety of the cabin. The roll of the waves did not make her feel ill, nor was she worried for the sake of her clothes. She felt liberated, away from the chatter of her sisters and the cloying attentions of her mother. Her father threw a coarse wrap around her and scolded her indulgently. She wrinkled her nose. The cabin reeked of damp clothes mingled with the passengers' steaming breath, the smells of wet dog, long-dead fish, the tang of sea salt and a ferryman's lunchtime sausage. Wrapped tight against the wind and rain, Ludevina stared out the window and thought only of the two days ahead of her.

Fog lay over the Tyrrhenian Sea, obliterating the horizon. There was nothing but water and a shifting swirl of white air. Vulcano appeared from nowhere, sulphurous and craggy. Then Lipari with its stepped dwellings and dark, bustling marina. Salina, the green island, came as a surprise: twin mountains reared into the centre and the villages spread over the rises.

It was near midday when they docked. Aluaro's tenants, Aurora and Stefano Palmerino and their son Aldo, waited awkwardly near the jetty and the little group made its way without speaking to the villa on the lower slopes of Salina.

The villa was grand by island standards but, despite the fact that their hosts had prepared their best rooms for Aluaro and his daughter, Ludevina was appalled by a plainness unknown in her circle in baroque Palermo. She waited, but the day failed to bring any excitement. By evening she was bored and restless, alone in the house at the edge of the ocean while her father drank wine with Stefano in the village. Aurora was once again in mourning for some relative. A stream of deaths and their accompanying rites gave a sombre framework to her days. She had worn widow's weeds since her early twenties. After providing her guests with their evening meal she again succumbed to grief and early sleep.

Evening mist coated the island in a purple glow. It seemed a living thing, this curling mass that wrapped around the buildings, softening the edges.

Ludevina walked to the edge of the terrace. Grey branches entwined the wooden supports, an occasional bud the only hint of a spring not far away.

Aldo returned from the vineyard late that evening. He climbed the stairs to the terrace two at a time and was startled by Ludevina. Caught between the light and the shadows, she appeared ghostly. He rubbed his forearm. '*Buona sera* Signorina Minieri. Where's Mamma?'

'Your mother's asleep. Your father said the death of your aunt has affected her deeply.'

Aldo grinned. 'Deaths! There's always a death for Mamma. They're her life.' He turned to Ludevina. 'How long will you stay?'

She lifted her chin and looked away from him at the now invisible sea.

'Only long enough for Papa to collect the rent and see to the business.'

Aldo noted her white skin and the curve of her neck. He went inside to gulp mouthfuls of pasta and oil-soaked bread and thought of nothing except the tall girl who stood still in the dusk on the terrace.

After he had eaten, Aldo returned carrying a flagon and two tumblers. Each evening he took his drink to the terrace where he could be alone. At twenty-three he still lived with his parents and worked with his father.

He offered Ludevina a tumbler. 'Would you like a drink? Our wines are famous, you know.'

'No thank you,' Ludevina said. 'Papa wouldn't want me to drink alone.' At home in Palermo they used fine-stemmed glassware.

'You're not alone. I'm here. Aren't you allowed to drink?'

Ludevina was not used to such blunt speech. 'Of course I am. At home we have a different wine for each course. I just don't feel like it, that's all.'

'Here, come on, just one drink to try our wine. We make it ourselves.'

Aldo pushed the tumbler at her and raised the flagon with his other hand. Ludevina did not want to appear unsophisticated. Surely one drink wouldn't hurt. She sipped and was surprised at the wine's sweetness. She expected it to be rough, in keeping with this man who drank two tumblers in succession and then poured himself a third. She drank the syrupy wine quickly and warmth crept through her.

It was just on nightfall. Aldo and Ludevina watched the mist settle and the sun and the moon exchange places. For a moment the island was alone in an indigo sea. Aldo moved closer to Ludevina. He cocked his head, encouraging her to look at him full in the face. He was grinning and she noticed that one corner of his mouth was glistening with wine. She wondered what it would be like to finger that soft flesh, and her heart beat faster. Embarrassed, she dropped her gaze and stared as Aldo walked his fingers along the upper railing until they were close to her own hands. Ludevina preened. This flirting was new to her; she was instantly flattered. In Palermo the young men were restrained by a crowd or a chaperone.

'Would you like to come down to the beach? The moon's bright and it's not at all cold.'

'I don't think Papa would approve. He told me to stay in the house.'

'Oh, come on. Papa again. Don't you make any decisions for yourself? We won't go far.' Aldo's tone was mocking. 'It's as good as daylight out there and they'll be at the tavern for hours yet.'

The wine, the white moon and Aldo's insistence overrode Aluaro Minieri's voice. When they reached the water's edge Ludevina sat down, took off her shoe and shook it to dislodge a pebble. Her pale blue dress glowed in the moonlight and as she leaned back on her hands its tight bodice curved over her breasts and into her waist. Aldo looked away, aroused by drink and desire. Then he sat beside her.

'Do you think you'll come here with your father again?'

'I might. Papa thought coming here would be a distraction for me. I've always been interested in his holdings. Mamma doesn't care much. She's too busy with the house and my brothers and sisters.'

'So are we a distraction?'

Ludevina blushed, suddenly aware of her superior tone. She went to speak but Aldo put up his hand to stop her.

'And is your curiosity satisfied?'

Ludevina breathed deeply and held her head high. She felt dizzy but she was Aluaro Minieri's daughter and would make sure this tenant knew that they were separated by more than the Tyrrhenian Sea. She was unprepared for her own response. Aldo was looking at her with a wry smile. She shivered and looked seaward. Aldo again dipped his head, forcing her to look at him until she could do nothing but smile. She felt his breath on her neck. Ludevina bit her lower lip and watched as Aldo ran his index finger the length of her thumb. He did not drop his gaze.

They made love while waves rammed the granite cliffs and wintry cloud drifts blocked out the light and the night grew colder. Afterwards, they were both embarrassed. Ludevina wriggled out from under Aldo's arm. She stood up and straightened her clothes.

'Where are you going?' Aldo said.

'I'm going back to the house. If I'm quick, I'll be back before Papa.' Ludevina left Aldo lying on the sand and sprinted across the beach.

'Wait,' Aldo called. 'I'll come with you.' But Ludevina was already halfway up the cliff, stumbling on the thick grasses and scratching her hands on the prickly pear.

Ahead of them, the villa was in darkness except for the lamp in the kitchen. Aluaro and Stefano did not appear to have returned. Aldo caught up with Ludevina just before she reached the house. He brushed at the back of her dress as they ran. Annoyed, she shrugged off his efforts to help her and he grabbed her by the waist and spun her around. He didn't understand this woman who had let him make love to her and now pushed him away.

A cold voice cut the air.

'Where have you been?' Aluaro walked through the kitchen door and stood with his legs apart and his arms folded. 'I said, where have you been?'

Ludevina froze and then pulled away from Aldo and ran to her father. 'Just to the beach, Papa. Just to see the moon.'

'What were you doing?'

'Nothing, Papa.'

'Why was he holding you?'

'I'—Ludevina hesitated—'fell and got dirt on my dress. Aldo was helping me to brush it off.'

She reached for her father's arm but he thrust her away. 'What were you doing?'

'Nothing, Papa.' Ludevina began to cry and her voice was shrill. 'There was nothing. Do you think I would have anything to do with such a peasant?' She gestured towards Aldo who did not move.

'I don't believe you.'

For Aluaro the event was written in the air. It was in the eyes of both young people, a dreaminess hinting at hidden things.

'There was nothing, Papa. He gave me wine. He made me go with him to the beach.'

'Go to your room.'

Aluaro turned to Aldo who stood with his head bowed. Aldo knew that he and Ludevina had broken the rules. He also understood the bonds of obligation.

Within three months Ludevina was married to Aldo and living in the villa on Salina. Each year Aluaro sent a deputy to make sure that the Palmerinos did their duty by his vineyard. After the marriage he deemed it of no concern whether Aldo continued to do his duty by Ludevina. She neither saw nor heard from her father or her family again.

In the early years of her marriage Ludevina openly linked herself with Persephone, that innocent young woman who was abducted from the shores of Sicily while picking flowers, to become mistress of the underworld. The analogy both amused and comforted her. It enlarged her fate. Ludevina never let it be forgotten that she had been forced to marry beneath her.

Contrary to expectations, no child was born of the first brief liaison. One year after their marriage, however, Ludevina bore a son, Nino. He was a dark-haired child with flashing eyes. She held her head high, for in bearing such a beautiful son she had done her duty. There would be no other children.

2

Angelina and Fortunato Coltelli lived directly below the Palmerino vineyards in a cubed house set back from the cliff above the bay. To reach his boat that lay sheltered in the granite-strewn harbour below the house, Fortunato had hewn a line of stone stairs. From the village beyond the house these steps were invisible, but seen from the water, they climbed in steep rises. Fortunato had painted each step a pastel colour, and his fellow fishermen accepted his flight of fancy just as they accepted the sun and the tides.

Angelina's cousin, Caterina, came after her own work to help prepare for the birth of the couple's first child. Fortunato was mending nets in the garden and smiled at her as she passed into the house. Caterina brought materials for stitching and stories to share with Angelina as they sat drinking coffee and eating sweet, crisp biscuits.

It was a pale afternoon on the cusp of autumn. There was no sun, only stretched, bleached clouds pulled across the sky by a howling wind.

Angelina, her attention caught by the low swooping of an eagle, dropped the cloth she was stitching. She stooped to pick it up and felt a sharp pain, and then another. Silenced by her fear she tried to stand upright. Caterina went to make her an infusion of rosemary tea and prayed it would quell the spasms rolling through Angelina's body.

Fortunato ran to the village to fetch Benedetta, the midwife, who came with her daughter, Lucia. He spent the next hour praying on the terrace, taunted by the wind and his fear. But Angelina's pain spiralled into contractions and within the hour a baby girl slipped into the world with limbs the size of tiny sausages. She was two months premature. She gave a feeble cry and was silent. Benedetta put aside her cloths and bowls of water and Caterina took up her rosary beads, calling for Fortunato to stand with her beside Angelina and their black-haired daughter. There was no longer any reason to continue the rites of childbirth.

It was then that Fortunato decided to go on a pilgrimage. He could do nothing amongst this debris of birth. He would leave the weeping women and journey to the church of the Madonna del Terzito to pray for his daughter's life. He understood that the Madonna listened and carried to God the prayers of the believers. Fortunato, like all the people of Salina, did not measure his life in days and hours, but by the cycles of festivals and miracles that shaped the year.

'I am her papa now,' he said proudly. 'From now on I am Papa Fortunato.'

That evening, Fortunato began his journey along the stony mule tracks that were scattered over the island like a fine carving. He stopped frequently to offer a plea heavenward, noticing all around him the reminders of earthly suffering: limp vines trailing over wooden trellises, oleanders blood-red in the evening light, rosemary bushes stiff and upright like perpetual penitents. He continued on with renewed vigour, oblivious to the sharp stones under his boots and to the wind that howled his fury and his pain.

When he saw the church's elegantly enchased metal cross, Fortunato cried out. 'Madonna!' There was no answer, only the swirling wind and air pungent with the scents of sea and herbs. He raised his voice. 'I have journeyed far to see you, to place my blessings at your feet and to ask you to grant me one more.'

Fortunato mounted the steep stairs to the church door. He wept when he entered but still stopped to take off his hat and genuflect.

'My Angelina is lying with our child,' he explained to the Madonna. 'She's been born early and is struggling to breathe.'

Fortunato remained on his knees. Tiny particles of dust played in the gloom. He let his eyes track a narrowing beam of light from the doorway to a point beyond the altar where it disappeared. Entranced he got up and began to follow it. He felt weightless and illuminated, seeing nothing but this light and its vanishing point. When he reached the altar rails and knelt to pray the light pulsated, intensifying until the church about him disappeared and he could hear the angels' sorrowing song. He felt the sweetest compassion and balm, and he saw a baby enclosed in light, lying in front of him on the stone floor.

Fortunato knew he had journeyed much further than the church of the Madonna del Terzito. For hours he leaned against the altar rails, the hypnotic rosary numbing his tongue and burring his lips. And when the morning light touched the sky, the angels lifted him up and carried him home, suspended in their song.

This, at any rate, is what he told the village folk. Some looked at him with awe, others with tolerance. They all knew what it was like to be suffused with the power of angels and saints. These revelations were part of the life of Salina.

Caterina claimed that when Fortunato returned his face was opalescent. She said that at the same time the child, who had been bluish with the effort for breath, began to change colour and fade into the soft almond tint of the newborn. It was only then that Angelina slept and Fortunato sat with Caterina and Benedetta drinking *malvasia* while keeping a silent vigil over the baby lying between them.

As first light rolled over the far reaches of the bay and crept towards the shore in layers of pink and yellow, Fortunato said with pride, as he would say many times in the years to follow, that the wail of his Delfina was loud enough to be heard on the other side of the island.

The news of the birth spread quickly, first in the village of Malfa and then to the nearby villages, even to the shepherds scattered throughout Valdichiesa.

Benedetta's daughter, Lucia, was charged with delivering the news in the village. She came panting into Ludevina's kitchen, triumphant with her announcement. She took a breath to steady her voice and began in the ingratiating tone expected by Ludevina. 'Signora Palmerino, Angelina and Fortunato have been blessed with a daughter.'

Ludevina counted the months. 'Then the baby won't survive.'

'Yes, yes, the baby is well. When Angelina delivered her child and it looked sure to die, Fortunato walked to the Sanctuary of the Madonna del Terzito and there he, he'—she fumbled for words—'was granted a miracle.'

Ludevina stared at the girl. She didn't believe in miracles. Miracles belonged to another time and place. 'The baby won't survive,' she repeated, and turned her back on Lucia.

Ludevina pulled Nino by the arm. The boy gave a shriek which he let slide to a roar before he felt the slap of his mother's palm on the back of his legs. He sat down on a rock, clamped his knees together, wrapped his arms around them and stared ahead of him. But it was futile. Ludevina did not bother to scold or to coax. She simply lifted him up and they continued on their way.

Just short of Angelina and Fortunato Coltelli's house she set him down and straightened his clothes. 'You will behave yourself. We are important people on this island and you will not shame your father and mother.' Nino didn't answer and she shook him roughly. 'Do you hear me?'

The boy nodded but refused to look at his mother. He was three years old and confused by her words. He only knew that if he acted against his mother's wishes, she would scream and slap.

Ludevina ignored his dropped eyelids and busied herself with a basket of cakes: airy, sugary morsels infused with her own mulled wine.

They picked their way between the boulders and the outcrops of prickly pear at the front of the house. When they entered the Coltellis' crowded kitchen there was a respectful quiet. Ludevina tossed her head and put her gift of cakes in the centre of the table, pushing aside the other plates of fruit and small covered baskets.

'Thank you so much,' said Caterina. 'Angelina will enjoy these. We know they're your specialty.' She bustled around the kitchen, preparing food and drink for the Coltellis' visitors.

Young Franco Gullo jumped to his feet and pulled out a chair. 'Sit down, Signora Palmerino. Here's a glass of wine,' he said. 'What an occasion this is! A real miracle. And look at your little boy. He's growing more like his father every day.'

Ludevina winced as she took Franco's seat. He held out a biscuit to Nino and sat back beside his wife, Gisella. Franco was thin and pale for an islander and the women laughed at him behind his back. He didn't look capable of a good day's work, let alone the fathering of a child. It was no surprise to them that Franco and Gisella had not conceived during three years of marriage.

'We've been in to see the baby,' said Gisella. 'She's so beautiful, so tiny.' She dropped her eyes and Franco placed his hand over his wife's.

Mario Rinaldi was watching from the far end of the oblong table and leaned forward with his glass raised. He and his wife, Gabriella, had heard the news and come quickly to Salina. The Rinaldis had chosen to live on the nearby island of Filicudi and were often not seen for months at a time. Over the years Mario had developed the knack of appearing at crucial moments. He said that he was forewarned of events by the wind, that he could read its breath. His friends believed him. He knew of the Gullos' childlessness and stepped in to prevent Ludevina demoralising the young couple. 'To Angelina and Fortunato's miracle child,' he said. He clinked his glass against Gabriella's cup of coffee and held it high. One by one the others picked up their glasses and cups. 'To the miracle child,' they toasted in unison.

Benedetta, still with rolled-up sleeves and a stained apron, plucked at Ludevina's hip. 'Come, come, Signora Palmerino. Come and see the miracle child.'

Ludevina let herself be drawn to the only other room in the house. Angelina was sleeping and beside her Fortunato cradled their baby in his brawny fisherman's arms.

He looked up as she approached and loosened the swaddling so that Ludevina could see the baby's face.

'Look what God has seen fit to grant us.'

The baby sucked at her lips, made a popping sound and then fretted softly.

Fortunato wore an otherworldly glow. Ludevina had seen that look before. She sighed but knew it enhanced her prestige to be in the presence of a miracle. 'You have a fine daughter. And with so much black hair for such a little one! Tell me, what will you name her?'

Fortunato raised the child and then lowered her. 'She will be called Delfina, Delfina Terzita. She is the fruit of the sea and the fruit of my prayers.'

'So you will name her in honour of fish and miracles,' said Ludevina. Her lip curled and she raised her eyebrows. 'Let's hope she lives up to her birthright.'

Holding his mother's skirts, Nino edged his way towards Fortunato and the baby. Fortunato motioned for him to come closer. Nino laid his little finger on the baby's palm, intrigued by the translucent, wrinkled flesh. In the slow, mesmeric movement peculiar to babies, Delfina flexed her fingers and curled them over Nino's own.

Delfina and Nino spent their childhood playing in the wind and the sun. Ludevina convinced herself that their class differences were offset by the island's perception of Delfina as a miracle, and she let them wander without interference.

It was the April of 1908 and Delfina was seven years old. She stood on the cliff above the beach where she and Nino often played. Next to her was a stocky boy a year younger than herself. He stood with his legs apart and his arms folded, braced like his fisherman father against the island winds.

'Wait here, Paolo. I'll go and find Nino,' said Delfina.

'Do you want me to come?'

'No, wait here. He'll be at the cave.'

Delfina skirted down through the spindly scrub to the water's edge. She shaded her eyes against the sun. She would have to run the length of the bay. She had a lot to tell Nino.

The cave was narrow, deep and gloomy. Delfina didn't want to go in alone. The children believed that the souls of drowned fishermen slept there at night and went out with the morning's flotilla to guide the day's catch. Delfina was convinced that some must stay behind.

'What are you scared of this time?'

Delfina ducked to avoid being poked with Nino's forked twig. 'We can't play yet,' she said.

'Why not?'

Delfina pointed to the boy waiting on the top of the cliff. 'That's Paolo Paschini. He's from Lipari. His father's gone to heaven and now he's living here with his aunt and uncle.'

'What about his mamma?'

'Papa said his mamma's with the angels. Papa said we have to let him play with us.'

Nino sized up Paolo and nodded.

Delfina signalled for Paolo to join them but the boy hesitated. Ten days earlier his father had told him to hurry and get their neighbour. Then a crowd of people had smothered him with tears and kisses and he was squeezed into a tight black suit and made to walk behind his father's coffin. He had done the same thing for his mother two years earlier. After the funeral his clothes and toys were packed into boxes. He said goodbye to his friends and he was rowed to Salina.

Delfina was now waving both arms. Paolo gritted his teeth and sped down the track and along the beach to the cave.

'You have to start there.' Nino pointed to the far end of the bay. 'And you have to have a twig, with sharp bits…'

Nino ran back towards the starting point, calling instructions as he went. 'Then you have to run to the cave and touch the inside wall. The last one has to tell what a dead soul looks like. And you have to tell it properly.' He gouged a mark in the sand and lined the three of them up behind it. 'Ready, set, go!' he yelled.

The children tore across the beach ignoring the sharp stones. Nino streaked ahead followed by Delfina and then Paolo. He arrived at the cave twenty metres ahead of the others and looked back triumphantly as Paolo lost his footing in a crab hole. Paolo righted himself and caught up with Delfina. As they neared the cave, Delfina gasped when a stone bit the flesh between her toes. Paolo spun around to check on her and stumbled again. Delfina passed him, touched the wall, and joined Nino at the mouth of the cave.

Nino grinned as Paolo drew near. Delfina's new friend was no competition. He grabbed him by the shoulders. Paolo wanted to grab him back but he knew already that life was like the sea, treacherous and requiring careful navigation. He stood still while Nino gloated. 'Now, touch the wall and tell us what a dead soul looks like?'

'That's not fair, Nino,' Delfina said. 'Paolo stopped to see if I was all right.'

'That's not part of the game,' Nino answered.

'I don't mind,' Paolo said. 'After all, I was the last one.'

Nino made a face at Delfina and went to push Paolo into the cave, but he had already disappeared inside.

Later that same year, just after his eleventh birthday, Nino went with Delfina and her mamma and papa to take part in the celebrations for the Madonna del Terzito. The Madonna's sanctuary nestled in the valley between the twin mountains and each July the people of Salina gave thanks to the Lady whose small bell called them to prayer. The Madonna was paraded through Malfa on a filigreed platform carried by four men, and garlands of flowers were piled around her feet. She was flanked by two sturdy putti in red and blue loincloths with solid gold wings and black crosses around their chubby necks. She bowed under a silver crown haloed with silver stars and two silver angels. Her arms were outstretched and her bell's clapper clinked. The priest heading the procession swayed in a trance of devotion. Throngs of people followed.

Nino worshipped, celebrated and ate with the rest of the people of Malfa and the other villages, and returned to Ludevina barefoot and dishevelled.

'You look like an island child,' his mother scolded. 'Isn't it enough that I have to be reminded of my fate every day without you acting like them?'

Ludevina's eyes clouded. At ordinary times in Salina's year she held herself apart from the islanders. By revelling in her accomplishments, she banished the guilt festering inside her. Festival days highlighted the differences between her childhood and her life now. She was horrified by the unrestrained enjoyment of the islanders. Now that Nino was eleven years old she could not control him completely. Ludevina looked at his grubby feet and rolled-up sleeves and her stomach churned.

Nino was perplexed. Why was his mother so cross this time? She never went to the festival anyway. She never followed the wobbling statue down the street or filled her belly from the laden tables. 'What is it, Mamma?' he said. 'What's wrong?'

'It's time you realised that the people of this island are peasants. When I was a child in Palermo I lived in a beautiful house with fine clothes and servants. You must become a man like your grandfather. Maybe one day he will come for you.'

Ludevina scrubbed at Nino's face and neck, regaling him for the first time with details of her childhood in Palermo. He must understand that he was special. She could not let him become like them.

Nino listened and felt the foundations of his life shift. His mother had always brushed aside his questions about her family. She was either too busy to talk to him or he was being a nuisance. Bursting with curiosity, he summoned up the courage to ask, 'Will my grandfather come to get me?'

Ludevina pushed him onto the chair and picked up a clean shirt. 'Your grandfather's too busy to come yet. He's an important man. But you should be ready for him when he does.'

Nino studied his mother. She was cross but also upset. Her eyes were wild. Her movements were jerky and she stared straight ahead as she folded and refolded his clothes. He wanted to ask her more questions but decided it would not be a good idea.

The next day he met Delfina near the yellow broom bush. She could read his confusion in the lines of his face and the rigid movements of his body as he dragged broom branches across the ground in front of him. 'Where's Paolo?' he said.

'He's gone fishing with Papa. He wants to learn to be a fisherman.'

Nino frowned and threw his branches on the ground. 'Last night Mamma told me that she was born in Palermo. She had a carriage, fine dresses and each Sunday they would walk on the marina and eat gelato. She says that grandfather was the finest man in all of Palermo.' Nino's face lit up.

Delfina propped her chin on her hands. She had never left Salina and Nino's connection with this outside world was incomprehensible.

'Mamma says that when she was a child they celebrated the feast of Santa Rosalia.'

'Who is she?'

Nino loved this part of his mother's story. 'She was a rich and beautiful lady from a noble family, who became a hermit and lived in a cave on the Monte Pellegrino near Palermo, where my family is from, and each year there is a festival in her honour.'

When Ludevina had told Nino these things he felt her slip from him and he wanted to pull her back.

'Mamma said that the chariot was like a great golden ship, and that as it moved towards the marina—that is where people like Mamma's family go to walk in the evenings—it shone with thousands of lighted candles.'

'Why is the procession so big? Why is she such a special saint?'

By this time Nino was facing the sea. He rocked from heel to toe. 'Santa Rosalia saved the city from a disease. It was called the Black Plague. So, she has to have an important procession.' Aware that he had omitted the best parts of his story, he backtracked. 'Everyone was sick. She appeared to a hunter. She showed him her blessed bones. People offered candles and flowers. And the city was cured.'

His voice had taken on the timbre of song and in the telling he seemed to go far beyond the waters that hurled themselves against the rocks below.

Delfina did not move. 'Is it bigger than our feast of the Madonna?'

'Mamma says the feasts here are for peasants.' Nino kicked at a tussock of grass. 'That Santa Rosalia brought about a real miracle, a grand miracle.'

'Papa says that I am a miracle.'

Nino turned to the girl sitting on the ground before him and he felt the fragmented parts of himself settle. He shook his head, pulled her up from the ground, and they raced towards the vineyards. In their wake the stories of saints and miracles whirled in the air like the litter from the fireworks that crackled and spat above Santa Rosalia's golden chariot.

3

The summer of 1914 had been exceptional in the Palmerinos' vineyards and their *cantina* was full. But now Ludevina was obliged to give away some of their wine against her wishes. She dragged Nino into the wine cellar, her face contorted with anger. A crate of empty bottles lay on the floor.

It had seemed like a good idea to Nino: to creep into Signor Reato's *cantina* after nightfall and take a crate of wine to share with his friends. No one would find out if they stored it in the cave. It was Paolo's fault that they were discovered. His uncle had smelled wine on his breath and followed his nephew. As usual, Paolo couldn't keep his mouth shut. His uncle carried the crate back to the Palmerinos' villa and dumped it on the floor of their cellar. He left Ludevina alone to deal with her son.

'How dare you do this to me,' Ludevina shouted. She slapped Nino and her fingers left red lines across his cheek. Nino rubbed his face to ease the sting. 'God punishes thieves. You're seventeen years old and should know better.' Ludevina smacked her son again and this time Nino's eyes watered. 'I've spoken to Padre Giovanni and he said that you must write a letter of apology to Signor Reato. Here, take these.' Ludevina thrust a notepad and pencil at Nino. It was not only the theft that made her angry. 'Signor Reato needed the wine you stole for his daughter's wedding. We'll have to replace it. Stupid, foolish boy. Bring the letter to me when you've finished.' Nino ducked to avoid another slap and slunk from the room.

Nino ran into a headwind all the way to the beach. Its rush against his body made him feel strong and alive. He picked a patch of shade between two rocks. They were pointed and thin like blades and towered either side of him.

For a while he fumed, cursing his mother and Paolo. Then he stared at the notepad before grinding the pencil through the first few sheets of paper. Still angry, he ripped them off and threw them away.

'Temper, temper,' a voice said.

Nino turned and saw Delfina gathering up the flying sheets. 'What's the matter?' she said.

Nino explained and she patted his hand. 'Poor Nino. It's quite easy really,' she said. 'You just put the pencil on the paper'—Nino was still holding the pencil and Delfina guided his hand over the paper—'and write "sorry".'

Nino laughed and said, 'Then I'll tell him his wine tasted rotten and gave us all a belly ache.'

'See, you feel better already,' Delfina said. 'Just do what your mother wants and don't go back to the villa for a while.'

Delfina cleared a patch between the pebbles and lay on her stomach. Out of the wind it was warm and dry. Beside her, Nino laboured over his letter.

At fourteen, Delfina had left girlhood behind. Her head was turned to one side and her eyes were half shut. Nino could tell she was awake by the way she was tapping her fingers on the sand. Her dress curved over her buttocks and fell between her legs. He inched forwards, meaning only to startle her. But, instead, he bent over and impulsively kissed her. Then he turned her over and took her face in his hands and his fingers were sure and quick as he pulled her to him and kissed her again, this time hard.

Delfina sat upright and they stared at each other. Nino was red-faced and surprised by what he'd done. It was as if some giant hand had cut the easy relationship they shared.

'I'd better go,' stammered Delfina.

She left Nino to finish his letter and wonder at what had happened.

That evening, Delfina said little during dinner and sat on the terrace, flicking at a string of drying peppers.

Angelina came and sat beside her. 'Is something wrong?' she said.

Delfina shook her head.

'Are you sure?' her mother said. 'Have you and Nino argued?' Delfina blushed.

'Ah,' she said, 'perhaps it wasn't an argument.'

Delfina shook her head again. 'No, Nino kissed me,' she said.

Angelina smiled. 'It's to be expected. You're both growing up. It just means that now you must be careful where you go together. And Ludevina or I must go with you. You know reputations get damaged easily.'

After that, Delfina and Nino still walked together but never far from either Ludevina or Angelina.

One November morning Nino was working with Aldo in the vineyards. For hours they had bent over the vines, trimming and twining the autumn growth. By midday they had zigzagged downhill and reached the end of the last row. This had been their pattern since Nino's childhood: he had climbed the slopes with the agility of a goat, brushing past the gorse and the broom, taking six steps to his father's two. Now he was a young man of twenty.

Aldo lay on his back, heedless of the stones. He closed his eyes against the sun and his voice was sleepy. 'You should lie down. Why stand when you can lie?'

Nino wasn't listening. His joints ached. He flexed his shoulders to ease the strain on his back. His eyes were fixed on a shadow that darkened the horizon. A placid sea frilled the island, rolling outwards in concentric circles. Salina seemed quieter and smaller now that summer had passed. Nino felt the island contract around him and he stretched his limbs again in defiance.

Aldo sat up and reached for his pipe. He tamped it down, then lit and sucked at the same time until a wisp of smoke spiralled upwards. He propped himself on his elbows and followed his son's gaze. 'What are you looking at?'

'A ship. There's another ship out there.'

'So what! There have been ships before and there'll be ships again,' Aldo said. 'What do you care about those ships and the traitors who leave on them? They were too lazy to keep trying. Seasons come and go. Some are good and some not. We've been lucky. The others should accept this blight on their vines. Things will change. They're already better than they were. Why can't everyone see that?'

Nino wasn't sure that things were better. He knew that Aldo had never forgiven his friend Umberto for leaving on the ship bound for America when phylloxera had decimated his vineyard. Nearly seventeen years later, Umberto's wife and children were still waiting for the signal to join him.

Nino knew about the phylloxera, the little parasite that sucked sap from the vines and left nothing but a dried husk. On the islands it wrought its destruction from underground, by building deformities into the plants' root systems until it killed them. When the food source dried up it scrambled to the surface, found another vine, descended to the roots and began all over again. In its search for food this small creature carried within its horny, transparent wing cases the power to move continents.

Nino bit back the words he wanted to say. Nothing would alter his father's opinion of either Umberto or the phylloxera. He stared towards the ship. 'But you can't blame people for trying their luck elsewhere,' he said. 'Look at Umberto. He's sent so much back to his family. Things have obviously gone well for him in America.'

The ground seemed harder now that Aldo was no longer young. He rubbed his elbows, looked over his vines, and admired their symmetry and the promise within their sculpted forms. He tapped his pipe against a stone and yawned. Then he waved one arm over the vineyard. 'This is a good day's work. I'm going back to the villa to rest.'

'I think I'll stay here for a while, Papa. If I finish those vines'—Nino pointed to a triangular set separate from the main body of the vineyard—'I won't have to return in the morning.'

Aldo rose, hooked his arm around Nino's shoulder and hugged him hard. 'I know you're restless, Nino,' he said. 'Phylloxera has made so many leave. And now we're losing our young men to the war.'

'I feel as if I'm not doing my duty,' Nino said, resisting the desire to break from his father's grasp. 'Down at the jetty the men talk of nothing else but the war. And I'm here doing what I've always done.'

'You are doing your duty,' Aldo insisted. 'If the government wants only sons to stay and work the land, it proves that what you do is important. We need our only son here!' He hugged Nino again and set off down the hill.

The ship on the horizon was heading towards the islands, an arc of foam splicing the water. Excitement flickered through Nino as he considered its destination: America, Australia, Venezuela? What was life like in these places? It was time to make decisions about his future. His nonno, Stefano, had died only months before. Nino watched Aurora wail and pace the length of the terrace, muttering that her husband had slipped between the cracks in the stone. After that she retired to her bedroom where she communed loudly with her Madonna and saints. The rituals of mourning made Nino impatient. Ludevina and Aldo now managed the villa and the vineyards and Ludevina had taken over the duties of the household.

Nino had always relied on Delfina whenever there was any change in his life. She would help him choose the right path.

While Nino spent his childhood on the slopes with his father, Delfina grew up in the embrace of Angelina and Fortunato. At seventeen she was aware that Nino looked at her with different eyes. She was slim but shapely and her black hair fell over her breasts and arms. She had seen Nino's approving glance rove the length of her body. She had seen his half smile and the way he bit his lip when they met and, although part of her liked this new tension between them ever since he had kissed her, she sensed a danger and yearned for times when things were less complicated.

At night, when Delfina lay in bed thinking about love and marriage, it seemed to her that there were three kinds of love. There was the love she felt for her mamma and papa, the love they all felt for God and the Madonna, and the love between a man and a woman. When Angelina told her daughter that marriage made lovemaking holy and children blessed, Delfina realised with shock that her mamma and papa felt this kind of love. She saw the looks between them and the fleeting touches of their hands. But surely it could not be the same yearning as when she wanted Nino to touch her.

It was late on a hot spring day and the sirocco blew in from Northern Africa, saturating the island with sticky heat. Delfina and Nino left Malfa and picked their way through the carpet of flowers on the upper side of a dusty track. Ludevina was gathering fennel and thyme on the lower side.

A gust caught at Delfina's skirt and she stopped to hold it down. The rush of air was cool against her but when it died away her dress clung to her skin and she plucked at it. Annoyed, she rubbed her hands the length of her neck and through her hair, catching her fingers in the tangle of curls around her hairline. She turned to see if Nino had gone ahead, but he was standing a short distance away, watching her. There was a look on his face Delfina had not seen before. She lowered her arms. 'Let's head towards the beach,' she said. 'It'll be cooler near the water in the shade of the cliffs.'

Before Delfina could move away, Nino covered the distance between them in three leaps. He grabbed her arm and slid his long fingers around her wrist. He lifted her other hand and placed his palm against hers. Smiling, he looked into her face and traced a line through the centre of her palm with his finger. A tremor ran through Delfina's body. 'Will you marry me?' he said. He curled his fingers through hers and drew her to him.

'We've always been together. I can't imagine being with anyone else. You know it's true. Don't you?'

Nino placed his hands behind her neck and pulled her to him and Delfina felt like she would burst with happiness. 'Yes, I will marry you,' she said. It was so like Nino to ask her in this impulsive way. Since childhood, she had watched him run through life. Shyly, she put her arms around his waist. 'But first you must ask Papa's consent.' The wind flicked them with grains of sand and small twigs, and they laughed as she ducked her head and Nino reached for the flying strands of her hair.

'Of course. I'll talk to him tomorrow after I tell Mamma and Papa.' Nino kissed the hair he had caught in his hands and ran his lips along its length until he reached her mouth.

There was no need for them to talk of hopes and dreams or plans. Exhilarated, Delfina saw their future: a jubilant wedding, laughing children, cooking for feast days and family occasions, her pantry filled with preserves like her mother's and her drawers stacked with hand-stitched embroidery. This love between a man and a woman was the most exciting of all and it belonged to her and Nino. Snug against Nino's chest, Delfina looked at the blue of the sky, and the blue of the sea, and thought of their future together on the island.

Ludevina, hovering nearby, noticed the embrace and hurried towards them. Hoisting her bag of herbs, she lumbered over the rocks and tussocks. When she had them clearly in her view she sat on the ground and proceeded to wind yarn from the pocket of her apron.

Nino sidled into Ludevina's kitchen as she was working a wad of dough. He crept up behind her and put his arms around his mother's waist. She jumped and pulled a piece off the soft mixture and gave it to him to eat. 'Here, try this,' she said. 'It's your favourite.'

Nino chewed the dough. He hoped his mother was in a good mood. 'Mamma. I've got something to tell you.' Nino's voice was unsteady and Ludevina turned towards him and rubbed her floury hands on her apron. 'I've asked Delfina to marry me.'

Ludevina's response was as quick as a slap. 'You can't marry her. She's the daughter of a fisherman.'

It wasn't possible. Her son couldn't marry beneath him. Her own marriage had been ignominious. If her son married an islander her dignity would suffer further. There would be a distasteful island wedding. She would be forced to accept Delfina and her family. She turned her back on Nino and began rolling the dough. Her voice was sharp. 'Remember that I am the daughter of Aluaro Minieri and you are the grandson of someone better than Fortunato Coltelli.'

There was a tense silence. Nino knew that his mother was unhappy and that she kept her distance from the islanders. After she had told him about her Palermo family, he'd listened for rumours in the village. He'd discovered only that his mother wasn't liked because she believed herself to be superior. So he was not surprised by her reaction now. He watched Ludevina stretch a rectangular slab the length of the bench and pick up a knife.

'Also, she was born early and on a night of shadows.' Ludevina ran the knife the length of the dough, severing it through to the tabletop.

'But Mamma, what has that got to do with anything? You know her birth was a miracle.'

Delfina's birth had given her a place in some celestial hierarchy. But this was not the status Ludevina wanted for the wife of her son. She continued slicing the yellow dough. The thin ribbons of pasta curled at each end and Nino resisted the old temptation to crush them with the flat of his finger. Later they would eat these fresh ribbons coated with a thick, warm sauce of red tomatoes and baby pink prawns.

'How do we know this is true? How do we know that she doesn't carry evil within her?'

Ludevina had played a trump card. Beads of perspiration glittered on her brow and her eyes narrowed. 'And look at her father! He dreamed of angels long before Delfina's birth. Married to a woman who says nothing and stitches pretty flowers on old pieces of cloth. Do you think that Delfina will be any different? All the miracles in the world will not make her a good wife.'

She sat down, threw her knife onto the table and let her hands fall into her lap. The memories returned to crush her. As she lowered her head, Ludevina saw a girl catapulting into a harder life, lulled by the night scents and a young man fresh from a vineyard. She gasped out loud and reached for Nino but her son stood firm. He would marry Delfina because she was part of him. As a child she had absorbed his confusion and pain.

'Be it on your head, my son,' Ludevina hissed.

She roused herself and stood up. She may have lost her Nino to this girl but her new authority within the family after Stefano's death would give her control over her daughter-in-law. It was just as well. Aurora would have been too soft on the girl.

Just before lunchtime the next day, Nino walked to the beach where Papa Fortunato moored his boat after the day's fishing. The bay was empty and a brilliant sun fused sea and sky in glinting electric flashes. From where he sat on the first of Fortunato's stone stairs, Nino heard the round of an old song long before he saw the boat enter the bay. He watched Fortunato and Paolo row towards the beach. Just short of the pebble bay, near the point where the pitted cliff face met the water, the two men jumped from the boat. They tied it to a jutting rock and waded to shore, the water slapping against their thighs.

Fortunato rubbed wet grit from his hands, looked up and saw Nino waiting for him instead of Delfina. He pulled off his boots and helped Paolo roll out the jumbled fishing net. When they had finished sorting their fishing tackle, Paolo picked up his flask and satchel, cooeed and waved at Nino, and set off towards home. Fortunato walked over to Nino who jumped to his feet. 'Has it been a good day's catch?' Nino said.

'Slow early on but things improved.' Fortunato opened his bag and showed Nino the flaccid rainbow-scaled fish.

Nino took a deep breath. 'I've something to ask you.'

'I thought you might.'

'I want to ask you if I can marry Delfina,' said Nino. His well-rehearsed words took him by surprise and he blushed.

Papa Fortunato pushed his hands deep into his pockets and scuffed at the coarse pebbles. 'Do you love Delfina and are you sure this is what she wants?'

'Yes, I do,' Nino said.

Fortunato and Angelina often talked about Nino and Delfina and the possibility of their marriage. From the moment Delfina closed her fingers over Nino's as a baby, the two had been inseparable. Delfina's miracle birth had strengthened Fortunato's acceptance of fate and again, despite misgivings, he let destiny take its course.

'I'll say "yes" on one condition,' he said. 'Delfina is our miracle and you must promise to take care of her.' Fortunato wished he could explain what happened to him all those years ago when the Madonna smiled on his tiny child. He wished he could tell Nino that Delfina was special. But he knew that the younger man would not understand.

'I'll look after her,' Nino said. 'Neither of us can imagine being with anyone else. I know this is what she wants.'

'Then come and help me carry up the rest of the nets,' said Fortunato.

From the top of the cliff, Paolo looked back at Fortunato and Nino. He guessed what had passed between them. Nino always got what he wanted. Paolo also loved Delfina but he had never dreamed of marrying her. He had come to Salina as an outsider and been quick to realise that the union of Nino and Delfina was written in island lore.

4

Delfina and Nino were married on the feast of San Lorenzo in August of 1918. They shared San Lorenzo's flower arches, flags and multi-coloured lights and heralded their wedding night with his fireworks.

It was late morning when Delfina slid the lawn dress over her head and moved to the mirror. She turned sideways and noted the fall of her gown.

'You must let me give you the material,' Ludevina had said to Angelina. 'Delfina is to be my daughter-in-law, after all.'

Ludevina could not let her son's future wife be married in her mother's dress. The cloth was coarse and, even though the embroidery was fine, there was the faint yellowing of age.

'I insist,' she said.

The new dress had full sleeves gathered at the wrists with slender ties. A collar defined its modest neckline and tiny covered buttons ran to a point just below the waist. When Delfina moved, the skirt swished.

Angelina entered her daughter's bedroom. 'It's time to go,' she said.

'Look, Mamma!' The two women admired the young bride's reflection. Satisfied, Angelina slipped her arm around her daughter's waist. 'You will remember what I told you?' she said.

'On your wedding night there is a little pain and some blood. After that it is easier and the love you have for each other brings its own pleasures.' She stroked her daughter's hair and her hand lingered on Delfina's cheek.

Delfina blushed. She was excited about the wedding night. If it was like the feelings she had when Nino pulled her close to him, it must be wonderful. She knew enough about her body to understand what her mother told her and held only the smallest fear. She believed her mother's promise that there were pleasures to look forward to.

Delfina loved Nino very much. Each time she was with him her daydreams of their future multiplied. The only doubt was the thought of living with Ludevina and Aldo. Delfina liked Aldo. He was quiet like her papa and his pipe always drooped from the corner of his mouth. Ludevina sometimes frightened her with her loud voice and harsh judgments. But Delfina was sure that Nino would take care of her.

Angelina stepped behind Delfina and tweaked the gathers of her daughter's veil into place. When the net lay in soft folds around Delfina's shoulders, Angelina sat on the edge of the bed. She was caught between wanting to prepare her daughter for marriage and being a harbinger of worry. 'Delfina,' she said.

Delfina left her reflection and turned to her mother.

'All men are different,' her mother continued. 'Nino's not like your father. He's always needed something to challenge him. Do you remember how competitive he was as a child? How he needed to win?'

'Yes,' Delfina nodded, 'but he's older now and shares the responsibility of the vineyard. He has plenty to keep him busy. And, he will be a married man.'

She turned back to the mirror and smiled at her mother's serious look.

After the solemn nuptial mass, the bridal party and guests walked to the Palmerino villa. Ludevina had offered her terrace for the celebrations after the ceremony and spread the tables with bowls of lemons and oranges and earthenware flagons of wine. Delfina and Nino sat in the centre of the longest table and Delfina looked up as a breeze rustled the sequence of dancing paper brides above her head. She was elated. She was like these paper brides, holding hands through time with the other women of Salina. She and Nino would have children and her daughters, in turn, would hold her hands.

When it was time for the guests to leave, Delfina and Nino stood at either side of the stairs to receive their good wishes and farewells. Paolo waited for the queue to dwindle before shaking Nino's hand. He turned to Delfina, embraced her and kissed her on both cheeks. She was surprised at the warmth and strength of his grasp; it was different from Nino's quicksilver fingers. When Delfina met her father and Paolo at the end of each day's fishing, she often walked the length of the bay with Paolo. His thoughtful presence and few words were a natural counterpoint to Nino's restless energy. She would miss these rituals now that she was a married woman.

'Congratulations, Delfina,' Paolo said. 'You and Nino were always meant to marry.'

When the last of the guests left, Ludevina took Delfina by the arm and led her to Nino's room in the villa. 'Wait here,' she said. She left Delfina perched on the edge of the bed.

Twenty minutes later, the door creaked open and Nino crossed the room and sat beside his wife. He was nervous and one of his legs jumped involuntarily. He put an arm around Delfina's waist and a hand on her knee. 'I do love you,' he said. 'You know that. Don't you? I always have.'

He kissed her and fumbled with the lowest of the loops that held the buttons of her dress. Delfina smiled at him. When Nino undid the last button, he slid the silken dress over her shoulders and kissed her breasts through the muslin petticoat. His breathing quickened. She let him roll her onto the bed and they lay beside each other. 'I love you too,' she whispered. Delfina had been waiting to say these words, and she really meant them. She reached over to turn out the lamp and heard a soft whoosh when the flame gutted. She struggled to free herself from her dress and lay still as Nino removed her underclothes.

When her husband slipped his hand and then his body between her legs, Delfina tried to relax. Angelina had said it was easier that way but Delfina's mouth prickled with fear. 'Nino,' she gasped. 'You're heavy.' She was frightened by the whine in her voice and grateful for the thin petticoat that covered her upper body.

She felt Nino tense and then push into her. There was a scalding pain. She bit her lip when Nino repeatedly thrust into her body. It was over as quickly as it had begun. Nino went slack against her and Delfina felt a warm trickle of liquid on her thighs and wondered if it were blood.

She reached for the nightdress on the side table and spread it over her. She felt as vulnerable as a lamb.

Nino propped himself up on his elbows and Delfina made herself look into his eyes. She thought that her husband looked pleased with himself, like after a good harvest or a decent meal.

She wasn't sure what to do next. She was filled with confusion and wondered if she were bruised. She was a woman now and might even have a baby. Delfina thought of her mother and held tightly to the promised pleasures.

Plucking up courage, she pulled Nino towards her and kissed him. 'I really do love you,' she said.

The following morning, Ludevina walked into Nino and Delfina's room without knocking. Nino had left for the vineyards with his father and Delfina was unpacking into the drawers and cupboards that had been emptied for her. Taking no notice of her daughter-in-law, Ludevina pulled back the bedding, stripped the bloodied sheets from the bed and marched out of the room.

Eight months after the wedding Ludevina approached Delfina as she tended the vegetable and flower beds overlooking the sea. The garden burgeoned with purple bougainvillea and gold-dusted hibiscus flowers as large as platters. Soon tall tomato plants would bear clusters of miniature fruits, some overripe and leaking a watery, seed-filled juice, while other parts of the plants held firmly to bunches of minute lime-green balls. All around, aromatic clusters of wild herbs had seeded and grown. Stumpy basil bushes and feathery stalks of parsley competed for space amongst the garlic and the onions. Chickens cackled around Delfina's feet. Behind the house the ordered lines of the lemon and orange grove were silhouetted against the late morning sun.

Ludevina stood for a moment, feet apart and hands on her hips. Then she rocked backwards, settling her squat figure. The sun was high and her shadow stunted. 'You've been married a good time. You have a duty. The duty of a married woman. To bring her husband's son into the world.' She bent over and her breath was hot on Delfina's neck. 'You are carrying a child?'

It was more threat than question. Delfina shook her head.

'Then I'll have to make some decisions. You must not disgrace us—even if you are a miracle child.'

Delfina understood that her failure to conceive was not her first error. She also knew that it would not be her last.

Near the women a young vine had sprouted pale shoots. Annoyed, Ludevina bunched them together and twisted them behind the mother plant.

A month after their conversation Ludevina again approached Delfina. 'You must go to La Grotta del Bue Marino, off the island of Filicudi. Aldo will row you there.'

Delfina knew she was serious; trips to other islands were not undertaken lightly.

'There you must ask the gods to help you conceive.'

Delfina inclined her head, knowing that a child already grew inside her, as yet just a wisp of life.

Aldo and Delfina set out alone in the fishing boat on a cloudless day. Delfina sat near the prow watching the little boat scythe the water. Shoals of fish swooped below the surface, their movements choreographed to some silent music.

Filicudi was a peaceful island of stone pathways. La Grotta del Bue Marino was wide and high enough for boats to sail into. Inside, light refracted off the damp walls illuminating deep crevices. The only sound was the occasional slap of water on the sides of the boat.

'They say that a sea monster once lived here,' Aldo said.

His unlit pipe hung from the side of his mouth and he did not mention the reason for their visit to this vast, primeval womb.

When Delfina bent over the prow and dipped her hand in the water, it came as no surprise to find that it was warm.

Once again, Delfina was gripped by pain. Soon it would tighten and spear her body, feeding off her fear like a malevolent beast. Over eighteen hours it had intensified until, at each peak, she screamed. There was no escape.

'If you don't hold yourself so tight the pain won't be as bad,' said Ludevina.

'Let her go,' said Lucia, the midwife, pushing her way between Ludevina and Delfina. 'She'll know what to do. Women always do—in the end.'

In her experience, and as her mother Benedetta had told her, the female relatives always interfered during labour, but Ludevina was worse than most. Lucia wished that Delfina's mother-in-law was like Angelina whose hand Delfina grasped. Angelina worked her fingers along her rosary beads with the other hand. She had placed a small plastic statue of the Madonna on the pillow above Delfina's head.

The Madonna stared sadly at the red forked tongue of a green snake that coiled around the small hemisphere on which she stood. She wore a voluminous cream gown pulled in at the waist with a gold girdle. Her head was draped in cream cloth and a turquoise cloak fell in symmetrical folds over her outstretched arms. Around her head was a wire corona with twelve evenly spaced stars.

'Breathe now.' Lucia read the pain on Delfina's face and manoeuvred her sideways in order to rub the small of her back. 'Remember, it will come and go like the tide.'

This time the pain subsided. Disoriented, Delfina thought it had stopped and tried to sit up. She felt Lucia's fingers probe

for the baby's head and saw her nod at Ludevina and Angelina
to wait at the far side of the room.

'Delfina, listen to me. Soon, the contractions will come
again and you'll want to push. When this happens you must
push hard, Delfina. Push your child into the world.' Lucia bent
over and stroked her forehead.

'I can't…'

'You must Delfina. Listen to me.'

'I can't!' Delfina was shrieking now. 'I won't. I'd rather die.
I don't care any more.'

Lucia took Delfina's face between her hands and focused
the labouring woman's gaze. In the darkness of transition,
Delfina's thoughts darted like fireflies. Where was Nino? Didn't
he love her? Why did Ludevina dislike her so much? Would
she ever feel like herself again? Lucia lulled her with words of
encouragement. Nino could not be here. This was women's
work. This was love. She must not be a selfish woman.

Then the pain returned and stemmed Delfina's thoughts.
She gritted her teeth and pushed.

'Push harder, Delfina.' Lucia was businesslike now. 'You
must push harder.'

Delfina bore down and believed that she would split open
and die. But, to her amazement, the baby slithered through her
and her scream was answered by a husky squall.

'It's a girl.' Lucia held the baby in the crook of one arm and
reached for a cloth with the other. 'And she has fair hair.'

Ludevina put her hand to own fair hair. 'Is she healthy?'

'Yes, yes, the baby is fine.' Lucia shrugged off Ludevina's
questions and gave the child to Delfina.

The baby writhed and whimpered. Delfina ran a finger over
her daughter's lips. She lay back, light-headed with exertion and

the rush of love for her child. So this was what her flesh and blood had made. She reached behind her for Angelina's Madonna and pressed the stiff little statue to her daughter's breast. Her mother joined her and the two women crossed themselves and their murmured prayers enveloped the newborn child.

When the afterbirth had been delivered and the room cleaned and tidied, Lucia waited. In truth, she was disappointed. The birth of Delfina's child had carried great possibilities. Lucia had secretly hoped that this child's birth would mirror that of the mother. There was little enough excitement on Salina. Ludevina muttered under her breath, placed some coins in Lucia's hand and pointed towards a wicker basket stuffed with produce and preserves.

Delfina was asleep when Nino came in from the vineyard at lunchtime. Their small bedroom had only one window and Ludevina had closed its shutters against the heat. The wooden slats cast thin shadows on the patch of sunlight in front of the window. The stone walls were bare and cool. Delfina's black hair was tangled and her face was white, like a plaster statue. In the soft light she looked childlike, one arm resting lightly on the baby who lay beside her, snuffling and trying in vain to flex her swaddled limbs.

Nino placed his index finger in the baby's palm. 'So, you are my child.'

In the quiet of the room Nino felt empty. He looked at his family and again felt life fragment, just as it had on the day Ludevina told him of her family in Palermo.

He joined Ludevina in the kitchen, and she kissed him and then held him at arm's length. 'It's good that the child is healthy but your first should have been a boy.'

Nino knew that with the birth of a daughter Delfina had added to her list of sins. He shrugged.

Ludevina was annoyed that she had been denied a grandson and Nino's indifference taunted her. 'I told you Delfina was born on a night of shadows. You need not expect her to do anything in its proper order.'

Nino did not respond.

Ludevina shifted the focus of her complaint. 'It's enough that this child is born just as I have the preparations for the feast of San Giuseppe.'

At the feast of San Giuseppe the whole village gathered to prepare a meal that would ensure the saint's protection of the impending harvest. Ludevina was known for her loaves shaped liked miniature animals, and her flowers whose doughy petals she mounted into an intricate parody of nature. Now there would be more to do, as the birth of a child must be properly celebrated. 'But what are you going to call this girl?' she grumbled.

'Delfina wants to call her Domenica,' Nino replied. 'She says it's the only name for a daughter born on a Sunday.' Nino knew Delfina's childlike devotions irritated Ludevina and that, in naming their baby after the Sabbath, she would again not endear herself. But to his surprise, his mother brightened.

Ludevina remembered that her father had often taken his family to the baroque church of San Domenico in Palermo. There, Ludevina prayed in front of the chapel consecrated to her beloved Santa Rosalia. Nino's daughter would bring her happy memories. Suddenly, although the workload would be heavy, adding the birth of a child to the harvest became a good thing. The village would see this as auspicious. Also, even though a girl, the baby was visible proof that her son could father a healthy child. 'So we'll call her Menica.' Ludevina announced. 'My little Menica.'

To her son and daughter-in-law's relief, Ludevina chose to see her granddaughter Menica as a lucky child, born just as the earth began to sprout. Menica became her grandmother's shadow, padding adoringly after the older woman who gave her almond cake and juicy grapes. At her second Easter, when she was just over a year old, she stood solemnly beside Ludevina as her nonna shaped Resurrection lambs from sweet almond paste. Menica carried her lamb until it melted under the heat of her hand and only its triumphant red flag remained.

Just after that Easter Delfina gave birth to Stella, as dark and quiet as her sister was fair and loud. Delfina named her after the first evening star.

5

All Sicily shrank under the August sun. People floated around the edges of their lives, too exhausted to carry out their daily rituals.

Aluaro Minieri nodded on his balcony. He was eighty-two and age had brought on a wasting disease that sucked the air from his lungs and left him gasping after the smallest exertion. During the long afternoons, his thoughts would turn to his family and he would mutter to himself. To think that I have five children…I have one son a priest. Aluaro ticked his middle finger against his thumb in a gesture of dismissal. It was expedient to have a priest in the family, but not productive.

Another son I lost to the cause. It was wise to heed the call of the Risorgimento, but foolish to pay the ultimate price. One daughter, not to put too fine a point on it, is ugly. And the other a nun. I have only the child of Ludevina.

When he reached this point he frowned and attempted to redirect his thoughts towards estate affairs. But his family's failings obsessed him until he thought he might burst.

It is unfair. This child, this son of my daughter should belong to me.

Pride, however, is an insidious thing and it had settled deep within Aluaro. He would never allow himself to see or acknowledge his grandson, even if it meant that his estate would pass to his other daughters and into the murky waters of a breakdown in primogeniture.

It was in this same hot month that his deputy returned from his annual visit to Salina with news that phylloxera had attacked the vineyards of Aldo and Ludevina. Aluaro planned his course of action and, three months later, again despatched the deputy to Salina.

Aldo shrugged his shoulders. 'I'm sure we can manage.' His brow was lined and his skin was as sallow as dried figs. The twelve days between Christmas and Epiphany served the islanders as meteorological portents for the months of the coming year. This year the predictions had not been auspicious.

Nino was leaning against the wall, biting on a piece of grass. 'Maybe this time the readings will be wrong?'

'No, my son. You know the forecasts we make between these holy days are never wrong. It has been difficult enough without the grapes. If we have rain in July and August, before harvest...' His voice faltered.

Now that phylloxera had decimated their vines, the Palmerino family would struggle to pay Aluaro Minieri his rent. They would have to rely on the profits from the citrus grove and whatever produce they could grow and sell. Aldo rubbed his forehead, pushing into his closed eyelids as if things might be different when he opened them again.

Nino watched his father from under lowered lids. He had harboured his secret since the arrival of Aluaro Minieri's deputy the previous November. He had held it at arm's length, watching to see if like a dream or a vision it changed shape or disappeared. But it had remained, stubborn and enticing, until one day he found he could not imagine his life without it and he felt unexpectedly exhilarated.

The deputy had arrived at midday on the Day of the Dead, the first of November. The Palmerino family was gathered at the cemetery where Ludevina had piled chrysanthemums into the urn in the centre of Stefano's grave. She had laid a cloth nearby and spread it with food and wine. In pride of place sat her ceremonial bread, moulded like two hands crossed on a breast with the fingers spread wide. Aurora pottered about, muttering prayers and singing snatches of childhood hymns.

Aluaro's deputy picked his way between the graves. 'I have a message for you Signor Palmerino, from Aluaro Minieri.'

Aldo was perplexed by the deputy's second visit for the year. He held out a warning hand to Ludevina who had rushed to stand beside him.

'Signor Minieri is very ill. He has given the matter I speak of great consideration. He has decided that these Salina holdings have become a burden. He wishes to sign them over to you and his daughter Ludevina. It is all written here'—he flourished an envelope—'and needs only your signature. I'll wait over there for your reply.'

Aldo was stunned. Before the deputy could hand him the envelope, Ludevina grabbed it. She always knew her father wouldn't forget her. She was still his favourite child. 'He must want to see me,' she said. 'There's so much I can help him with if he's ill.' She began to shake and cry.

The deputy looked at her with distaste. 'Your father doesn't want to see you. That's why he sent me.'

Winded, Ludevina slumped to the ground.

Aldo straightened his shoulders. He wanted the deputy to go so that he could tend to Ludevina. 'There is no need to wait,' he said. 'Tell Signor Minieri that I am honoured.'

The deputy looked past the family group, taking no notice of Ludevina. 'Your son isn't here?'

'My son had work to finish.' Aldo nodded towards the cemetery's iron gates. 'He'll be here shortly.'

The two men farewelled formally and the deputy walked towards the gates. He encountered Nino just outside the cemetery, and Nino was taken aback by this man who pulled him to one side. No one saw the package he slipped into Nino's hand.

Now, two months later, while Aldo lamented his crops, Nino became agitated. The early January sky was leaden and rain fell in sparse, heavy drops. The two men were standing at the top of the citrus grove. Below them white foam dashed against the cliff edges and sent spray into the sky.

'Papa, I have something to tell you.' Nino hesitated. 'You remember when my grandfather's deputy came the second time last year.'

'Ah! The time he gave your mother and me the full worry of this vineyard.'

Aldo's pride in ownership had faded along with his vines.

'He gave me something else.' Nino pulled the package from his pocket and held it towards Aldo. 'He gave me enough money to go away if I needed to.'

Aldo blanched. 'He gave you money! Where does he want you to go?'

'Yes, Papa. He said that I should go away before the phylloxera destroys the islands. He's concerned, Papa. After all, I'm his grandson.' Nino savoured the words.

'You can't leave us now,' said Aldo. 'We need you here to build up the grove and the crops. And what about Delfina and the girls?'

'I've got to go, Papa. I can earn money and send it to you and then you won't have to work so hard.' Nino was excited. 'I've decided to go to Australia. I've heard there is land for the taking. Delfina and the children can join me when I'm settled.'

Aldo was stunned. 'So you are just like the others,' he muttered. But Nino was not listening.

The thick stone walls did not muffle Ludevina's frenzy. Delfina and Nino could hear her from their room on the other side of the villa. Nino opened the shutters and sat with his back to his wife and children, his feet on the windowsill, smoking one cigarette after another. The window framed a black night sky sprinkled with stars. The moon was invisible and without it the stars appeared random and unfixed. Menica and Stella looped around each other in their bed and listened while their mother told them a story of mighty deeds and munificent gods; a story that began in a far away place and travelled the immense distance to where they lay.

When they were finally asleep, Delfina padded across the floor and stood behind her husband.

'You know I must go,' he said, without looking at her.

There was a crash, followed by quiet. Delfina watched Nino grimace. Ludevina's earlier words hung between them. This new world, she had screamed, was like a siren that called but promised nothing. And, once gone, would Nino ever return? Did he not remember that his family was from Palermo? How could he leave Salina when there were so many troubles? And his wife and children? And his duty to the woman who had given him life?

Delfina placed one hand on her husband's shoulder. In bed, he had often spoken of friends who had taken their chances. He spoke not of dreams but of fortunes, not of possibilities but of certainties. She was not surprised. He turned towards her and she placed a hand on his cheek and told him what he wanted to hear, 'It's in your nature to move forward.'

Nino grabbed her by the arms and held her tightly. 'I'll send for you when I've made our fortune.'

Delfina nodded and then raised her head to look out the window. Night had deepened and with it the brilliance of the stars.

With the help of Aluaro's deputy, Nino had booked his passage to Australia before telling Aldo of his plans. Less than two weeks after their conversation, Nino stood in a queue near the jetty at Santa Marina with the other migrants. A uniformed official scrutinised each person's papers and let them return to family and friends. The scattered groups along the seafront watched the rising winter waves and prayed for calm waters.

A tight-lipped Ludevina poked Aldo with her finger. 'It's your fault that Nino's going,' she said. 'If you'd built up the grove earlier, before the phylloxera struck, Nino could have stayed. But he's a good boy. He'll come back and show you what a real man can do.'

Ludevina would not admit that Nino had chosen to leave Salina. Nor would she blame her father for providing the money for him to go. She was convinced that Aluaro had come to Nino's rescue. Instead, she found her scapegoat in Aldo. 'You're a fool,' she muttered.

She turned towards Delfina. 'And you.' Her voice was dangerously calm. 'If you were more of a woman, Nino wouldn't want to leave.'

Delfina felt Aurora's hand clasp hers. She knew Aurora would go to her room when they returned to the villa and console herself with the relics that linked her with her God. But Delfina didn't know how she would console herself. Nino's absence would take away the buffer between her and Ludevina. She stared at the grey ship dwarfing the horizon and busied herself with Menica and Stella, who were splashing in the shallows. 'Your father's about to leave on the big ship,' she said as she pulled the little girls from their game. 'Come on. Let's see who can give him the biggest hug.'

Nino returned with his papers just as the request came to board the rowing boat. He paused, looked at his family and there was a last scramble for hugs and kisses.

Ludevina threw her arms around Nino and howled. When Nino turned towards Delfina, Ludevina wrenched him back and held him fast. He pulled away but let his mother hold one hand while he put his free arm around his wife's neck, pulling her close to kiss her. 'It won't be long before I send for you,' he whispered.

'I know,' Delfina said. 'I love you. Don't forget us when you're in Australia.' She was trying to be light-hearted and was disturbed at her own anxiety.

Menica and Stella clung to Nino's ankles and he bent to cuddle them. Menica stamped her foot and sulked. 'I don't want you to go, Papa,' she said. She began to cry.

'Come on,' said Ludevina. 'Come to Nonna.' Ludevina dropped Nino's hand and cradled her sobbing granddaughter.

Stella wiped at her running nose with the back of her hand. She knew something was not right and there were tears in the corners of her wide eyes.

As Nino leaped into the rowing boat, Aldo rushed forward and slapped his son's back. 'Come back to us. Won't you?' he said. Nino waved his hat when the sailors pushed the boat into deeper water.

Angelina and Fortunato stood apart from the Palmerinos. They had said their goodbyes earlier. When the boat was just a speck in the water they walked back to their house and wept for their daughter and her children.

6

Each day Delfina set off with her daughters on the back of the grunting mule to collect capers or whatever was in season. In summer the girls scampered along the rough tracks, laughing at the billowing clouds of dust and sending falls of pebbles trickling over the cliffs. When it was wet or the frost sharp they stayed close to their mother and the mule. Menica was the stronger, short and purposeful. Stella quickly grew taller than her older sister but moved as if she did not quite trust the ground beneath her feet. They clung to their mother and were happy to be children between the mountains and the sea with their mother set like Mary on a small mule.

In the spring of 1924 a boy from the village ran breathless into the villa waving an envelope. Ludevina snatched the letter, clutched at her breast and sank onto a chair. It was from Nino and was addressed, as usual, to the Palmerino family. Nino had not written for six months when he first left for Australia. After that, the family heard from him every two weeks. But in his second year away the letters became less frequent, first a month, then six weeks apart.

Delfina was shelling peas into a large enamel dish. She kept working, popping green peas from their pods. Finally, Ludevina went to the drawer for a knife, slid the blade under the flap of the envelope and took out the letter. She stood with her back to the window, the thin paper held up to the light. From the other side of the room, Delfina could make out short sentences written in smudged, dark ink. Ludevina read in silence.

'What does he say this time, Mamma? Is he well? Does he still have work?'

'Yes, yes he's well,' said Ludevina. 'He sends his mother his love and says he has work in the orchards.'

Delfina was frustrated. Ludevina did not let her read Nino's letters to the family. She fed her family tit-bits of information and brushed aside Delfina's inquiries as to whether Nino had received her own letters. She consoled herself with the knowledge that in Australia she would be free from Ludevina's unpredictable moods. 'Is he still living with the other workers? Does he say when he'll send for us?'

'None of that matters. My Nino's a good boy! He'll do what's right. He'll be a success and then come home to his family.'

Ludevina rummaged amongst the pile of sewing crammed into a wicker basket in the corner of the room. She pulled out a strip of red fabric and tied it around the letter.

That evening, when the children were asleep, Delfina walked along the cliff, watching the sea tumble against the rocks below. The wind whipped sand against her legs. Her hair flicked her face and her thin red dress was no protection against the sudden return to winter. Delfina thought of the letter. This time she was angry. Nino had abandoned her. Surely, if he loved her, he would have sent for her by now? Turning inland, she passed the outskirts of Malfa, and stopped when she neared Paolo's home. He had recently moved into a two-roomed house of his own. He was sitting outside, mending nets in the waning light. She watched as his fingers made the broken net whole. He suddenly seemed more substantial than anything else in her world.

Delfina faced the sea and watched the last of the yellow spring light slip into the void beyond the ocean. In its final moments the sun flung shimmering beams across the water and turned the nearby fields lime-green, as if this flamboyant display could prolong its life.

Also caught by the drama, Paolo looked up from the net he was mending. As he turned back to his work he noticed Delfina. She had changed. Life with Ludevina had neither hardened nor fractured her spirit, but it had shaped her in the same way as a picture is defined by the space around it. Her mouth was always slightly pursed as if she were trying to make sense of a contrary world. She stared out to sea while her children chased the tides and collected shells on the pebbly beach. She had turned inwards, like her father, relying on some sense of wonder within her.

Fat drops of rain began to fall. Delfina was standing with her back to Paolo, her dress splattered with blood-coloured raindrops. She fumbled impatiently in her pocket, then tied up her black hair with a length of cloth. She turned sideways and there was tension in her straight back and anguish in her face. She was rubbing a twig of rosemary between her fingers, lifting it every so often to inhale its scent.

Paolo stood up, hesitated, then dropped his net and walked towards her. 'A penny for your thoughts,' he said. 'What are you trying to remember?'

Delfina was puzzled and then smiled. 'Oh, of course, the rosemary,' she said. 'I was thinking of the game we played as children, daring each other to describe what a dead soul looks like.' She turned back to the sea. 'I was remembering what it was like to be a child, and then I was trying to remember Nino—clearly. It seems so long and he seems so far away.'

The wind slowed, pulled up by the chill of coming rain. Soon the sky would open and sleeting rain would soak them to the skin. Paolo pointed towards his house. 'We can shelter inside if you like.' Paolo bundled his nets and followed her.

Delfina stood near the window, watching the rain. In between downpours a brilliant rainbow arced over the bay and she called Paolo over to see it. He went and stood behind her. Delfina turned and reached to pull him closer, directing his face to the window with the flat of her hand. His skin felt smooth. At this hour of the day Nino's face had prickled with stubble. Self-conscious, she removed her hand, suddenly aware of an intense longing. Nino had needed her and she had always been there for him. She had expected to be lonely in his absence but not to wonder if need and love were different.

Paolo felt something stir in the woman beside him and when he reached for her it was not with Nino's hungry hands. His tender and inexpert fingers moved from her face to her body like a blind man. He smelled of brine and fish and in his arms she felt like an island, like Salina, suspended and safe.

The shock of their bodies' embrace stopped them short. Delfina pressed her hands to Paolo's chest, pushing him away. She looked at the floor. 'This should not happen.'

She was crying, tears as heavy as the raindrops outside.

Paolo wiped her cheeks with his fingers. 'Perhaps this is how it was meant to be?'

'No, it can't happen. Nothing can change.' And then Delfina stopped. She felt a quick rush of fear followed by the knowledge that she had taken a new path and, in spite of her Madonna and her God and the crucifix on the wall, she let Paolo put his arm around her shoulders and lead her to the bed under the window.

Later she lay with her head on his chest. Paolo was sleeping and his breathing was light. She sat up and ran her fingers down his cheek. He had reached through her shadows and wrapped himself around her and a rainbow had lighted their lovemaking. He was safe and made her feel strong, yet she knew she could not allow herself to love him. Delfina's family held her like an anchor.

Paolo stirred and reached for her but Delfina looked away. 'This can never happen again,' she said.

Paolo nodded. 'I know. This will be our secret, our own miracle.'

He pulled her to him and hugged her fiercely and Delfina arched her neck to see his face. They understood that this small island would keep them apart.

Eight weeks later, Delfina counted the days since she had last bled. At first she blamed the delay on her anxiety but, when another two weeks passed, she acknowledged the truth.

7

Autumn came late that year and a hot sun still blazed in late September. Delfina was in her fifth month and her belly was swelling. She kept out of Ludevina's way and wore loose clothing.

In early October, Ludevina eyed her warily. 'You haven't bled for a while. Are you ill?'

There had been no rags drying and she had noticed that Delfina was pale and her face thinner. Suddenly Ludevina knew. Her face contorted and she grabbed Delfina's arms and shook her.

'You're pregnant. Aren't you?'

She pushed her to the ground, lifted up Delfina's dress and pressed her hand hard on her belly. 'You whore!' There was pleasure in her voice. 'I told Nino you carried the seeds of evil. Now you will give birth to evil.'

Delfina did not move as Ludevina, with deliberate menace, pushed up the sleeves of her daughter-in-law's cardigan. Ludevina's nails were sharp and she dragged them the length of Delfina's forearms until the blood rose. She slapped her hard and Delfina fell backwards.

'Who's the father?' she demanded. Of her long ago evening with Aldo, Ludevina recalled only that she had not fallen pregnant. The islanders had been surprised at the hasty wedding but her father ensured that there was no hint of scandal.

Ludevina glared at Delfina. 'You tell me,' she screamed. 'Who is the father?'

Delfina shook her head, terrified. 'I'll never tell anyone,' she said. 'Especially you.' There was nowhere to run and she held fiercely to the memory of her lovemaking with Paolo. Her thoughts were incoherent and blood was congealing on her forearms, but she knew one thing for certain: this was Paolo's child and in that there could be no shame. Ludevina grabbed Delfina's arm and dragged her to her room. Before she shut the door on her, she bit on her bottom lip and eyed Delfina. 'So, even miracles can go wrong,' she snarled.

For days Ludevina prowled the perimeters of the house wailing at the turns of fate and calling on the saints and angels to deliver her. Then she decided what to do. She would send Delfina away for the last months of the pregnancy. If she was careful it could be kept a secret and the baby, well, that was easily disposed of.

Mario moored his boat onto a rock jutting from the cliff face and waded the short distance to shore. Ludevina was waiting for him, and when she told him of her plan, he frowned. 'What about her children?'

'What about them?' she said. 'They are Nino's children. They have their grandmother. If Delfina goes with you it will be good for all of us. Your wife needs someone to care for her. Her illness must be difficult for you, especially alone on Filicudi. And for us the benefits are obvious. We can keep the baby hidden. With any luck this birth will be like its mother's but maybe this time the child won't survive.'

Mario winced. He knew that Gabriella needed help but had not considered seeking it from a forlorn and pregnant young woman. He also knew that someone had to help Delfina. 'All right. She can come to us, but on one condition.'

Ludevina's eyes narrowed. She mistrusted Mario's vision of himself as a father to the islands.

'When the child is born it will be sent away. Do you understand me? This child will be born and will live.' He emphasised the last word. 'Franco and Gisella Gullo's vines have died. They have no children. The baby will go with them when they leave for America. Do you hear me?'

'The child would be better off dead,' repeated Ludevina. 'I'll make sure it's taken from Delfina straight after its birth. None of us want to be reminded of her shame.' Ludevina nodded and strode back to the villa.

Delfina walked under a faded blue sky to the front of the Coltellis' house and stood on the terrace. She had spent her childhood here, watching the sea and helping her mother cut and stack vegetables for pickling in bottles of all shapes and sizes. At the height of summer, Delfina set vermilion tomatoes to dry on a tiered wooden rack. Her childhood had been blissful. She pushed up her sleeves. Thin raised weals ran the length of both forearms. She ran a hand over her hard belly. 'What a way to come into the world,' she whispered to her child. Her heart sank as she thought of her baby's uncertain future. She took a deep breath and walked in the front door. 'Mamma, it's me,' she called.

Angelina put down her sewing when her daughter entered the room. 'Have a look,' she said. She held up a blue dress, its yoke quilted with bright flowers. 'I've made dresses for Menica and Stella.'

Delfina took no notice. 'Mamma,' she said, 'I've got something to tell you and then I have to tell Papa.'

'What is it? What's wrong? Are the girls all right?' There was panic in Angelina's voice.

'Mamma. Just listen,' Delfina pleaded. She took her mother's hand. Her breathing was ragged. 'Don't say anything until I've finished.' She lowered her eyes and said, 'I'm going to have a baby.' Her mother paled and dropped her hands into her lap. 'It's Paolo's child, Mamma,' Delfina said.

Angelina leaned forward with her hands outstretched. The blue dress fell from her lap. Delfina crouched at her mother's knee and Angelina cradled her while she cried. When Delfina was spent, her mother smoothed her hair and face. 'Why has this happened?' she said.

'I was so lonely.'

'What will happen now? Ludevina? What did she say?' Angelina rubbed her hand across her forehead.

'Ludevina is sending me to stay with Mario and Gabriella on Filicudi. The baby will be born there. But Ludevina won't tell me what she has planned for my child. She's sending me away before anyone finds out I'm pregnant.'

A shadow crossed the doorway. Startled, both women looked up.

Fortunato was weeping when he took his daughter in his arms. It hurt him to know that he could do little for Delfina. On her marriage, he had given her into the care of the Palmerinos. She was Nino's wife and Aldo and Ludevina's daughter-in-law. The future of Delfina and her baby was their decision.

Fortunato arranged for Delfina to meet Paolo on the beach the next morning.

Delfina took Paolo's hand and held it to her belly. She watched his face go pale. She nodded.

'Our baby?'

Delfina nodded again.

'I'll look after you. Please, let me look after you and our child,' begged Paolo.

Delfina pushed away his hand and shook her head. 'I came here because Papa said you have a right to know,' she said. 'But this will be the last time we meet in private. I've a husband and children. If I come to you, too many people will suffer.' Her voice wavered. 'Ludevina is sending me away. I have to go.'

'Fortunato told me you were going to help Gabriella. I'll visit you on Filicudi.' Paolo was agitated now.

'No!' Delfina spoke firmly. 'No one must know that you are the father. Especially Ludevina.' Paolo reached for her but she backed away. By keeping her secret, Delfina fought to preserve the memories of their time together and protect her family. 'Don't follow me,' she said.

The defiance in her voice stopped him.

Mario collected Delfina in late October. Bruised clouds hung in the sky and the air was humid with a coming storm.

'Hurry up! Mario will be waiting,' urged Ludevina. 'He'll want to leave before the storm arrives.' She was watching Delfina pack clothes into a bag. Menica and Stella played nearby.

Menica tugged at Delfina. 'Where are you going?'

Delfina bent down and cupped the child's face in her hands. 'I have to go away for a while. There is a very sick lady and I have to take care of her.'

'What about me? Can I come too?'

'No, you will stay here with Nonna.' She stroked her daughter's cheek. 'And I'll be back soon.'

Sensing her mother's unease, Stella moved towards Delfina but was hooked back into the silence of her grandmother's black skirt. Ludevina then pulled Menica to her and ushered both children from the room.

She closed the door behind them. 'You're no mother to my son's children. It would be fitting if you were to die in childbirth,' she snapped. 'You'll come back to this house—but not with your bastard child. You're not so much of a miracle now, are you?'

Panic sliced through Delfina. She had felt the child kick in her womb and was horrified that Ludevina might contrive to put an end to this new life. After Nino left, the children had filled her days and she knew now that, during her enforced absence on Filicudi, Ludevina would try to take them from her too. Could she plan with Mario and Gabriella to leave her baby with someone on the island? Ludevina taunted her that she would have to be her own midwife. Gabriella couldn't be much help and Filicudi was remote. Delfina was distraught for her daughters; if anything happened to her, they would be left with Ludevina.

Mario rowed to Filicudi Porto and then he and Delfina took the coastal donkey tracks towards Capo Graziano. Gabriella was a sickly woman whose indeterminate illness returned periodically, leaving her bedridden. Delfina would help with the chores now done by women from the nearby hamlet, and wait for the birth of her child.

Three months passed and Delfina's time was close. It was late afternoon and a pale semicircle of moon lay on the horizon. Delfina, Mario and Gabriella sat on the small terrace. Mario and his wife had come to love the young woman thrust at them so suddenly. As Gabriella had watched Delfina lapse into a sad acceptance of her situation, she had felt her own strength return. But she understood that for both of them it would be a brief remission.

'Did you know that in ancient times the women of this island made a pact with the moon to determine the sex of their unborn baby?' she said. 'And they had the gift of being in many places at once.'

'That would be a handy thing for any mother,' said Delfina. She was stitching with the colours of her island. A pile of children's clothes lay beside her, embroidered with dots of yellow broom and red geranium.

Gabriella was distressed by what she knew must follow. She exchanged glances with Mario.

'Delfina.' Mario cleared his throat. 'Gabriella and I know you have often asked us this, and Ludevina made me promise not to tell you, but now we think some promises have to be broken. When your baby is born, it will be sent away with Franco and Gisella Gullo. They'll take the child to America. You must somehow prepare for this.' His voice faltered. He did not tell her that Ludevina had wanted to dispose of the child.

Delfina closed her eyes. A tremor ran through her body. Surely no one could do this to her. Panicked, she decided to tell them the truth.

'Mario, I must trust someone.' She reached for his arm. 'This child is Paolo's. I want you to promise that you will tell him what is going to happen to his child. I want you to tell him that I love him and that I'm sorry.' Memories of Paolo filled her mind but she would not allow herself to recall his touch or smell his fisherman's dampness. 'But I can't speak to him,' she said.

She turned to Gabriella and gestured at the moon.

'I want my child to be a boy. I want my child to be like his father. And, if I can be like those ancient women'—she was crying—'I will never be separated from him.'

Delfina's son was born on a cold January day. Gabriella and two women from the hamlet delivered the boy with ease. As dawn broke, Delfina held her son and wondered how her life could continue.

She spent only two weeks with her baby and she did not name him. While he remained unnamed he was still part of her. She carried him along the terraced tracks of the island and pointed out the vines, the olives, the carob trees and the weather-beaten red rocks. While he sucked, she traced the veins of his body with her forefinger and slid her hands over his flesh, forging her memories.

Mario rowed Delfina and her son from Filicudi to Salina in the early evening. As they rowed, Delfina watched the island of Panarea turn purple under the darkening sky. Dew settled on their clothes and hair. Delfina brushed droplets from the surface of her son's blanket and blew warmth on his face. She watched it change to a rosebud pink and then back to pearly white. He was perfect and exquisite and a deep grief settled inside her. She did not try to stop herself from crying.

Just before they reached Salina, Mario laid down his oars and put his arms around her. Delfina moaned and Mario flinched at her pain. The baby fidgeted and cried at his mother's wail. The three sat together while the boat rocked on the winter swell and the twin breasts of the mountains loomed over them.

When they moored at Salina and stepped from the boat, the baby whimpered and Delfina stumbled against Mario. He held them again before he walked with them to Ludevina's villa.

When Ludevina answered Mario's knock at the door he hesitated, his arm around Delfina and the baby. But Ludevina dismissed him with curt thanks.

Ludevina blocked the doorway to the villa. She folded her arms over her bosom and her gaze lingered on the baby in Delfina's arms. His blanket had loosened and he was waving wrinkled red fists in the air. Delfina struggled to enfold his tiny arms.

'Cover it up,' Ludevina scowled. 'No one wants to see your bastard.' She gripped Delfina's upper arm. 'Come on. You'll stay in your room until morning.'

'Where are Menica and Stella?' Delfina cried, as Ludevina pushed her along the hallway. Now that she was close to them again, her fears for them increased. What had Ludevina told them? Would they have forgotten her?

'You don't think I'll let you see them yet, do you?' Ludevina said. 'Not until the child's gone in the morning. I've sent them away for the night.'

Delfina and Nino's bedroom smelled musty. Delfina sat on the knitted counterpane. The baby fretted in her arms. Ludevina dropped Delfina's bag on the floor and kicked it against the wall. Then she walked from the room and locked the door behind her.

Delfina was agitated. She did not want to say goodbye to her child in this cold room. She walked to the window and flung open the shutters. Holding tightly to her son, she climbed on to the wide windowsill and jumped the short distance to the ground. She hurried along the deserted track between the villa and the sea and sat down on the highest point, near the edge of a cliff to the left of the village of Malfa. She cradled her son in her arms.

'You've taken her to the villa—with my son?' Paolo said. He was pacing up and down his front room. 'I must go to her. I must see my baby.' Paolo grabbed his coat and headed for the door.

Mario rushed forward and held him. 'You must let things be,' he said. 'Delfina does not want to speak to you. But she wanted me to tell you that she loves you and she's sorry for what's going to happen.'

'What are you talking about? What's going to happen? If Delfina loved me, she'd want to see me.' Paolo was shouting.

'Listen to me! Ludevina has arranged for your son to leave in the morning with Franco and Gisella Gullo. He will go with them to America.' For a moment Mario thought Paolo might fall and tightened his grip. 'Paolo,' he continued, 'we all know about tradition and the family. Delfina is giving you freedom and protecting those she loves. If Ludevina finds out that you are the baby's father it will cause everyone more pain. Leave Delfina alone. Be grateful to her.'

'If she loved me she wouldn't do this,' Paolo repeated. He felt helpless. He had respected Delfina's wishes and not gone to Filicudi. Then he had believed they would have time together when she returned with the baby. Now this, too, had been taken from him. He sank into a chair and covered his face with his hands.

Around Delfina and her son the wind harried the fields with frantic gusts, bringing with it the night scents of salt and animal manure. The light changed from blue to indigo in a single brushstroke and clouds scattered in loose threads.

Delfina felt the shift of day to night. The air was silent, and then came the clicking of the cicadas and the boom of the night sea. The wind whipped her hair, a heavy mass as sleek as wet kelp and uncut since the day of her birth. She heard the first evening bells. It was always like this, and always would be. She had grown up with bells. Church bells summoning her to Mass, joyous strains calling her to pray the Angelus, the solemn knell of funeral bells. Bells that chimed the songs of centuries.

Delfina crossed herself and thought of her Madonna, serene above the entrance to the church of the Madonna del Terzito. By now the twin volcanoes of Valdichiesa would have cast their shadows over her, and she would be protected between the two domes of her church while bells rang though the valley.

Suddenly, five kilometres away, on the volcanic island of Stromboli, there was a low rumbling. Aeolus' son, wearied by his banishment beneath the mountain, was becoming restless. Delfina was used to these protests.

'*Si lamenta,*' the island folk said, 'he groans and it is all his own fault.'

The ringing of the bells merged with the volcanic rumbling.

Delfina held her baby in her arms, swathed in layers of soft blanket. The boy strained against his bindings and closed his eyes against the wind. His nose was the flat, unformed nose of the newborn, and the puckered skin of his lips was speckled with blistery milk spots. Delfina nestled him to her. 'You are my gift,' she whispered. 'You must always remember that you are my gift. You were conceived in loneliness and when you were born you brought joy.'

She stopped to see the effect of her words. The baby's bleary eyes opened and looked at her.

'I went to him, your father, long after my husband left for Australia. Long after my Nino left me to wait and wonder. And Paolo came to me and you were born, my gift.'

The child in Delfina's arms gave a faint cry.

'Now they want to take you away. They say that I've disgraced the family, but I know that I've done none of these things.'

She lifted the baby high above her head as if to show him the extent of his world, and then she rocked him in her arms.

A restless darkness filled with scudding clouds moved into the curve of the bay. Every so often a single cloud fragmented and streaked the face of the moon. The wind whistled as it slipped in and out of rocky crevices and mountain slopes. Delfina sat still and the child slept, untroubled by the wind and the call of the future. She watched her son and inhaled his warmth and vanilla scent. She watched his eyelids flicker and his hands clench and unclench. She watched her son and, in the privacy of the dark, continued her conversation, her head held high and her face set towards the sea.

'You will be,' she said, 'as strong as this wind. It won't matter where they send you because you'll return to me each time the wind blows.'

She looked at the child defiantly. The baby opened his eyes again, made a sucking noise and searched for her breast. A sudden wind piled up the clouds, briefly interring the white moon and its waxen light. In the blackness Delfina fed her son and said her goodbye to him.

Long after midnight she and the child returned to the house and slept in the shuttered room she had shared with Nino.

Light came early to Salina, creeping upwards until the sky lay serene and blue. The local fishermen had long gone out and the bay was empty except for a single wooden boat. In the boat sat Franco and Gisella Gullo, bound together in reluctant acceptance of their misfortune. They sat in their boat terrified that some evil might take away their unexpected good luck.

Delfina stood on the beach with her son in one arm and a hessian bag filled with his belongings in the other. Every so often the boy mewled, nuzzled her breast and then lapsed into silence. Delfina flinched as Ludevina's words sawed through the morning air.

'Go on, hand him over,' Ludevina said. 'He doesn't belong to us. You have disgraced us and it is by the will of God that we need not be reminded of it every day of our lives.'

Delfina handed her child and the bag to Gisella and then dropped her arms to her side. Gisella did not look up and immediately began rearranging the swaddling as if to begin the task of exorcising Delfina from her son. This new son of the Gullos would spend his first ten months in Milazzo. He and his parents would then take the train to Messina, the boat across the straits and board a ship off Reggio di Calabria. He would go to America to begin a new life; a life where he would never be surrounded by aqua waters and feel the breath of Aeolus against his skin.

'You,' Ludevina shouted, 'you can go now. There is work to be done if you are to keep things fit for my Nino.'

Delfina turned and walked towards the villa, feeling her child brush by her with each breath of wind. She did not weep but understood that the thread binding her past to her future had been broken.

Paolo watched the little boat rock its way out to sea. The woman he loved would not see or speak to him and had let his child be taken away. Yet he knew that Delfina had no choice.

Paolo forced his attention back onto a heap of tangled fishing nets. At the other end of the tangle sat Fortunato Coltelli, patiently untwisting the knotted ropes with his gnarled hands. He was in agony for his daughter, for the grandson he had lost, and for the man beside him. He stopped his work and looked up at Paolo. 'You know, all will come full circle in the end. It might not be as we wish. But of what consequence are our wishes?'

8

On the feast of the Madonna del Terzito, Delfina and her daughters watched as the Madonna trundled down the street. When the statue wobbled past, Delfina gazed at the blush on her face, at her carmine lips, her eyes shadowed in pain and her fine arched brows. The Virgin's black hair was parted in the centre and swept down her back. It was July and six months after Delfina's return from Filicudi. *Why did this happen to me?* She appealed to the statue. *Tell me what to do!* The Madonna would understand. She had also lost a son. What did the Madonna do when her son was taken away? She hadn't run from her troubles but had been at the foot of her son's cross.

Stella tugged at Delfina. 'When can I give her these?' She was holding a bunch of wilting flowers.

'Soon,' said Delfina, 'when she's inside the church. We have to follow those people at the end.' She pointed to where the procession thinned. 'Then we all go into the church for Mass. You can give them to her when she goes past us down the aisle.'

Delfina and the children sat in a back pew. Menica tucked her hands under her legs and rocked back and forth. Delfina stilled her and the girl kicked out angrily.

'Nonna doesn't like coming here,' she whispered from behind her hand.

'How do you know? Did she tell you?'

Menica didn't like questions.

'When did she say this to you?' Delfina persisted. 'You know how important our Madonna is—and why we come here on her special day.'

The men carrying the structure laboured down the aisle. When it drew near, Delfina held on to Stella as she teetered forward with her bouquet of flowers. The Madonna's head tilted towards Delfina and, as the two women exchanged glances, Delfina understood that she must leave Salina with her daughters and go to Nino. In her love for Paolo, she had stepped outside the boundaries of her island. While she stayed, she would have to fight the temptation to go to him. And, every time she walked to the beach, she saw not only his house, where their son was conceived, but also her lost child being rowed out to sea.

While she was on Filicudi, her daughters had changed. Menica had avoided her nonna's heavy hand by learning to beguile Ludevina, but Stella had become withdrawn. In order to hold her family and her beliefs together, Delfina couldn't wait for Nino any longer.

Delfina followed her mother and father into their bedroom. With Angelina's help, Fortunato pulled out the loose stone in the floor. He plunged his hand into the cavity and pulled out a wad of notes. Breathing heavily, he sat on the bed and counted them into Delfina's hand.

That evening, when the girls were asleep in bed, Delfina wrote to Nino.

Dear Nino,

I must write this letter while I still have the courage.

    I'm coming to Australia, Nino, and bringing Menica and Stella. We've been apart for too long and the children need you. I'm scared but please don't try to change my mind. By the time I hear from you, everything will be arranged and it will be too late.

    Papa has lent us the money for our fares and says we don't need to repay him. But I know you'll want to give the money back as soon as possible. Don't be angry with me for this. Papa just wants to help us. He's also going to organise our tickets and other things we'll need. I'll write again when we've set dates and times.

    I won't tell your mother until just before we leave, so please say nothing in your letters to her. If she finds out too soon, things here will be very difficult. I know she won't be happy but I'll do as much as I can for her and Aldo before we go. Just make sure you send your reply to this letter to my father.

    Also, don't worry if things are not ready for our arrival. Just being together will be enough.

    With love from your wife,

Delfina Palmerino

It was three weeks before Christmas and so far the winter had been mild, most days tempered by a liquid sun. Mario usually visited Salina each month to meet with Delfina and bring her news of Gabriella. But his wife had been ill since August and he had remained on Filicudi until now.

He climbed to the terraced slopes high above Malfa and waited. Only people who truly understood their land could have fashioned such symmetry in the hillsides. He was troubled and chewed on the end of his pipe, stopping every so often to hawk spittle. The years had bent his back and greyed the curls on his neck. He sat in the lee of a chestnut tree, his face to the sun and his eyes screwed in concentration. He watched as an early winter shadow fell over the village below.

A familiar voice came from behind him. 'What's wrong?'

Mario jerked his head and flinched as the muscles in his neck protested. 'Madonna, these bones are not what they used to be.'

Delfina laughed and bent to stroke her mule's neck. 'It's so good to see you.'

'Ah, it's you, is it? The miracle child.'

'My mother-in-law tells me I'm not so much of a miracle now,' said Delfina as she dismounted and sat beside him. 'Tell me, what's worrying you? Is it Gabriella?'

'She's much better now but the pain has been severe and I didn't want to leave her.'

He placed a hand on Delfina's shoulder. 'What will you do, Delfina?'

'I can't hide anything from you, can I?'

In a moment Mario understood. 'Ah, so you will leave us too? Do you know that the population of our islands has almost halved? I sometimes think that Stromboli, without the weight of its people, will erupt in a fiery blaze. There'll be no one left to keep the god where he belongs. But these are the thoughts of an old man, don't you think?'

Delfina smiled. 'Try to understand, Mario,' she said. 'If I go to Australia I'll be with Nino and far away from Ludevina. She taunts me about my son and I don't want her destroying my memories of him. And then there's Paolo. Each day I see him walk along the cliff top to my father's house and I feel so sad. I must take the children and leave Salina. I must go to Nino and find whatever fate awaits me.'

Mario looked at her. 'Yes. You must go. I know that,' he said. 'And in these troubled times our families will lose daughters as well as fathers and sons.' His smile was wan. 'Soon it'll be left to the grandparents to do all the chores.'

Mario stretched out his legs and leaned backwards on his palms. Delfina's jaw was set and her body hunched as if she were about to run a race. He saw that her face was now haunted by her losses.

Wisdom was his burden: to understand more than other people, to know that recent history had shuffled the deck so often that things were no longer in order; the ace had taken the place of the king, the club of the diamond.

Delfina scrambled to her feet and shook out her bunched skirts. Mario rose and pressed her hand between his callused palms. Delfina felt the bones roll under his grasp.

'Perhaps when you find your fate you will bring it back to our islands,' he said. 'You will bring it back here and it will belong to all of us.'

Delfina mounted the mule, tapped its sides with her heels, and they made their way down the rocky path. She looked backwards just before the path curved seaward. Mario had settled on the ground in the spitting rain. Gusts of wind threw cloud shadows every which way. Mario's hands fumbled through the sign of the cross; his eyes were shut and his lips moved silently.

Three days later Delfina got up at daybreak. She watched the mid-winter sun lighten the sky and slip away, chastened. She moved quietly through the morning's chores, the children asleep and Ludevina still in bed. From her room, Ludevina's high-pitched voice called instructions and reminders at regular intervals.

In winter the garden yielded only a few vegetables wet with dew and a handful of wild geranium flowers, their loose, brightly-coloured heads nodding on stiff stalks. Sodden bougainvillea drooped over a rickety wire trellis, their purple splendour reduced to daubs of colour under the leaden sky.

Delfina stood looking out to sea and wondered what Australia would be like. It, too, was an island. But she knew it was large and that Nino lived inland, near a long river. She was used to the smell of salt on the wind and couldn't imagine living without the ocean. She crushed some sprigs of mint and smelled their sweetness. She was confident that Nino would take them to church. Her Madonna belonged to Salina, but she would take her statue of the Madonna to Australia and, each year, they would celebrate her feast day. When Ludevina began banging pots in the kitchen, Delfina sighed and walked back to the house.

Menica and Stella ran to meet their mother at the kitchen door. Ludevina turned from the sink, saw Delfina and was silent.

Delfina summoned up the courage gathered along with the fruits from the garden. 'Mamma, I want to go to Nino. I know he said he'd call for me when the time was right, but it's been three years.'

Ludevina whirled around. Her skirt flapped against her legs. 'What makes you think that my son will want you now? He has made plans. You shouldn't interrupt them.' Ludevina had taken care that Nino did not find out about Delfina's son. She was terrified that her daughter-in-law would reveal her secret, and that her Nino would be shamed.

'I know that he'd want his daughters,' Delfina said. 'I know that it's time to rebuild our life.'

'Are we going to see Papa?' Menica's eyes were bright. She was curious about her father.

'Be quiet,' snapped Ludevina. 'I'm talking to your mother. You and Stella take your toys and go to your bedroom.'

Menica pouted. She tugged Stella from the floor and wrenched her arm. Stella squealed and Delfina bent to console her.

Ludevina took no notice of the crying child. 'What will become of us, left here to look after the vineyards and the orchard?'

'Nino's been gone a long time. We need to be with him.' Delfina was flustered. She was comforting Stella who sobbed quietly while Menica sulked.

Ludevina thought of the house without Menica and Stella, of the daily tasks that would fall to her in the absence of her daughter-in-law, of her son hard at work in Australia. Anger ballooned inside her. She was again to be abandoned by those who should love and respect her. First her father, then Nino, now Delfina. While her daughter-in-law remained on Salina, Nino was not lost to her. It irked Ludevina to think that she remained in touch with her son through the woman he had married. She would be left with Aldo and Aurora, just as in those first empty days of her marriage.

Turning her back on Delfina, she pushed both hands hard against the sink. 'And how will you pay for this? In his letters Nino tells me he hasn't enough money for you to go to Australia yet.' She set to slicing potatoes with speed and precision.

Ludevina hoarded the letters from Nino in her room. Once she'd read and re-read each letter, she put it on the table near her bed, and every night before sleep she placed her right hand on the pile and recited her novena.

'Papa will pay for us to go.' Delfina's voice did not falter.

Ludevina dropped the knife. The blade hung in mid-air before clattering to the sink.

'Like father, like daughter. You have no notion of how a wife should behave,' Ludevina snarled. 'Look what you've done to my son. If you go you must keep that bastard child a secret. You are a Palmerino and must protect the honour of the family. You must promise that you will be silent. You must promise, promise me! Promise me!'

She clawed Delfina's arms, glaring at her with wild eyes, her face clenched and distorted. Delfina stood still and stared. Menica and Stella cowered, wide-eyed, against the wall.

'Promise me!' Ludevina screamed. 'If you don't, I will do whatever is necessary to stop you from going. I will not have my son a cuckold.'

In the wake of this outburst, her silence was unforgiving. Ludevina knew that in denying the child she was acting just as her father had done all those years ago. But she had to protect her son from the knowledge that his wife had loved another man.

'I won't tell him,' Delfina whispered, and with these words she said another goodbye to her son. She looked straight at Ludevina. 'But I will go to Australia.'

The two women stood facing each other: the older woman was bound by ties that coiled back through centuries, the younger woman was caught in a time where the past no longer held sway.

'One day I'll find out who the father is.' Ludevina swiped her arm across the bench top. A pan hit the floor with a dull metallic thud, followed by another and another until her fury was spent and the two women remained motionless, eyeing each other across the littered kitchen floor.

In early January, four days after the feast of the Epiphany, Delfina waited for Paolo to return from his morning's fishing with Fortunato. She had not once done this since her return from Filicudi. She huddled against the cliff for protection from the wind. When the two men moored their boat and saw her, Fortunato looked from Delfina to Paolo and hesitated. Then he walked slowly towards his stone stairs and climbed them without looking back.

As Paolo neared her, Delfina rose and held out her hands. 'I've come to say goodbye, Paolo. You know I'm doing the right thing.'

Paolo did not take her hands.

'Will you stay here?' she said. Her voice cracked and she dropped her hands to her sides.

'For a while, at least,' Paolo said. 'One day I'll know what to do.'

Distressed by his reserve, Delfina put her arms around him and caught her breath at the familiar smell. His body relaxed and he rested his head on her shoulder.

'I would have done anything for you,' he said.

'And because you loved me, you listened when I asked you to do nothing.' She put a finger to his lips to stop him from replying. They sat together on the beach until the tide rose and flooded the pebbles around their feet.

9

Delfina and her daughters left Salina late on a bitter winter's day. The *Osterley* was waiting in deep water directly out from the island. This time, the wooden rowing boat left from the Malfa jetty instead of the main port of Santa Marina. The boat hugged the coast before turning seaward and the island's high granite walls loomed over them.

Menica and Stella whimpered with fear as they watched Fortunato, Angelina and Aldo shrink from view. Ludevina had not come to say goodbye. Delfina fought the dread that she might never see her parents again. She pressed her hand to her mouth to stifle her cry and bent over her daughters. 'Wave your hands at Nonno and Nonna. Wave goodbye,' she said. 'Blow lots of kisses to everyone.' Menica and Stella waved and blew butterfly kisses until their family was out of sight.

The climb from their wooden boat into the *Osterley* was like crossing the universe. Waves butted the ocean liner and the smaller boat rocked wildly. The men's lanterns sent restless, liquid reflections skittering across the inky sea. Delfina and the children inched their way through the black towards the side of their small boat. This sea was the sea of the sirens, the same waters and the same winds that had taunted Ulysses on his journey home to Ithaca.

The three held fast to their suitcases as they were splashed by the salt water. The children shivered in the night air despite woollen coats and their mother's protective arms. They were like papier mâché figures, moulded by the sea and the night, and fragile in the wind. They waited silently to be helped into the ocean liner.

Stella was four years old and a solemn child. The darkness accentuated the whites of her brown eyes and the mist frizzed her black hair. Delfina ached for Stella's tentative steps and the way the child's hand grasped her own.

Menica was almost six and had listened to her nonna. She knew how to breast the wind that whipped the little boat and tossed them about like dolls. She found it easier to stay upright when facing forward.

Stella had not spoken since leaving Malfa and her frightened words in the wind were like the piping of a piccolo amid full orchestra. 'He's not happy, the volcano's not happy.'

The low rumblings of Stromboli came from somewhere behind them.

'What do you mean?' Delfina croaked, unable to stifle her own misgivings.

Stella's eyes were fixed on the blackness. Her panic escalated with each grumble of the volcano. Her fingers dug into Delfina's arm and she pressed close to her mother. 'Bad things happen when the volcano's sad.'

'It's not sad,' Menica said. 'It's only the devils from hell rumbling around the inside because they can't escape.' She was laughing and shaping her arms into huge devil's horns.

Stella shrieked and covered her face with her hands.

Delfina caught Menica's mischievous smile and frowned at her. Then she turned to Stella. 'There are no devils. They say that once upon a time a god did bad things and was locked away inside the volcano. These grumblings are his cries and those spurts of ash and lava are his protests.' She stroked Stella's cheek and looked over her shoulder. The upper reaches of Stromboli glowed with an unnatural light.

How easy it was to slip between worlds. With a groan from the engines and a hiss of steam, Delfina and her children entered the hybrid world of life on a ship. She watched the islands dissolve into sea space. Suddenly there was a loud thud. She turned and saw Stromboli shoot a jet of volcanic red and yellow. Fragments of light hovered, outlining the now distant islands in a theatrical flourish of farewell. There was another thud, another smaller jet, and the islands disappeared.

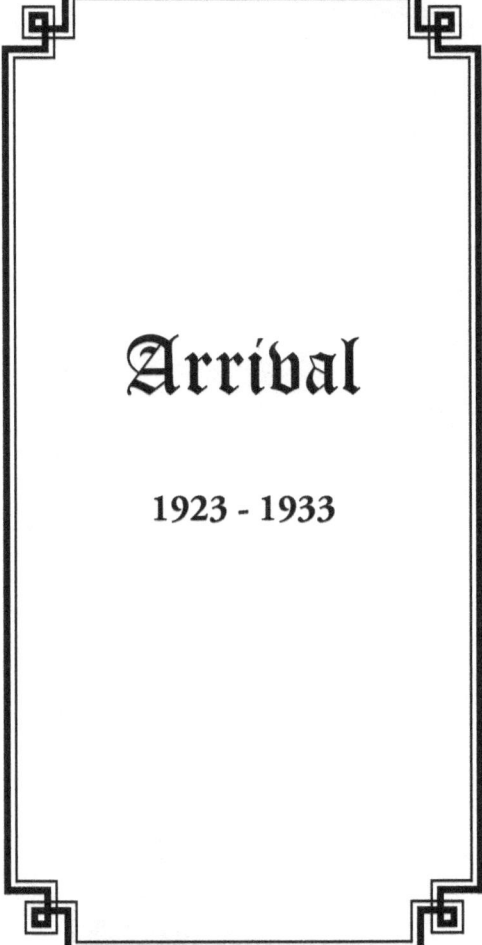

Arrival

1923 - 1933

10

Sergeant Henry Blackman stood sentinel at the entrance of the Mildura police station. He was an impressive figure, six feet four inches tall, and seventeen stone. Despite the summer he wore full police uniform, a lightweight helmet the only concession to the claustrophobic heat. His left forearm lay across the small of his back. His right arm hung rigid by his side. There was good reason for this protection of his left arm. Henry had arrived in Mildura in 1888, a year after the Chaffey brothers established an irrigation settlement they hoped would rival the Etiwanda and Ontario colonies in Canada. The local lads resented the threat Henry posed to their freedom and determined to retain their supremacy. They set up a fight between the new constable and a district hero with a renowned 'dirty right'. No one knew about Henry's 'dirty left'. The young constable made his name on the first day.

It was Christmas Day of 1924 and there had been no incidents. To mark the occasion, Henry Blackman allowed himself some systematic reflection. In the evening darkness, he ran through his thirty plus years patrolling the banks of the impassive Murray River as it flowed through Mildura.

The town of Mildura sprawled across the edge of the desert on the Victorian side of the river. It was 350 miles from the sea and twelve hours by train from the city of Melbourne. A car journey was hazardous on the unreliable roads and there were traps for the unwary on the uninhabited stretches of countryside. Mildura's main streets were planted with gum trees and pepper trees and many were named after the fruits that flourished in the red earth and the long hours of sunshine. Traditional Victorian brick buildings stood beside weatherboard shops and hotels with wide, shady verandahs. The orchards and vineyards surrounding the town attracted droves of immigrants and itinerant workers.

There had been no police station in the early years and Henry had maintained a precarious law and order from his rooms at the Murray Boarding House. To his relief, his wife, Alice, got on well with Henrietta Simmons, a buxom woman who ran the complex of detached rooms with miserly efficiency. There was no lock-up, only a chain and a set of handcuffs. This had seemed to Henry both inhumane and impractical. He thought it much better to arrange a fight between the antagonists and let them sort it out on the riverbank. His landlady baulked at having felons chained to the trees in her garden and was relieved at the arrival of the new portable lock-up. She had overseen its placement in a far corner of the barren yard. An endless parade of petty criminals was further punished by the stench of old cabbage and the odour of congealed mutton drifting up from the fly-blown compost heap.

The years had brought the usual mix of suicides and drownings and parents who kept children from school during the picking season. All these misdemeanours Henry Blackman duly punished in the Court of Petty Sessions at the Langtree Hall. He was thrilled when the witness box and the dock arrived in 1892, and each night had them carried to the police station, rather than leave them in a public hall. He was called in when wooden buildings, tinder dry and lined with crisp hessian, exploded into flames and there was no help except for wet bags and tin buckets. He refereed personal feuds, and did his best to walk the cultural tightrope after different nationalities had filtered into the community. Henry's bête noire, however, was sly grog.

Mildura was not a temperance society. Alcohol could be freely and legally consumed in private; hotels were unable to obtain liquor licences and constantly sought a way around this difficulty. Henry knew that all circuitous routes to problem-solving created their own problems: at the turn of the century the lack of licensed hotels brought about the formation of clubs. Mildura merchant houses acted as agents, buying in whisky and beer for sale in these clubs and the proliferating sly grog shanties. In these unsupervised environments the rough and undesirable mixed with the down and out, each fuelled by a river of alcohol. Even after the parliament, which sat in its grand bluestone house in Melbourne, passed a law in 1916 which made it easier for hotels to gain a licence, the sly grog trade continued.

The foreigners were the main problem in Henry's view. They might have drunk diluted wine from childhood but they buckled under the caustic brews cooked up in sly grog shops. Henry yawned, squared his shoulders and felt his spine stretch. Out of the corner of his eye, he saw a figure lurch down the street into the full glare of the electric streetlight.

Confused by the light, Nino Palmerino threw up his arms to steady himself but fell face forward, spread-eagled across the luminous pool.

Henry recognised the young man from Italy. The thin fellow who lived like a dog at the edge of the workers' compound. The one who worked from dawn to dusk. Five minutes passed and still Nino did not move. Henry liked to give the fellows a head start. He was not averse to letting them crawl off into the desert. He stood for a while longer, pitying the misfortune of the man to have staggered into Madden Avenue and collapsed under his very nose. Perhaps a short stint would do him good, sober him up—until next time. A token arrest would show everyone that Henry did not tolerate drunkenness in the streets. He collected the keys to the lock-up and set off down the street, absentmindedly booting a beer bottle into the gutter.

Nino had arrived in Australia the previous summer. His enthusiasm got him through the hardships of the sea voyage and the protracted train journey to the outpost of Mildura. Stranded in the wide main street of town, Nino had looked left and right. To his right the Grand Hotel simmered quietly, a pale yellow building on top of mud-coloured earth. It was different from the buildings of his childhood, which appeared to grow from their surroundings. In the eyes of the wiry young man, the Grand Hotel, sitting proudly on the desert earth, had conquered its surroundings and heralded his own future. Nino felt anticipation fizz through his intestines like a firecracker.

The next two months he spent in the orchards harvesting peaches and apricots. He spread these out in the sun until their sweet liquid centres stiffened. Day after day, amidst the heat and the sticky little flies, he kept his head down and his mind on the future. He thought often of Delfina and his daughters. He was sorry he had missed their baby years, and realised he might not recognise them when he saw them again. But he was sure they would flourish in Australia. As soon as they were old enough, he would send them to school so they could be like the Australian children he saw romping in the river. And Delfina in Australia? It was all right for him to battle in this desert, but would his dark-haired island wife cope with the heat and the isolation?

Less often, his thoughts turned to Ludevina and Aldo. He knew he would probably never see them again. He pushed his fears aside and concentrated on earning the money to bring his wife and children to Mildura. In his imagination he put them in fine clothes and set them in a cottage on the outskirts of town. When the picking season ended Nino had enough saved to buy an axe and a shovel. For all the itinerant workers, these tools were more precious than gold.

At first he slept rough, curling up at night under a blanket. Itinerant workers moved in packs across the country. In Mildura they lived in temporary dwellings near the river, just outside the town centre.

One evening a man with sinewy arms and a brusque laugh saw Nino asleep under newspapers beside the fence that surrounded their camp. He walked over and kicked him with his foot. 'Hey, dago, ain't you got nowhere to sleep?'

Nino sat upright.

'You're on our place, you know. Get outa here quick smart before I wallop you a good one. You're letting down the tone of the place.'

Tiger Bailey turned to his laughing mates for their approval.

Nino stood up and his sheets of newspaper scattered.

He still wore his trousers but had taken off his shirt. His rib bones were visible under his vest.

It must have been the much-mended shoes placed side by side or the small box of provisions with the upside-down mug that made Tiger turn back to his mates.

A short time later he returned with a blanket. 'Hey, wog, me and the boys think you can stay.'

After that, Nino spent his nights in the safety of the compound. When the weather was clear, he slept beneath a stringy gum tree. When it rained or the wind blew dust and grit into his nose and eyes he leaned a piece of tin against the compound fence and pressed himself to the ground. It was quiet at night with only the rustle of the gum and the crackle of the dying fire. That was when he wrote to the family, and dreamed of seeing them again.

In late November Nino sat under a tree outside the entrance to the workers' compound. The morning sun blasted his face. The horizon merged desert and sky into a thin line with no end and no beginning. The yellow-blue perspective thrilled Nino. The past year had been difficult, but through hard work he had scrimped and hoarded a tidy sum. He had a job and a place to sleep. The shade from the gum tree thinned as the sun rose higher and Nino got up and ambled towards the riverbank, content that, so far, all had gone as planned.

When a man lounged into the middle distance, Nino shaded his eyes and squinted through the heat haze.

'Hey, Nino, my friend,' a voice finally called. 'How's it going? How's life for a fellow countryman in this new land?'

It was a familiar Sicilian dialect, but it was not until the man was almost upon him that Nino recognised Alfredo di Nola. He had seen him only twice. On the first occasion he had been inciting workers to protest and on the second he had been lying in a ditch.

Alfredo leaned against the fence, cursing as the tin seared his bare shoulder. 'How's work in the orchard, my friend?'

He did not look Nino in the eye but stared past him towards the hotel. The upward inflection of his sentence dropped to a tone of menace with the last two words.

'Work is work, you know how it is,' said Nino.

'Enough savings yet?'

Nino had heard the rumours about Alfredo and his men. Even though they were fellow Sicilians, Nino was aware that a man alone was not safe. This was one of the reasons he remained close to the workers and their compound. Fear prickled at the back of his neck and he swallowed hard.

'It's hard to save,' said Alfredo. 'Hard to save enough to bring a wife and children here.'

'Yes, it's hard to save, hard to think too far ahead.'

'I know it is, I know it is.' Alfredo patted Nino's back and let a comradely sigh drift between them.

For a short time neither man spoke. The silence and heat filled Nino with foreboding.

Alfredo tapped against the fence with one hand. 'We're always in need of workers, you know. There's always room for another of our Sicilian brothers. The work is hard and the hours long but the rewards are good—for those who put in that little extra. And there is always the pleasure of being with those from home.'

When Nino did not answer, Alfredo pulled out a wad of notes and shuffled them between his nicotine-stained fingers. 'Think about it, my friend. Think about it. Your wife. You miss her, yes?'

Nino thought of Delfina. Alfredo's words had changed her from a formless memory to a full-bodied woman.

'I can see that I'm right,' he grinned. 'You live in the compound, don't you? With the council workers? I suppose your evenings are enjoyable enough?'

'They've been good to me. They let me sleep near the fence. We talk sometimes.'

Alfredo lit a cigarette, watched it slowly burn, and flicked ash.

'We have huts for our men, and every evening there is a campfire and much singing. The stories we hear. Like the day Luigi cooked a hare in the dark and discovered too late that it was teeming with maggots! Ah, the stories...'

Alfredo was laughing as he sauntered away.

A short time later Nino picked up his empty cup and three bank notes caught in the breeze.

There was no single reason for Nino's decision to ignore Alfredo. He told himself that, in his situation, it was sensible to be wary. After all, no one knew better than a Sicilian that there were dangers in store for the unwary who crossed boundaries in society without being sure of what lay on the other side. Nino's boundary ended at the compound fence. At the end of another day cutting the Mallee scrub, or processing the fruits that grew incongruously in this dry place, the sight of Tiger and his mates was comforting. In the evening, they sat around the campfire and Nino learned about the way of life in his new country. If he moved away from this security, he faced the risk of getting into trouble through simple misunderstandings. He also knew that Alfredo reckoned on the opposite.

Christmas Day arrived, clear and still. Nino watched a group of local women walk to church accompanied by their menfolk. They wore pale, belted dresses, their laughing faces turned to the sunshine. Their arms were slender beneath capped shoulders, and they wore short gloves and prim hats. The men who could afford them wore suits. Nino thought of Salina, of the church with the pierced and prostrate body of Christ lying in its glass coffin, and the cloying scent of candles and incense in the damp air. He thought of the mumbling old women, their faces obscured by headscarves, and the young women, hanging behind with bowed heads. He bent forward and clutched his stomach, pushing hard until the pain took over from the memories.

A breeze brought cries of 'Oh, my dress' and 'Hold onto your hat' as the dust plumed and fanned outwards. The men's elaborate attempts to shield the dresses and hats brought more laughter and some scolding, and the group moved down the road and out of Nino's sight.

Nino thought to follow them into the church but, in the early days of heat and sand, there seemed no God to answer to in Australia. God had not followed him on the boat from Salina or on the train from Melbourne. He had not appeared in the sticky sun-drenched orchards or spoken to him as long days became star-filled nights. Nino's childhood had overflowed with threats of hell coupled with promises of heavenly salvation. He could still hear Ludevina's voice. 'If you do not honour your mother and father, Nino, you will be damned to the flames forever.' And, if the day had been a good one, 'My beautiful boy; a good son will drift to God as surely as the spring winds blow away the still cold of winter.'

Instead of going to church he ate lamb and potatoes for lunch with Tiger and the others, sitting around a eucalypt, its thin branches piled with gaudy red and green streamers. They drank sly grog and by evening they lay together in a heap, slurping beer or whisky as the sky faded to silver-blue.

'Where ya going?' said Tiger.

'Just taking a walk,' said Nino. He was very drunk.

'Don't go out there, you'll get into trouble.' Tiger attempted to stand up but fell backwards among the slumped bodies.

Nino walked along the tin boundary fence of the compound, through the gate and onto the road, aware only of the cool air with its hint of moisture. He didn't even see Sergeant Henry Blackman before he keeled over.

Morning sunlight streamed through the barred window of the lock-up. Hot and yellow, it was broken only by the black rods of shadow cast by the bars. There was no escape from the sun.

The previous night Nino had dreamed of his family and Salina. In his dream each aspect of his life formed its own discrete section. Each of these sections was separated by a grid system that crisscrossed with mathematical precision. From his vantage point within the dream, Nino noted that this grid system was not unlike the roads that divided the flat Mildura town centre.

He saw a boy, all wire and bone, running across a backdrop of vines while mountains soared above him and the sea roared below. The boy did not stop running but trod the same path again and again. He saw a girl, light like a bird, her dark hair blowing in the wind. Every so often a gust lifted her and she teetered forward like the smallest Babushka doll. She occupied the centre space of her section flanked by symmetrical mountains. He saw two children sitting at a table, absorbed in making biscuits. A stream of doughy animals with startled raisin eyes spilled onto the floor. He saw Ludevina and Aldo, Aurora and Stefano, dancing around a graveyard feast, faster and faster, until the scene blurred.

Then there was the village of Pollara, buried in mountain shadows. Above Pollara loomed the slopes of the Monte dei Porri covered in prickly pear. On the beach, grey pitted pumice cliffs reared over the black sand. There was Lingua, open to the sea, where the setting sun threw beams of orange iridescence over white stone houses, and etched the distant fishing trawlers in black. There was Santa Marina, a small bustling port. There was no order in this grid, only a jumble of fishing nets and small colourful boats, and men singing the same refrain. Finally, Malfa slept within a frame of grapes. Nino watched the grapes shrink through a palette of greens and purples until they dropped and Malfa was framed by twigs.

Nino slipped from his dream as if through honey. As he woke, images flickered like the badly projected films shown nightly in Mildura's Wonderland Theatre. Slowly the figures in the grids subsided, leaving his eyes patterned with black crisscrossed lines. In between the lines the spaces were empty.

The suffocating sun combined with the pain that pounded at Nino's temples, each dull thud carrying the force of a punch. He was unable to move and lay on his back, wavering in and out of consciousness. At one point he heard the soft bustle of skirts as Alice Blackman refilled his water jug. When she left, the clean scent of lavender cut the air.

Even Henry had put his head around the door, although he usually left such ministering to his wife. He returned to the front desk. Christmas interrupted the usual mechanisms of law and order. Henry thought it a shame to hold Nino until January returned things to normal. He pondered his next move. It appeared that Boxing Day would be a repeat of Christmas Day. The weather was unrelenting and Henry was glad there was little to do.

Around lunchtime footsteps crunched on the gravel road outside the police station. There was a rap at the door and in strolled Alfredo di Nola. His skin was tanned to the texture of fine, brown leather.

Henry ran through what he knew about Alfredo. He seemed a pleasant enough fellow. He was known to be a hard worker but there had been some rumours. Nothing definite came to mind.

The man had not spent time either in the lock-up or in jail and Henry tried to judge fairly. He jumped to his feet, walked around the desk, and fronted Alfredo. 'What can I do for you?'

Alfredo adopted a mix of deference and formality. 'You are holding Nino Palmerino, I believe?'

'And if I am…'

'I would like to pay his bail.'

Henry did not normally allow bail, preferring to let the system take its course, but it was the holiday season and the court sessions were infrequent. Without understanding it, he acknowledged the web of Sicilian brotherhood. Finally, he thought of Alice who was helping a family whose breadwinner had been crushed under a tractor. It had been a drain on funds and a little extra would go to a good cause.

Henry had learned early that negotiation signified weakness. He named a hefty sum, which Alfredo placed on the desk. The pair walked to the lock-up without another word.

Nino heard the rattle of the lock and sat up dizzily.

'Come with me, my friend,' Alfredo took his arm, 'we have better places to be than here.'

Alfredo's words were unexpectedly comforting. The day had clouded over and the usual clear skies were now a dull grey. In the distance an orderly flock of birds veered sideways before swooping upwards to become dots in the vast desert sky. Nino clung to Alfredo's arm, aware that if he tried to stand alone he would fall over.

In Sicily honour was bound into a complex system of debt and debtor. This network of brotherhood had travelled the oceans and grown with Mildura's flourishing vineyards. It was as intricate as the tendrils of the vine itself.

'You'll come and work for me, won't you?' Alfredo said as the two men walked through the centre of town.

'*Si*,' replied Nino, and with this word he shifted allegiances from the compound with its foreign but clear rules to the cryptic familiarity of his own people.

Tiger shrugged and then affected a staccato. 'You-people-are-all-the-same. This is a new country. We give you a chance, we eat together,' he sneered, 'but you wogs stick together. You don't want anyone else.'

How could Nino explain brotherhood? How could he tell of a past that pulled and repelled at the same time?

Nino handed Tiger his neatly folded frayed blanket.

Tiger turned on his heel and disappeared behind the compound fence.

Nino was drawn back into the world he had left behind, where wives and children far away came to life in a haze of homemade wine, and where duty, in all its guises, kept him vigilant.

'These men here, these men, the ones on the edge of the town'—Alfredo put a map on the table and ran a finger over a group of houses on the edge of the Mildura settlement—'we're lucky to have fellow countrymen who have done so well.'

Nino knew what was coming next. He could smell the unmistakable odour of greed under Alfredo's guise of fellow feeling.

'Perhaps they have a little to spare for us, a small token for the ones who have made things possible for them? And these people here'—Alfredo pointed to the streets on the map where tin shanties battled with the heat, the sand and the red mud—'they have such trouble understanding how to behave in a new country. It is our duty to help them. I'm sure they know what it means to have friends; I know you do. You might pay them a visit, Nino, perhaps suggest a little generosity?'

Alfredo handed Nino a list of addresses and patted him on the back. 'It is only a little generosity, my friend, a keeping of things within the family, a small contribution.'

11

The ship's dining room smelled of sea and sweat and boiled mutton. On their first night out from the islands, Delfina and her daughters stared at the pale meat buried under watery gravy, and the overcooked vegetables leached of colour and texture.

Menica picked up a spoonful of peas. They were boiled to an olive green and oozed from their split skins. 'Mamma, I don't want this. I want food like we have at home.'

'It won't always be like this,' Delfina soothed. 'When we get to Australia things will be like home. This ship comes from a different place and they eat different food. That's all.'

Delfina thought of her mother's cooking, brilliant with the reds and purples of island fruits and vegetables. On special occasions Angelina had stuffed shiny capsicums with rice and the white-orange of seafood.

Delfina, Menica and Stella were the only travellers leaving from Salina. There were other passengers on board from Lipari and Panarea but Delfina's tentative inquiries revealed no one she knew. Each day as the *Osterley* drew further from home, Delfina's anxiety grew. She had hoped that her imminent reunion with Nino would somehow make up for the loss of her son, her family and Salina. But, on the ocean liner, she relived her losses. She realised that her husband might have changed.

She felt inconsolable at the separation from her parents and yearned for her green island instead of this churning sea. At night, she recalled Paolo's last touch but knew he was no longer part of her life. And, worst of all was the knowledge that her baby son was on another ship, in another ocean, and she would never see him again.

Fearful of her emotions and the strangers who surrounded her, Delfina disappeared into her cabin. She unwrapped her statue of the Madonna del Terzito from its layers of tissue paper and she and the children prayed to her each night. She left the cabin only for meals and to check on Menica, who soon overcame her revulsion for the food and grew chubby and windswept. Menica joined the children who patrolled the decks in packs or skipped with long sailors' ropes. She returned to her mother in the evening, laughing and full of stories. Stella observed them all from a distance. Delfina watched with sadness as her ghostly child withdrew further into herself. She rarely joined the other children, preferring to spend her time playing solitary games in their cabin.

Stella was drawing on a large square of paper: her mother, Menica and herself were stick figures on blue wavy lines. Satisfied, she looked up at Delfina. 'Mamma, where did I come from?'

'What did you say?'

Stella sensed her mother's agitation and picked up her pencil. She looked down at her drawing and began to scribble quickly. 'I said "where did I come from?" '

Delfina took her daughter's hands in her own. 'You come from Salina. And before you came from Salina you came from God.'

'Where will I go when I die?'

Delfina pulled her child close. 'You will go to God and the circle will be complete.' She held Stella and rocked back and forth. For the first time since leaving Salina, her childhood God surrounded her and her daughter and stopped them from falling.

On the high seas many passengers succumbed to seasickness and Delfina spent long hours lying on her bunk while the waters heaved and bile burned her stomach. The world rolled beneath her and she felt powerless. She could not tolerate the porridge and puddings and became gaunt and light-headed with illness. Weakened, she feared for her daughters' childhoods and recalled her own for comfort.

She was a child of seven or eight years old, and it was a dew-drenched summer morning. She had gone with Fortunato and Angelina to Lipari to visit a master net-maker. Lipari was only four kilometres from Salina, and Delfina loved its Norman fortifications set on high embankments and its Greek and Roman ruins on remote promontories. Papa often took her walking through the island and told her that they lived in paradise.

The family rowed across in the early morning just as the sun was struggling through the layer of mist coating the landscape. The world was powdered in blue. There were no clear lines: islands, mountains and sea merged one into the other. They rowed in silence and watched darts of sunlight break the water's surface. Delfina would not have been surprised if Jesus with his bleeding heart had appeared above the boat in a halo of light, or if Mary of the downcast eyes had hovered with her hands held out to the family in entreaty. She would not have been surprised by any of these things. She was young and her world was infinite.

Fortunato and Angelina crossed themselves and bowed their heads after they had secured the ropes to the jetty's wooden poles. They looked at each other, nodded and uttered a prayer of thanks to their Madonna for the safe journey. Delfina knew that her parents would then shift the burden of their care to Lipari's Saint Bartholomew. Inside his cathedral, on the left-hand side of the altar, sat an empty brass-trimmed reliquary where the dusty bones of this martyred saint had once lain in an anatomical muddle. The people of Lipari believed so strongly in their saint that even the removal of his mortal remains to the town of Benevento centuries ago had not shaken their belief in his presence.

Fortunato exchanged greetings with the fishermen. There were few people around at this hour. They climbed up through the maze of alleys flanked with yellow and white stone houses and shops. It was too early for business and the hawkers had not yet begun to call their wares. The streets lay in wait for the shrill gossip and the smell of the early morning catch. Angelina stopped to peer into the wicker baskets outside the shops and stalls. Delfina plucked wild geraniums from the roadside until her palms bulged with slim stems topped by tiny heads of petals. Fortunato had a spring in his step. This promenade through the town made him feel lucky to be living on these islands.

After their walk, they continued to the home of Giuseppe Rocca. Giuseppe's house sat above the beach at Porto delle Genti, a little way from the Marina Corta. Here he wove his nets, bearing in mind the size of the fish and the soul of the fisherman. Worked into these nets were intricate designs featuring sea creatures and mythical sea people. Giuseppe's wife was a rotund woman with ruddy cheeks and grey hair pulled tightly back in a bun. She greeted them effusively, hurried off to her kitchen, and returned minutes later with fresh milk and sesame-coated biscuits.

'And so Giuseppe,' Fortunato said, 'what do you have for me this time?'

Giuseppe cocked his head and grinned: theirs had been a long and affectionate alliance. He lifted his arms and spun them across his head in a circle finishing with his palms open towards Fortunato. 'I swear by the bones of Saint Bartholomew that my nets are the best value in the islands.'

Fortunato laughed. 'Can I believe such a thing when the bones of your saint have been long gone?'

'At least they were here,' Giuseppe said, 'and would I dare to swear by such a saint, if what I say is untrue? Our Bartholomew's bones are more solid than your lady's tinkling bell.'

Fortunato made to cuff him lightly. Their camaraderie was as strong as the knots dotting Giuseppe's nets.

Saint Bartholomew was endowed with a particular mystique, thanks to his origins far away in the East. In imitation of Christ he took up his staff and wandered into the wilderness. Many believed that those who sheltered and provided a burial place for a martyr would stand next to him or her on the Day of Judgment and receive intercession. The island of Lipari had reached out to Saint Bartholomew and saw itself favoured by God.

Delfina was sitting at the table, nibbling sesame seeds from the top of her biscuit. She watched as Giuseppe unfolded his nets reverently on the wooden table. Neptune with his trident grimaced at her. On another net Ulysses was bound to the mast of his ship in order to rebuff the call of the Sirens. On a third the chameleon Proteus slipped through the hands that tried to hold him fast.

'These are fine indeed.' Fortunato traced the patterns with his fingers. He chose two nets and placed his money on the table. There was no need to bargain.

As they left Giuseppe's house a fierce wind blew in from the sea. Delfina's hair flicked her face and made her eyes smart. Her dress flapped against her legs. Angelina laughed and bunched her daughter's hair with her hands, holding her close so that it didn't pull. Fortunato told her that Bartholomew meant gift of God, son of he who moves the waters, so he was a fitting patron for this island awash with the forces of the wind. As they rowed from Lipari to Salina, Delfina snuggled close to her mother. When the sun slipped behind Panarea, her floating consciousness heard the crystalline notes of a bell as light as a fingernail on glass, and she knew that she was going home.

The cabin was dark when Delfina woke from her fitful sleep. Lipari still floated before her eyes and she reached to hold down her dress against the wind. She shook her head and squinted in an effort to focus on her sleeping daughters. Then she looked towards the door hoping for a sliver of light from the outside. There was nothing, only the dark and the engines. She felt hot and perspiration beaded on her forehead. She wished she could push out the walls and let in some air. She lay back on her bunk and told herself that she was between worlds and must be patient, but her heart was beating fast and cold gnawed at her stomach.

Doctor Ferranti shifted his attention from Delfina to her daughters. 'Elena, can you find someone to look after the children? They can't stay here.' He shook his head and turned back to Delfina.

Elena took Menica and Stella by the hands. She was a nurse who had boarded in Sicily, assisting the ship's doctor to subsidise her fare to Australia. She had watched Delfina and her children's first meal in the dining room with sympathy. After Delfina had been absent from meals for a week, she worried about the two unkempt little girls who sidled to and from the dining room alone. Then she insisted that Doctor Ferranti check on Delfina.

Elena thought for a moment and bent over the girls. 'While your mamma is sick you can come and stay with me and my cousin. She has a little girl about the same size as you'—Elena patted Stella's head—'and you'll be able to play together.'

'What about Mamma?' Menica demanded. 'Where will Mamma go?'

'Your mamma will stay here and the doctor will look after her. I'll bring you to see her every day.'

Four weeks into the journey Delfina had felt ill and weak. At first she was unsure what was happening, and put her bilious stomach down to sadness. When the rasping cough began and pain shredded every breath, she slid into a fever. Within days pneumonia hacked at her lungs.

Delfina reached out and grasped the doctor's wrist. He was rummaging in his bag and turned quickly, surprised at the strength in her thin arms. Her eyes were glassy and, even though she was looking straight at him, the doctor felt her gaze was focused elsewhere. He bent forward to hear her words.

'Give him to me. Please, let me have him.'

Doctor Ferranti motioned to Elena. 'She wants to see her children. Let them come a little closer, only enough so she can see them.'

Menica went first, followed by Stella.

Delfina shook her head fiercely and made to brush them away.

The doctor leaned forward again to catch Delfina's whispered words.

'Let me see him, please.'

He turned to Elena. 'She has a very high temperature. I think she's confused. Take the girls away and bring them back in the morning to see their mother.'

He stared at Delfina. There was something about her illness that worried him. She was a woman with a secret and he knew from long experience that it was much harder for people with secrets to get well.

Delfina's ashen face and sunken eyes terrified her daughters. The two children clung to each other. Elena led them away.

Delfina sweated and tossed on her narrow bunk. Memories of the islands and her childhood floated just out of reach, but made surreal by illness. She was under siege: fever burning her flesh, hallucinations searing her mind.

She was sitting on her father's knee while he threaded peppers until they hung from ceiling to floor.

Papa Fortunato always began with the same words. 'I believe I am a witness to another miracle from the Madonna.'

In the quiet of the evening, Fortunato and Delfina were silhouetted by the fire and the past.

'Long, long ago when the emperors with their swords and their idols ruled God's city of Rome and Christians laid down their lives, a hermit came to Salina for refuge.'

'What is a hermit, Papa?' Delfina always asked this question.

'A hermit is a man who is touched by God.'

'Is that bad, Papa? Did God hurt him?'

'No, the touch of God is light, like a feather on the heart. It doesn't hurt. It's just that some men can't bear to see this honour given to another.'

She was six years old but Delfina understood. After all, didn't Antonio, the village lunatic, yell and shake his fist on feast days and pick the heads off the bulbs that grew outside the sanctuary?

'The hermit brought with him an image of the Madonna. He lived in Valdichiesa, between the peaks of our twin volcanoes, in a hut made from dried grasses and branches. He prayed to the image, which he placed in a natural grotto in the hillside. We call this the first site of the Madonna.' Fortunato always said this with extra emphasis. 'Those who believed came from afar to pray with the hermit. They rowed from Lipari and together with the hermit they erected a stone building for our glorious lady. They came from as far away as Sicilia, Calabria, Napoli.' As he mentioned each place Fortunato raised his arms higher into the air.

'They were like the kings who came to see Jesus,' Delfina added.

'Yes,' Fortunato nodded, 'they too were holy pilgrims. But we are born to be tried, born to rebuild.'

Delfina snuggled closer.

'Hundreds of years ago an earthquake struck our green island and the sanctuary fell to the ground, but we were not discouraged.'

'But you were not born,' Delfina said.

'Those who believe do not belong to any particular time. That is the joy of belief. Time is human and prevents some men from seeing God. They think only of their life on this earth.'

'Our Padre Giovanni says that we'll live forever,' Delfina said proudly. 'He says there is another world.' She hoped that this world would be just like Salina with its hillsides covered in flowers, its purple-blue sea, and its islands always visible on the horizon.

Fortunato patted Delfina's head. 'Some fifty years later the sanctuary was rebuilt, larger and more beautiful than ever.' Fortunato crossed himself several times. 'His Holiness consecrated it to the Madonna.'

'What happened then, Papa?'

'This was the second site of the sanctuary. Centuries passed and our island was invaded again and again. People scattered and returned but the sanctuary became a ruin and was covered with shrubs, grasses and flowers. On the twenty-third of July, in 1622, some men from Lipari were clearing land at a site near the old sanctuary. A man named Alfonso Mercorella was alone while the others took logs to the shore. He heard the sound of a small bell and saw a beautiful woman carrying this bell in her right hand. He moved nearer to the woman and its tinkling became clearer. But the woman disappeared. The other men agreed to clear the area in the hope of finding her again; instead they found the ruins of the old sanctuary, built almost a thousand years before. On a freestanding stone, near what looked like the original altar, was a picture of Mercorella's vision. It was another miracle. The Madonna had led them to the third site of the sanctuary.'

Fortunato crossed himself again. 'Of course, the sanctuary of the Madonna del Terzito was rebuilt and stands to this day.'

'And your miracle, Papa?' This was Delfina's favourite part.

Her papa put his hand under her chin and lifted up her face. 'I prayed in the church the day you were born without breath.'

'Did you see the lady, Papa?'

'Alas, no, but I felt her breath on the air and carried it home to you.'

Delfina's fever broke in the early hours of the following morning, scythed from her as if with a knife blade. She heard again the whirr of the engines, the rhythmic slapping of the sea at the sides of the ship, and the whimpering of her two small girls. She waited for the anxiety or the fever, but they had been replaced by emptiness.

In the following days Delfina slipped between sleeping and waking. Her skin was now the colour of bone and stretched over her cheekbones. She lay on her bunk relieved of feverish visions but stranded by weakness, no longer sweating, but parched. The knife-blade had removed not only the fever but also the past. She tried to conjure up the images that had soothed her, but in their place there were only the white walls of the cabin and the muffled thump-thump of the ship's engines.

Doctor Ferranti still visited daily. The resilience of these displaced people always amazed him. When he was convinced that Delfina would not relapse, he sent Elena to bring Menica and Stella to the cabin. The two girls crept towards Delfina. This new life was full of prohibitions and for the period of her illness their mother had become one of them.

'It's all right. Your mother's weak but she'll soon be well. You must be gentle and try to help her. Go to her.' Elena pushed the girls forward and joined the doctor near the cabin door. 'Poor little things. We can only hope that life is better for them in Australia. Apparently she has a husband there.'

'At least she will get to Australia,' Doctor Ferranti said. 'I heard last night that recently a boat carrying some migrants bound for America capsized off the coast of Reggio di Calabria and they all drowned, every last one. May they rest in peace.'

Menica and Stella sat beside Delfina but their mother said nothing. Delfina had heard the doctor's words and thought only of her baby she had put on the boat with Franco and Gisella Gullo. She had not even given him a name, and his first days had been a series of leave-takings. He had never felt his father's embrace. He had been forced from her and then from Salina. Delfina did not have the strength to press for details about the drownings. Her memories of her son were too fragile to face the possibility of his death. She lay still and let them think her illness had made her cry.

She listened in the night for her daughters' snuffling. She clung to them, insisting that they not leave the cabin. Elena brought their meals and was even more perplexed by Delfina's withdrawal.

Delfina could not tell anyone about the pain that possessed her. Days passed while the sea heaved around them and they drifted like ghosts around the edges of their own lives. Many times she thought of Fortunato and Angelina, and of Paolo, but she now knew there were places where God seemed absent.

'It's Australia! We're here! Come! Come! Everyone up on deck!'

A deckhand ran through the ship yelling at the top of his voice. People rushed out of cabins and called to each other to hurry.

Delfina heard the calls and reached for a cardigan. As she slipped it over her shoulders, she fingered the sharp set of her collarbone and the hollow below.

'Mamma! Quick! Quick!' Menica and Stella burst into the cabin and pulled at Delfina's arms. 'Come, Mamma, quickly!'

Delfina laughed. 'Why are we in such a hurry?' she teased.

'It's Aus-tral-i-a.' Menica was jumping up and down, enunciating a syllable per jump.

'It *is* Australia,' Stella echoed.

The promised land was no more than a darker colour breaking the line of the horizon. Morning mist turned the ocean grey like the sunless sky. Delfina watched the land gain form. She felt no joy but only the dullness that comes at the end of a long ordeal.

The ship berthed at Port Melbourne pier at the end of the summer of 1926. Delfina waited on the deck with her daughters.

On each side stretched an expanse of beach with yellow sand and rows of buildings flanking the shore. Unlike her islands, the land appeared to have no contour. She had heard of the vast spaces and their sense of freedom. The passengers on board had spoken of little else. But Delfina felt as if someone had removed the arms that had cradled her since birth and she had come to a universe without end.

There was a soft bump as the ship nudged the pier. Overcome with excitement, Menica and Stella ran from one section of the railings to the other, bobbing up and down between the passengers who crammed two deep along the side of the ship. Delfina and the children were at the back of the throng. Those around them were calling out the names of relatives and friends. The trip had been too long and the hopes were too high to waste a single minute. Every so often a gasp or a strangled saintly evocation testified to some longed-for reunion. A quick sign of the cross, a flood of tears, hugs and kisses, and then the first steps in a new land.

Delfina watched the paper streamers float before they fell to the ground. She craned her neck to keep the girls in sight, pulling nervously at the buttons of her cardigan.

A deep male voice cut through the babble. 'Delfina!'

Delfina started. At the sound of their mother's name, Menica and Stella stopped running. The three of them turned to search the swarm of faces on the pier below.

'Delfina, here, over here!'

Nino stood to the left of the crowd. He wore a pinstriped suit, a white shirt and a crimson tie. His hair was slicked back off his forehead and he had grown a moustache. He tapped the ash from his cigarette with his forefinger and rocked from heel to toe, as if this slight elevation would lift him high enough to see above the crowd. Through the mass of people and the falling multi-coloured streamers the young husband and wife looked at each other for the first time in three and a half years. Nino saw a thin, pale woman in an ill-fitting dress, at odds with the black-haired beauty of his memories. Delfina saw a man who was still wiry but heavier than the boy who had left her on her island. She tugged at the girls to take notice of the man on the pier.

'There's your father. Look! Look!' Delfina leaned over the ship's railing to point. Stella looked towards Nino but was distracted by the tension in her mother. Menica looked her father up and down and approved of the smile that played behind his black moustache.

Delfina straightened her crumpled skirt and smoothed the loose strands of hair from her face. She took a deep breath and grasped the hands of her daughters as they worked their way towards the gangplank.

Nino struggled through the crowd. 'You're here at last,' he called. He reached his family and embraced Delfina. 'I've missed you so much,' he whispered. Menica and Stella clung to their mother's legs.

Delfina smelt her husband's unfamiliar shaving cream and for a moment felt like a stranger. He took her face in his hands and kissed her. 'I've missed you too,' she said. Tears ran down her cheeks. She had so much to tell him but she would save her words until they were alone. She squatted beside the girls. 'Say hello to Papa,' she said.

'My! Are these my daughters?' As Nino let her go and bent to greet his children, Delfina's hand lingered on her husband's suit.

Nino reached for Menica who let him hug her. Stella resisted him and glanced at her mother for reassurance. 'It's your

Papa, Stella,' she said. 'This is the place Papa came to when you were a baby. Now we're all going to be together.'

Delfina looked up at Nino. 'It's been a long time,' she said. 'For them. For all of us.'

12

The train edged forward and then shunted backwards. It came to a standstill with a belch of steam and the squeal of brakes. Despite the summer, the night air was cold. Delfina shivered. The train's black bulk hid the stars, foreign, misplaced stars which spread out like a rash. Delfina felt like a small animal that had travelled far from its territory. Where did she belong in this dry and foreign land?

She watched Nino through lowered eyes. It had been twelve hours between the ship's arrival and the train's departure for Mildura. Delfina was numb with exhaustion. Terror waited at the edges of her thoughts ready to pounce if she let down her guard.

Nino's voice cut through air that was heavy with smoke and steam. Particles of grit smudged his face and bare arms. 'Hurry up! If you don't get on it'll leave without you!'

He heaved the last of their bags and cases onto the train and reached for the children. Menica lifted her arms towards her father and thrust her body forward. Nino grinned and swung her into the carriage. She laughed. 'Mamma, come on, quickly! Listen, the train sounds just like our volcano!'

Nino rested for a moment before reaching down for Stella. He had taken off his jacket, pushed up his shirtsleeves and now leaned on the side of the train, his thumbs tucked behind his braces. Delfina recognised her husband's suppressed energy. She also noticed an easy confidence she didn't recognise.

When Stella didn't respond to her father's beckoning, Nino leaped from the doorway of the carriage, landing with a thud beside her. 'Come on little one. We're waiting for you!' Grabbing her by the arms, he hoisted her up. She was as stiff as a peg doll and from the doorway looked back desperately for her mother.

Delfina picked up her carry bag. It was the first time she had been close to a train and she walked uncertainly. Nino sensed her fear and took her hand. He had not touched her since that morning. She looked at him and blushed as their fingers interlocked. Nino's fingers were slimmer than she remembered and his hands were bony. She caught her breath and wondered at how this intimate act could make them seem like strangers.

Salvatore di Maggio watched Nino's efforts to board his family. He slouched against the train's green leather bench, his legs spread over two seats. His hands were jammed into his pockets and he was alert with curiosity. This was not the first Sicilian woman he had seen arrive in Australia. They all wore the same expression, a mix of apprehension and awkwardness. Then most of them disappeared into the backgrounds of their husbands' lives. He turned to his companion, 'What do you think of her?'

Gaspare flicked ash from the compartment window and drummed his fingers on the glass. 'Simple enough! No problems there.'

Stella hesitated at the compartment door before edging along the bench to her sister. Menica was leaning out the window which she had pushed up until the metal clips clicked into place and she was sure it would not fall. As she edged towards Menica,

Stella kept one hand on the bench and both eyes on the two men opposite. Gaspare was almost bald and his head was shiny with sweat. His fat belly bulged over the top of his trousers. Stella's grave eyes widened and one forefinger went to her mouth.

'Pretty little thing,' Gaspare observed, 'which is more than you can say for the mother. She's as scrawny as a skinned rabbit. Nino told Alfredo she was, well, you know…' He made a few lewd gestures.

Salvatore shifted in his seat. 'Enough Gaspare, the kid's still watching. How do you think Nino went?'

'He should be all right. Giorgio thought he could get away with it; he thought moving to Melbourne meant he didn't have to pay.'

'Does Alfredo always follow them up?' Salvatore said.

'Depends. Our Giorgio's made himself a bit of money.' Gaspare bit his lip and raised his eyebrows. 'In the early days we gave him money and advice. He shouldn't have forgotten this. Nino is proving to be good at persuasion.'

'Where did you put the money?'

'Don't worry. Once he'd done the job I put it somewhere safe. Nino was too busy worrying about the wife and kids. That'll keep him busy for a while. Skinny or not, she's still a woman. And if that's not enough there are always the others.' Gaspare winked and grinned.

Delfina stood in the doorway, dazed, blocking Nino's entrance to the train. There was a whistle and the train spewed out coal dust and steam before lurching forward. Nino shouted and jumped aboard, pushing Delfina into the compartment. 'Move in! What do you want? To leave me on the station?'

Delfina looked at him blankly and tears ran down her cheeks.

Salvatore and Gaspare looked away. The two girls stared at their parents, then swivelled back to watch the new land gather speed out their window.

Nino pointed towards the seat and Delfina sat down. She felt as if every step she took was into the unknown, and almost every word she heard was incomprehensible. Perched on the edge of the bench, stiff with panic, she clutched her bag and tried to stifle her tears.

'Sit back,' Nino said.

Delfina did not move.

It was only then that Nino realised he had been speaking to his wife in English.

There were four carriages in total, three for the second-class passengers and the fourth for first. When Delfina crept down the corridor, she noticed the sleeping berths and the gloved women. She lowered her head and pulled her cardigan closer to her.

The journey to Mildura was a night of noise and jolting, punctuated by whistles and the singsong calls of guards and porters. No one entered their small compartment, so the Palmerino family and their two companions had the luxury of sharing a space meant for eight. Nino, Delfina and the girls sat along one wall while Salvatore and Gaspare occupied the opposite bench. As the train steamed away from the scattered city lights and the black ribbons of roads, it stopped intermittently on the brink of a crossroad or ground into an empty station. When they were delayed at a town called Maryborough, Delfina watched a car chug along the road followed by two whinnying horses and their riders. The road tapered until it disappeared into the night. She watched the car and its entourage grow smaller until they too vanished.

The children fell asleep, undeterred by the upright seats. They curled into tight balls using Nino and Delfina as pillows. Above their heads an elaborate pressed metal lantern shed a harsh glare on their pinched faces.

Salvatore stayed awake for a long time. He watched Nino nod against the window while his young wife sat erect, staring at the landscape. When Gaspare's snores intensified, Salvatore kicked him, but his companion only mumbled and started snoring again. Salvatore felt sorry for Delfina and bent forward to catch her eye. 'Are you all right?' he said. 'Would you like a drink?' He held out a flask.

Delfina shook her head and leaned back against the bench.

Salvatore took a swig from the flask. He knew it was hard to settle into a new life and Delfina did not seem like a robust woman.

Around midnight Delfina fell into an uneasy dream in which ships and trains, cars and horses flashed by. She woke with each jolt of the train, and more distorted images lumbered across her field of vision. The hills of the Great Dividing Range, the one variation on the landscape, had passed by under cover of darkness.

Near five in the morning, a rosy smear near the horizon paled to pink, then to turquoise, before dissolving into the bleached blue of an outback summer day. Delfina watched the morning unfold against the flat landscape. Dry paddocks stretched into the distance. Dusty sheep grazed the dun coloured earth. Delfina felt exposed and breathless.

Suddenly there was a childish whimper. Stella stretched out her legs, pushing hard against Delfina. She rubbed her eyes and sat up, bewildered by the light and the movement of the train. 'Are we home yet?'

Delfina lifted the child's head into a more comfortable position. 'No, not for a little while.'

'I don't want to go any more. I want to get off!' Stella's voice rose, a childish singsong in the island dialect she had only just begun to master. 'I want to get off the train.'

Delfina looked at Nino. He was staring at the child sobbing in her lap.

'She's such a baby!' Menica rolled her eyes.

'You're a big girl and she's only little,' Delfina scolded. 'Hush now, both of you, we'll soon be home.'

Panic spiralled inside her: she did not know where home was. She turned to Nino for reassurance.

'Where will we live?' she asked.

'We have a house on a fruit block, a way out of town. There's quite a bit of land and it's near the river.'

'What's a fruit block?' Delfina asked.

Nino thought for a moment. 'The land around Mildura is sold in lots large enough to plant fruit trees or vines. So they call it a fruit block.' He raised his eyebrows and shrugged.

He didn't tell Delfina about the lack of water and the ferocity of the heat. All this would be obvious soon enough. And he didn't want her to appear any more frightened. He had to keep face in front of Salvatore and Gaspare. Instead he told the girls about the orchards with peaches and apricots and little bush flies.

'Can I help you pick the fruit?' Menica said. 'Like I help Nonno at home?'

'No, not like home. Mildura is much bigger than Salina and I have other work to do besides the orchards. You'll stay with Mamma and help her in the house.'

Menica frowned. 'When we arrive, can I go down to the sea?'

'There's no sea. The sea's a long way from Mildura.'

No sea. It was not possible. On Salina, Menica had gone down to the sea many times each day. She pushed her feet hard against the opposite bench and screwed up her face.

No sea. The words rang in Delfina's ears. Of course, she had studied her father's map and knew that Mildura was a long way inland. But she was exhausted and fearful and she grasped her arms across her stomach and pushed down, struggling with the realisation that she had not come to the end of her journey but was only just beginning.

Nino did not explain further and Delfina did not ask. He was irritable. He turned back to the window and lit a cigarette. Post and wire fences rolled past, the only dividing lines between vast paddocks. Occasionally the train changed direction and the amber landscape moved through a palette of golds and browns, or some longer wheat-coloured wild grass shimmered in the wind.

Battling boredom, the men exchanged phrases in their own dialect peppered with disjointed Australian idioms. Delfina strained to understand. She clung to the few recognisable phrases, but the meaning remained lost. Nino had taken on another life and another language. Their past could only be spoken of in old words.

13

The train pulled into Mildura station a few minutes after nine o'clock. It was so open. So flat. Delfina stood as if paralysed while the dust, as soft and yellow as powdered mustard, eddied around her feet and dissolved in the hot air. She licked her lips. The road ahead was brown and the houses were built from sun-bleached wood. The dry heat made Delfina feel as if she had stepped into an oven; it sapped what was left of her energy. Across from the station gum trees stretched into the distance, their thin grey leaves languid. Behind the trees the Murray River lay immobile, deep and wide, yellow and brown, the gum trees mirrored across its width.

No one took any notice of the young woman shivering in the heat. The area around the station was bustling; cargo was delivered and family, friends or the latest batch of workers were collected. Stella and Menica wandered here and there examining their surroundings. They rubbed the talc-like dust between their fingers and walked to the edge of the road to watch the cars being cranked, and the boxes loaded onto trucks or drays. Delfina heard Nino exchanging greetings with people while he heaved their belongings onto a rickety cart.

A great deal had changed for Nino since he went to work for Alfredo di Nola. He had found the lure of a brotherhood irresistible. It was not that he clung to his past. He embraced the wide land that stretched forever, devoid of the sudden dips into shadow that could trap a man and prevent him from moving forward. No, the past was simply that—the past. What he wanted was the security of a hierarchy. In Australia there was work but he lacked a sense of place and the possibility of power. He shared this need with the other men who came with their dreams and their plans and found themselves cast as outsiders. They each tried old ways in the new land, understanding that some would fit and some would not.

Nino finished loading the bags and walked over to Delfina. Gaspare and Salvatore joined them.

Gaspare ground his butt under his foot and looked straight at Delfina. 'So, what do you think? Do you think you'll like it here?'

Delfina gaped at him with eyes that were bloodshot with fatigue. How could she tell this stranger that all she felt was thirst? She longed to hear the rush of the sea, to feel the morning air damp with mist, when even the driest days of summer were tempered by water. There was nowhere to hide in this flat land around her. There were no mountains tumbling with stones thrown by capricious volcanoes. No grottoes and shrines filled with offerings of flowers and food by black-clad women and laughing children. And, strangest of all, there was nowhere to climb. There was nowhere to view the world from on high and feel that God was in his heaven.

'It'll be good to be home. The children are tired.'

'You'll settle in quickly, make a home for our Nino here! Won't she, Nino, eh!' Duty done, Gaspare dismissed Delfina from his mind. He put his arm around Nino's shoulders. 'You did a great job in Melbourne,' he said. 'Just think of the money.' He rubbed his fingers under Nino's nose and Nino laughed.

At that moment a black car pulled up. A door banged and Alfredo di Nola joined the group on the roadside. 'How did it go?'

Alfredo spoke to Gaspare but he was watching Nino. It was the first time he had trusted Nino to carry out a job. The arrival of Nino's family had tied in well and he knew that Gaspare and Salvatore's experience would see it done properly.

'My friend here,' Gaspare pointed to Nino, 'has done well. You'll be pleased.' He took a wad of notes from his pocket and gave them to Alfredo.

Alfredo shuffled the notes like a pack of cards and, with a showman's sleight of hand, removed three from the centre and gave them to Nino. His eyes shifted to Delfina and his relief was visible: a fragile and displaced wife would cause no bother to Nino. 'Buy a little trinket for the wife.'

Alfredo shook Nino's hand and slapped him on the back. Then he bowed to Delfina before walking swiftly back to the car.

Gaspare ground another cigarette under his heel and looked about for Salvatore. 'Eh, Salvatore, what are you doing? Hurry up!'

Salvatore was squatting on the ground tossing pebbles into the air and trying to catch them on the back of his hands. The two girls squatted near him, watching intently.

'He's a kid, this one, what do I do, eh?' Gaspare mocked.

Salvatore stood up, dusting his palms, and the two men headed off in the direction of the Grand Hotel.

Across from the station Henry Blackman watched the exchange. He was two months off retiring and was tired of fighting the sly grog trade, and of keeping an eye on the migrants drawn to the vineyards and the orchards. Now there was a new menace: a little bit of Sicily in Australia. Henry Blackman was secretly glad to leave that particular problem to the next sergeant.

He pitied the slight woman who had not moved during the men's dealings. He knew the poor thing would disappear inside one of the tin shanties on the newly created fruit blocks and never be seen or heard of again. There's little else you could do when your husband was up to no good and you didn't speak the language.

Henry thought of his own Alice, jolly in her full skirts and large sun hat, chivvying the locals who found themselves in the lock-up. There was no nonsense about Alice. He was sure she would enjoy their retirement. She would flourish in the cool of the mountains just as she had in the desert heat. Henry cast one more glance at the scene opposite him. He resolved to prepare an eleventh hour report for his replacement.

The Palmerino family climbed into the cart and settled amongst the luggage for the slow journey to the fruit block. They passed along the wide streets of Mildura. Through the open doors of the department stores Delfina glimpsed huge floor spaces bordered by wooden counters. Outside, aproned storekeepers kept the dust at bay with wide straw brooms. Colourful painted signs hung overhead: J.H. Shilliday, Cash Storekeeper, Grocer, Ironmonger, Draper & Timber Merchant, General Storekeeper; George A. Nash, Federal Cash Store, Baker & Grocer; Jones, Livery & Bait, Stables. She reached towards Nino for an explanation. He was talking to a man running alongside their cart and signalled impatiently that he would tell her later. The morning was in full swing and the roads and footpaths were dotted with shoppers, jinkers and carts. People wore broad-brimmed hats, and some of the better dressed carried parasols. Everything seemed enormous to Delfina. The sun, the shops, the wide streets. Even the people appeared large, with their hats and their sauntering stride. Stella and Menica withdrew into a watchful silence.

The family headed north-west. For a while they travelled parallel to the sleepy river. They passed low dense scrub, its desert green under a shroud of dust. Despite the jerking of the cart, Delfina and the girls fell asleep, leaving Nino with a mounting anxiety. He looked at the woman by his side. She had changed, and part of her was not really here at all. He frowned in irritation; she would always be waiting at the end of his day, flanked by these two silent children. The children filled him with alarm. Stella was a stranger and Menica was just like his mother.

Nino did not dwell on these thoughts; in Australia he had learned to manoeuvre. He turned his mind to his last conversation with Alfredo, and the memory of his boss's praise made him grin with pleasure.

Nino's work for Alfredo had enabled him to purchase a ten-acre block. One boundary ran along the Murray River and the remainder formed a triangle as it veered inland. He had built their hut not far from the water's edge, an amateur but effective mix of waterproof hessian and galvanised iron, supported by solid Murray pine posts. Hessian walls divided the shack into two bedrooms and a living area. The windows were covered with fly-wire. There was nothing to keep out the heat and the cold. Concrete coated the floor. A single tall gum tree behind the hut cast stringy shade. At the side Nino had built a pergola and vines trailed over its supports.

Delfina awoke when the cart lurched to a stop. Both Stella and Menica stayed asleep.

Nino lit another cigarette and stared ahead.

Delfina climbed down from the cart and walked towards the hut. She stopped near the pergola to finger the vines. She ran her thumb and forefinger along their downy tendrils and the scent of sea spray stung her nostrils. She lifted her head and looked about wildly, but there was only the sluggish river and the eerie calls of desert birds.

Menica lay on her back in bed, her arms folded behind her head. Out the window she could see the moon swinging in the sky like a ball surrounded by twinkling stars. Beside her Stella squirmed and sighed, missing the warmth of her mother's body.

Exasperated, Menica jabbed her elbow at her sister. 'Stay still!'

The little girl cried in pain.

'Shut up, you baby! Mamma will wake up.' Menica pulled the bedclothes over her sister's head and held them hard.

Stella flailed against the thin coverings. Her cry became a wail, then a shriek.

'Stop it.' Menica was losing patience. 'You cry all the time: in the boat, on the train, here.' Her voice rose and she, too, began to cry. 'Shut up, you b-a-b-y.'

Stella broke free from the bedding and pummelled Menica with closed fists. She did not stop shrieking. Her mouth was twisted and red weals were erupting where the blanket had rubbed against her face.

A man's voice came from the next room. 'Be quiet and go to sleep. If I have to come in, there'll be trouble. Do you hear me?'

The squabbling sisters sat still, wiped away their tears and waited.

Through the hessian walls they heard their mother's low voice and their father's sharp response. Delfina appeared in the doorway. Stella flung herself out of the blanket, across the room and against her mother. Menica sulked on the bed.

Delfina sat with her daughters while high cloud drifted over the face of the moon.

Pale under her wild black halo of hair, Stella looked up at her mother. 'Why don't you sleep with us, like you always do?'

'Because we're in Australia, your father is here, and it's my duty to be with him.'

Stella chewed on the end of her finger. Menica spoke for both of them. 'That's stupid.'

Delfina had no answer: have I done this because I'm dutiful? Is that my reason to come halfway across the world? Is that reason enough?

From the other room came Nino's faint snores. Stella giggled and Menica glared at her.

'Come on you two, back to bed,' Delfina said.

She tucked the girls under the blankets and went back to her seat at the window. The unknown stars in the unknown sky reached their zenith and the paddocks blazed with a yellow night-light. She sat until her fear subsided into resignation.

It was two in the morning when she returned to her room. Nino lay perfectly still. She crept to the side of the bed and stood as close as she could without waking him. They had made love before they went to sleep, awkwardly, like two strangers. Afterwards, Delfina wanted Nino to hold her but they lay side by side and, before long, she heard his breathing deepen and knew he was asleep. In the moonlight she could make out the dark shadows on his cheeks above the thick moustache. She peered closer. His fingertips were stained with nicotine, yet his nails were white and manicured. He had never cared about nails at home. Just like his clothes. She glanced over to where his pants lay folded pleat to pleat over a wooden box, and his underwear lay in a neat pile on the floor.

She tiptoed back to her own side of the bed and reached for the bag that had not been out of her sight since she left Salina. She opened the clasp and felt inside. At first she couldn't find it and the panic, which seemed to come so easily now, welled up from her belly. But it was there, and with great care she took out her statue of the Virgin Mary. Mary was stained from her journey: her turquoise cloak rubbed and worn. As she sat on the edge of the bed twisting the halo of stars back into its spherical shape, Delfina prayed silently that she would not yet be sent a child.

14

Delfina dumped her basket on the kitchen floor. She had been in Mildura now for three years and establishing her garden had been hard work. It was Easter Monday and she had been up since dawn. In the grey light she had scattered grain for the scrawny fowls and watched them cluck and peck at the unyielding surface. She liked their jerky nervous hobbling as the hens hurried towards her. No matter how hard you work this Mallee ground, Delfina thought, it resists. The new country had sun and vines and tomatoes like Salina but there was no subsoil when she dug into the ground. No one had planted anything here before her.

Menica's voice cut into her reverie. 'Mamma! She smells!'

Stella stood in the doorway holding out a sodden heap of clothing.

Menica, her nose wrinkled in disgust, stood behind her. 'She's wet the bed and I'm not sleeping in the same room as her any more. When are we going to have breakfast?'

Stella was looking at the floor. Menica went to continue her diatribe but Delfina moved swiftly across the room.

She reached for the tin tub hanging on the kitchen wall and poured in water from the kettle on the stove. A thin stream trickled onto the bottom of the tub.

'I don't want to have a bath with her.'

'You have to. We don't have much water. There's no choice.'

Delfina was exasperated. The river flowed past their block but water was still unreliable and delivered by a fickle pumping system. She watched as Stella, mute with shame, climbed into the tub. Surely she would stop wetting the bed soon. It had continued since their arrival in Mildura.

In the warm water the sisters soon forgot their differences. They splashed and their laughter rang out. Delfina was jittery from her early rising and willed the diversion to continue. The girls had brought home their school reports for their parents to read over the Easter break. When her daughters were in bed, Delfina deciphered them with difficulty. Menica's marks were high, her exercise books neat with cursive script and ticked with red pen. Stella still printed, and the teacher said she should participate more in the games. Outside the kitchen window, Delfina watched the Australian sun edge lazily upward, livid yellow in an eggshell sky. When it reached the kitchen window the fly-wire screen threw sharp rhomboid patterns across the concrete floor.

Menica grew sick of the bath and climbed out. 'School starts again on Wednesday,' she said, towelling herself dry. 'Miss Price said I can use the inkwell after Easter.'

'You are clever,' said Delfina, 'and so is my Stella here.' She put one arm around each damp daughter and they laughed at the moist patches on her apron.

'I have a good idea.' Delfina knelt in front of Stella. 'If you have two dry nights in a row, I will make some *biscotti regina* to share at school on your birthday. Would you like that?'

Stella brightened, but Menica pulled away. 'Can I have some too?'

'Of course,' Delfina prattled, 'I meant you to have some too—you are doing so well in everything.'

Delfina had spent most of their three years in Mildura on the fruit block. Nino tried to teach his wife the new language, but her hesitation frustrated him. On the few occasions she accompanied him to town, he introduced her to the wives of his workmates. They were from many places and their faces were etched with stories they could only exchange in halting English. Between husbands, children and work, each woman could withdraw into the comfort of a private memory: photographs stored in a cardboard box, linen embroidered by lamplight in a distant country, recipes prepared by mothers and grandmothers. They were too shy to share their memories, as if to tell them would be to commit an offence.

It was different for their children. For them the new language was an adventure and they rolled the sounds around their mouths like lollies, sucking confidently for the meaning. Delfina envied Menica who moved between Italian and English as she played, until the words became interchangeable. Stella was more deliberate. She did not mingle her languages but kept them separate, summoning each when it was required.

As she cleaned up after the girls' bath, Delfina remembered the ingredients of Angelina's recipe. She did not have any anise, but the children wouldn't notice if she substituted extra lemon zest in the *biscotti regina*.

Delfina put on her sun hat and walked to the edge of her vegetable garden. She was surprised and pleased at how much she'd grown. This year she could set up a stall by the roadside to sell the fruit and vegetables they did not need. It would raise a little money that she could set aside for her daughters.

She had planned her garden carefully, watching the patterns of the sun each day to find the right positions for growing: where it leached the ground and where the shadows lessened the late afternoon heat. In the early days her garden had been her retreat.

Now she was content. In the warmth of early morning, the dew still coated the tomatoes and the peppers, and the yellow zucchini flowers shone like miniature suns against the rampant foliage. A cluster of thumb-size fruit promised a sure harvest. Delfina sprayed the crop with the garlic mix she prepared herself and checked the strawberry net for signs of insects, raising it high enough to deter the birds. She fingered the fruit that lay on the bed of yellow straw and picked the few weeds that had seeded between the rows. The glistening tomatoes made her most proud. She had to watch them closely, to catch them before the sun burst their skins, and juice and seed spilled out.

She threaded her way along the rows, gathering the damaged and overripe fruits into a basket. She could hear the clucking of the hens, and Stella and Menica who sat on the steps in the shade of the house and arranged strips of colourful fabric around some wooden peg dolls. When they weren't at school, the girls were usually happy playing all day together.

'You must do as I tell you,' Menica sternly told her doll. She picked up a piece of peacock blue silk and began to wrap it around the peg. 'I'm going to give you to Martha at school.'

'You can't do that. That's my material.' Stella grabbed at the fabric and Menica held it out of her sister's reach. 'Give it to me,' Stella whined.

'Mamma said I could have this piece. Yours was the red one. Remember?' Menica poked out her tongue and Stella slunk away.

From where she was listening, Delfina could only see the top of Menica's fair head. She stopped for a moment to watch her daughters.

What have I done, she thought. Will my girls forget the land where they were born, or will it return to them only in dreams and snatches of memory? She shifted the heavy basket to her other arm and walked towards the house.

Stella had gone to stand in the fretted shade of the eucalypt. She raised her arms and looked up at the doll clasped between her hands. She moved to and fro; she and the doll engaged in a slow dance. A breeze flickered the eucalypt shadows. It was quiet in the garden. Small insects thrummed. Oblivious to her mother and sister, Stella glared at the doll. 'Look,' she demanded, 'this is our beautiful garden. This is our house. This is A-u-s-t-r-a-l-i-a.'

She pronounced each letter with a short exhalation. Then she moved the doll from side to side, turning the stiff body in its blue checked dress.

Caught in the acid rush of memory, Delfina felt cold with fear. She fought the image of the lost child she had held aloft so that, blown through by the Salina wind, he would not forget his homeland.

Later, before the heat led them all to the edge of the river, she cooked tomatoes, onions and garlic and for a time imagined herself back within the safety of her mother's stone walls. The presence of her baby lingered. If she let herself she could still feel his softness and smell his newborn scent. But she remembered her illness on the ship and the talk of the capsized boat, and she knew in her heart that her son was dead.

15

Revived by their dunking in the shallows of the river, Menica and Stella were playing at the back of the house. Delfina was prowling the perimeter of the yard as she did every day. She squinted and shaded her face with her hand. In the distance she made out a woman gliding towards her, her scarlet garments startling in the grey landscape. Beside the woman a child hopped and skipped. Every so often he bent to pick up something and the woman stopped until he was ready to go on.

'I've been meaning to visit you for ages,' the woman said when they drew near. She had a musical voice. 'My name is Shuja. My husband and I moved from Mildura to our fruit block six months ago. It's on the far side of Matthew Langdon's property, so it's a bit of a walk.'

Shuja must be Indian, thought Delfina. In her scarlet sari with its gold trim she was like an exotic bird. A dark caste mark lay between her kohl-lined eyes.

'My family arrived here not long after they discovered gold in Victoria'—she reached towards Delfina—'but you're here all alone.'

'I am not alone,' Delfina said. 'I have my daughters.'

'Ah, but the language. It's a problem.' Shuja clasped Delfina's hands between her own brown hands. 'I hope we can be friends. Tell me your name.'

'I am Delfina Palmerino. I come from Salina, an island at the bottom of Italy.'

'Such a beautiful name,' said Shuja. 'And you've come such a long way.'

'Which part of India is your family from?' Delfina asked shyly.

'My grandfather was a schoolteacher in Calcutta. He heard they were picking nuggets of gold from the ground in Australia.' Shuja laughed. 'He brought his wife and son, my father, to try his luck. When my grandfather died, my father came to Mildura and did the mail run—you know, the letters and parcels that are delivered to the fruit blocks and farmers. We've been here ever since.'

'Does your husband deliver the mail too?' Delfina asked.

'Not any more. George worked with his father until he died late last year. His father bought our block when Henry Williams' store got the mail contract back in the 1880s and he knew he'd have steady work. Up until now, it's never been farmed. We've great plans for it. But that's enough about me. Who are these young ladies?'

Menica and Stella had appeared from the back of the house. They stopped at the sight of Shuja.

'My daughters,' Delfina said proudly. 'This is Menica, and this is Stella.'

'Ah, yes, your daughters. Let me introduce you to Enrico. Enrico, come here!'

The boy was tracing patterns in the dust, a series of arches fanning outwards. At Shuja's call he dropped his stick and ran to her side.

The child was now close enough for Delfina to see that he was not related to Shuja. He was tall and thin, about six or seven years old, a few years older than her own son would have been by now. They were an incongruous pair, this sombre child and this vivid woman.

'I take care of him,' said Shuja. 'His mother's unwell and his father thinks it's good for Enrico to spend time away. Like you, they're new to this country. But for me it's not so new.' She turned to the boy. 'Enrico, this is Menica and Stella.'

Enrico held out his hand.

Menica stared and then turned away.

Delfina bent over her. 'What is the matter with you?'

Menica answered in rapid-fire Italian, full of scorn. 'He's a boy! And I'm sick of babies! Papa said I'm a big girl now. I don't want to make friends with babies.'

Delfina blushed and Enrico stared with his mouth open.

Shuja did not need a translation. She walked forward and took Menica's hand from behind her back. Her bracelets glinted in the sun. 'So you are the elder daughter. This is, I think, very important.'

Menica felt the faint pressure of Shuja's hand and smelled her heady scent of incense and flowers. Her sari shimmered in the sun. She reached forward to touch the cloth but Shuja had already turned towards Stella.

Timidly, Stella held out her hand, first to Shuja and then to Enrico. 'Do you want to play with my dolls?' she asked. 'I have three and you can have one of them.'

Menica snorted. 'Boys don't play with dolls.'

Enrico nodded at Stella and the two went off towards the river.

Menica stomped after them.

Shuja sighed. 'It's so hard for my poor Enrico. We looked after him when we lived in Mildura and his father still brings him to us now that we've moved out here.'

Delfina was too shy to ask questions.

Shuja read her thoughts. 'Ah, I should explain a little. His mother's name is Francesca. His father said she never recovered from a tragedy when she was young. The memory of it returns and she must go to bed until she is well again. I don't know what happened. He came to me with Enrico in his arms. He was worried and needed someone to care for him while he worked. Together we look after Enrico, and Francesca can rest. Since then, I've become his other mother.'

'How often do you look after him?' Delfina asked.

'As often as necessary. Sometimes at my home and sometimes in his own,' said Shuja. 'After Easter he'll be going to school so he'll come every day. When his father told me this, I knew I must come to see you. I've waited too long. Now we shall be friends and Enrico can meet your daughters before his first day at school.'

Delfina smiled but said nothing. She could never tell Shuja that her own son had drowned near a dark beach. She was filled with resentment for this Francesca who left her child to the care of others, and with grief for the son whose touch she would never feel.

Fay Price opened the schoolroom door, hoping for fresh air. Despite it being April, the box-like weatherboard school, built to accommodate the children of settlers and workers to the west of Mildura, was baking. Fay smoothed her dirndl skirt and ran a finger under her damp collar. At least the children won't have enough energy to play up, she thought. She saw Delfina approach and looked at her watch. There was an hour until home time. She sighed: Fay did not speak Italian and Delfina's English was hesitant. Conversations were difficult and Fay had to hold herself back from correcting. That morning too, the new Italian assistant priest from Sacred Heart Church had given religious instruction in the storeroom to her few Roman Catholic pupils.

Fay heard Pietro Silvi lauding the catechism in what she thought was also imprecise language.

Delfina was carrying a cardboard carton covered with a red checked cloth. She climbed onto the verandah and held out the box. 'Today is the birthday of Stella.' Delfina measured her words. 'She is eight years old. I bring these for the children.'

'How nice!' exclaimed Fay. 'It's been so hot today and a surprise will be good.' She took the box and gestured for Delfina to follow her, but Delfina shook her head and waited outside. If only this mother would make an effort to join in, Fay thought.

Delfina heard the strains of 'Happy Birthday' and tiptoed to the window. Stella was distributing the sweet biscuits to her classmates. She had managed four dry nights and her confidence had grown. Delfina heard Fay Price's voice above the chatter. 'Because it's Stella's birthday, you can go out and play until home time!' There was a cheer from the children.

Delfina waited for Shuja to come for Enrico and they walked back together as far as the crossroad. Delfina, Menica and Stella dawdled towards the block in the mid-afternoon heat. Felled tea-tree branches were piled in heaps on the cleared land.

'Father Silvi came today,' said Stella, as she hopped from one patch of shade to another.

Delfina had not met the priest. Each time she went to Mildura she visited Sacred Heart Church but there were no relics or paintings, only a bare cross and some wrinkled prints under glass. Delfina tried to pray there but was relieved that they didn't go into town every Sunday. Instead she observed the Sabbath in her front room with her daughters: she pulled down the blinds, lit candles and lost herself in the mysteries of the rosary.

Stella paused under a tree. 'Where's Werrimull, Mamma?'

'It's not far from here. We could walk there but it would take a while. Why do you want to know?'

'Father Silvi said that a woman saw the Blessed Virgin near Werrimull. Didn't he, Menica?'

Menica nodded and continued reciting her multiplication tables.

'Who is this woman?' said Delfina. 'What's her name?'

'Menica, do you remember?' Stella tugged at her sister.

'Now look what you've done,' said Menica. 'I've lost count.'

'Do you know, Menica?' Delfina insisted.

'I think her name's something like Cecilia Vivianti. Father Silvi said she was young when it happened and now she's very old. He's a bit strange,' said Menica, wrinkling her nose. 'He got really excited and said that he wants to build a church in the place where it happened.'

'Mamma, can we go to the church?' Stella said.

'Of course, we will. When it's built!' Delfina put her arms around Stella and swung her around.

'Seven sixes are forty-two,' declared Menica.

Delfina smiled to herself. She was pleased that this land allowed for incarnations. Cecilia Vivianti's vision confirmed that there were other devout women who survived in this desert.

'Is it all right if I tell Enrico's father to come here for him this afternoon?'

It was early morning. Shuja was sitting at the table in Delfina's kitchen frowning at a piece of board cut from the side of a packing case. Beside her was a tin of whitewash and a straggly brush.

Delfina often thought about the poor boy and the watchful father who negotiated the care of his wife and son. 'Of course, now that he's at school and we're working together.'

Shuja nodded and smiled up at Delfina. She glistened: the golden, filigreed rings were heavy in her ears, her hair was polished and drawn back from her forehead, and the whites of her eyes shone.

'I think we should list all the fruit and vegetables. It's better that way, easier for you and the customer.'

Delfina remembered the rough wooden signs in Salina—*capperi, pomodori*—painted in crooked reds and greens. There were so many signs and it was such a small island; she often wondered if there were enough people to buy all the produce advertised on the roadsides. 'Then I'll need a lot of signs; I'll have different things to sell each time.'

Shuja pursed her lips. 'We should just write Fresh Fruit and Vegetables. Keep it very simple. Yes?'

She waved her brush through the air like a baton. She left it poised and raised her eyebrows.

Delfina laughed and nodded.

With her tongue between her teeth as she focused, Shuja drew thick white letters on the brown surface and each letter ended with a curved serif. When she finished she stood by the window and held the sign up. 'There. What do you think?'

The two women smiled across the littered kitchen table.

While Shuja fussed over her sign, Delfina arranged goods on large pieces of board set in the shade outside the kitchen door. She had saved her favourite basket for her masterstroke, a sample selection of all her goods for sale.

She positioned the mottled green of the zucchini, with their yellow ends in symmetrical waves, so they would accent the curve and polish of the peppers. The tomatoes were her favourites: mounds of red, sweet fruits with skins like filled balloons. In the winter, she thought, I will have oranges next to mandarins next to lemons. Their colours will be brilliant against the winter sky. She was thrilled by her own plans.

It was mid-morning when the two women, helped by the children, carried their goods to the roadside. They had chosen a spot under an old eucalypt, its thick trunk and wide canopy offering some protection from the sun. Shuja added chutneys to Delfina's stall, mysterious, spicy offerings with chunks of fruit and vegetables. The day slipped by, broken only by the infrequent carts rumbling home to more remote blocks, or by the itinerant workers moving between the water locks or the stations further to the west. Once a car approached and a well-dressed woman took off her gloves to finger the produce. She bought tomatoes and peppers, and patted the heads of the three chattering children.

Late in the afternoon Shuja and Delfina, trailed by the children, returned what was left of their goods to the house.

'We are clever. Yes?' Shuja demanded.

Delfina smiled and jingled the few coins in the bottom of her apron pocket.

Shuja watched Delfina as she made coffee on the stove. Her cheeks were flushed. She wore her hair in a ponytail at the nape of her neck. It reached well below her waist. She had put on the weight lost during her journey from the islands and her body once again curved under the thin cotton dress. 'You look well!' Shuja exclaimed.

Delfina turned. 'It's so much better now. When I first came here I was miserable. Everything was different: the weather, the food, the language. At times I thought I'd die.'

'But you didn't, did you? And look at what we've done.' Shuja hugged her friend.

Delfina smiled. Shuja smelled of sandalwood and oranges. 'I've met you,' she said. She put down her spoon and swirled Shuja around by the waist. 'I have my garden and we have success. And you've taught me so much of this English language.' She jingled the coins again.

Shuja sat down, breathless and laughing. 'I'm so pleased. And our meeting has also been good for the children. Look at Enrico. He can't wait to come here. He is in love, I think, with Stella. They are alike those two, living in a world of dreams.'

'Sometimes I think Stella is lucky. She's like I was as a child. It's as if she has never changed countries.'

'She is different from Menica. I can see that. The one always reaching out for the new and the other reaching inward for, I don't know what? Enrico too is a thoughtful one. His future is already deep inside him. It doesn't matter what we do. We can't alter this fact.' Shuja paused. 'When I have children, I wonder what they'll be like and where they'll belong—with an Indian mother and an English father who've both lived all their lives in Australia!'

'You'd like children?' ventured Delfina.

'Of course. But we've been married for four years and haven't been lucky yet.' Shuja shrugged. 'There's plenty of time, and while I wait I have Enrico.'

The two women turned to watch the children playing in their usual spot on the house steps. Enrico had gouged two perfectly proportioned figures in the dust with a sharp stick. Stella was watching him, her hands between her knees. Menica rocked on her heels, looking into the distance and frowning.

Just as the sun began to fall behind the gum trees there were three sharp raps at the front door, followed by a musical rat-a-tat-tat-tat.

Delfina was pouring the saucepan of coffee into her best cups.

'I'll go,' said Shuja. 'It'll be Enrico's father.'

A man's heavy footfall followed the padding of Shuja's bare feet. When Nino's work with Alfredo brought in extra money, he had added two rooms either side of a narrow hallway, which then opened into the original kitchen. Delfina gasped with surprise when she saw Salvatore di Maggio come down the hallway. Since that torturous train ride from Melbourne three years ago she hadn't seen Salvatore or Gaspare again. From the brief comments she gleaned from Nino, she knew both men still worked for Alfredo di Nola.

Salvatore stepped forward and held out his hand. He spoke in English. 'How do you do? Nino told me you had done a lot to the place. It's looking good.' He waved his arm to encompass the house, yard and block. 'And how are your two daughters? Have they learned to balance the stones on their knuckles?' He pretended to flip a stone from the palm to the back of his hand.

'They play, as always, while we worry about them,' said Delfina.

Salvatore caught sight of his son through the door and called, 'Enrico!'

The boy ran up the steps into the house.

'I didn't know Enrico was your son.' Delfina could not keep the surprise out of her voice.

'He is my son, yes.' He looked fondly at the boy. 'But he's really the son of my wife's cousin. His parents died when he was very young. My wife's not well. Australia is difficult for her. These are two reasons why Enrico always looks so solemn. Don't you, my son?' He ruffled the boy's hair.

Shuja's almond eyes flashed from Delfina to Salvatore. 'You know each other?'

After Delfina had explained, she picked up the saucepan. 'Will you have coffee with us? This afternoon we are celebrating.'

'Why not?' Salvatore walked around the table and sat in the chair opposite the kitchen window. 'What is this celebration?'

The two women interrupted each other if a detail was left out of their story.

'Where did you hold this stall? There's only the house and the chicken shed.'

Shuja clapped her hands. 'We are resourceful women, we do not need a building.' She took Salvatore to the front door and pointed out the big gum.

'You sheltered under the tree? All day? Ah, this is no good. I will build you a proper stall with a roof. Nino will have some planks and tools. No, there will be no argument. It is my gift to you for looking after Enrico.'

When they returned to the kitchen, Salvatore raised his coffee cup in a toast. The sun flashed though the open front door and down the narrow hallway, spreading yellow inside the kitchen.

Delfina rose and pulled the door closed. 'The sun, it's so strong here,' she sighed. 'It's everywhere all the time.'

'You're right,' said Shuja. 'I'm used to it. But my mother always complained that she couldn't breathe in the dry air.'

'Yes, water's precious here,' said Salvatore. 'This is a dry country. We're not used to it and it's not used to us. We're all new actors in a new play. It's as if the sun gets things wrong and throws light or shade where they're not meant to be.'

Delfina was staring straight ahead. 'In the morning on Salina the sun is bold. It plays with the bright colours of the houses and the flowers and splashes off the sea. In the middle of the day we rest while the sun makes the grapes grow. In the early evening it finds the tombs on the hillsides and warms the bones of the old ones, not too much or too little.'

Shuja and Salvatore exchanged glances. Salvatore was embarrassed. 'So, we have a poet amongst us,' he exclaimed. 'There is a lot for us here too, you know. '

Delfina laughed self-consciously. She poured thin streams of coffee into their cups and the three of them sat at the table while the sun dropped behind the horizon.

Three days later Salvatore was admiring his work; he pushed his palms into his sides and arched his back to ease the ache. At the sound of a car on the gravel at the front of the house, he looked around.

Nino slammed the car door shut and waved. 'A good job, my friend!'

Salvatore touched his hand to his hat, clapped his heels to attention, and both men grinned.

The stall was about twelve feet wide and six feet deep. At the front it was high enough to enable the women to walk around, but its sloping roof meant that the back of the stall was useful only for storage. The front wall was built to half height and Salvatore had fixed a counter to the top. There was a narrow doorway in the right side wall. The stall was built from bleached fence palings and stood on the verge separating Nino and Delfina's property from the road.

Nino strode towards Salvatore through the tussocks. He stopped short of the stall and plucked some grass seeds from his socks. The two men listened to the eerie rustling as the afternoon breeze blew in from the desert.

'Do you want to do something with the rest of your land?' Salvatore found it hard to understand how, apart from Delfina's efforts, Nino's fruit block remained largely virgin.

'One day, perhaps. But for now I'm busy. With Alfredo there's always a lot to do and no time for all this.' Nino flicked his hand in a gesture of dismissal. 'I'll leave it to the woman. She's good at growing things. Although she's not so good at growing babies.' Nino saw Enrico walking towards them and lowered his voice. 'I would like a son.'

Salvatore slapped Nino's back and spoke too loudly. 'There's plenty of time, my friend.'

Enrico dragged his stick behind him as he walked, leaving a thin red line in the dirt. Nino slipped into Italian. 'Sometimes I think it was a different woman who came to Australia, that something happened on the ship.'

Salvatore let him speak. It was not like Nino to be reflective.

'Delfina always thought a lot. After all, she's Fortunato's daughter.' He struggled for words. 'I know she was ill on the journey but I think only part of her came here. She's like a shadow. She hardly speaks and spends all her time in the garden. She won't go into Mildura.'

He remembered the loyalty he owed his wife and stopped.

Delfina's words of a few days ago came back to Salvatore. 'We are not the same as we were in our old countries,' he said. 'Some find the new difficult.'

'What of this paradise and all it has to offer us? For me it is full of possibilities. So many that I don't know where to begin. Perhaps this is why I haven't grown the grapes.' Nino chuckled.

'Then you are lucky. For many it is a Garden of Eden with snakes in every corner.' Salvatore turned to the stall. 'So, you like my work?'

Nino grinned. 'The women will think you are a god!'

'And that, my friend, is how it should be.' Salvatore bowed.

Delfina had made an arrangement with the neighbours: they supplied her with excess produce, rather than see it rot in the sun. She repaid them with sewing and small commissions of embroidery, and so her island flowers graced the cloths and pillowslips of the Mallee. Sometimes she was obliged to share the proceeds of her stall, but Delfina stashed most of the money she made in a tin beneath some broken concrete in the kitchen. Nino did not ask about this money. It remained in the tin, her talisman and her insurance against life turning upside down.

Delfina became known locally as the pretty, dark-haired woman who lived out of town and sold produce every day from the roadside. The other women were called Pete's wife or Jack's woman, but Delfina's name wasn't linked with Nino's.

The letter arrived just as the first frost greyed the red Mildura soil. It was July 1933. The icy shards crunched underfoot and evaporated in the watery sun. Beside the long flat roads, the rows of unpruned vines looked grotesque. Soon the seasonal workers would arrive and shear them back to the trunk. In contrast the orange trees bent double, their glossy leaves choked with perfect golden globes. The streets and paddocks lay still under the wide winter skies.

Delfina was walking beside the river. She passed their block and moved into the open country. In her hand she held the letter, the thin, creased pages filled with Papa Fortunato's words:

> *To our dearest Miracle Child,*
>
> *I write to you from our terrace. The waves crash below me and your mother is sewing in her chair. You have been gone so long now. Let me see, it has been at least a thousand years! I often try to see your Australia in my*

mind but it's not easy when the seasons are opposite. This doesn't matter because I can always see you running through the fields of red poppies, your baby feet pounding the earth. But I am growing sentimental and maybe you, in your new country, will think your old father a fool.

I will tell you the news of Salina. Aldo and Ludevina are no longer growing the vines, so these are withering on the slopes. Sometimes I think it was not only the people who left our islands but also the vines. Ludevina's ravings have become worse. Her mind is no longer clear and poor Aldo has a hard time. Recently a girl from the village has been going to help them. Tell Nino gently. He will be worried about his mother.

Aurora died early in the spring. It took Aldo weeks to clean out her room. There were so many relics—bits of plant and bone and cloth. Our poor padre still mutters as he sorts through the piles but he is not throwing anything out. How is he to know what is real? Of course there was great wailing, even more than usual—so many of the young have gone and we cannot afford to lose our elders.

Mario and Gabriella send their love. Gabriella's illness now confines her to bed and Mario does not visit Salina as often as he once did. When he comes, he rides a mule to Valdichiesa to pray. He says that he is getting too old for taverns and must think of the afterlife.

Your mother is well. She sends much love. She includes the recipes that you wanted and asks if you have difficulty getting the ingredients. The fruits and vegetables in our cupboard pile high as there are only the two of us to eat them. Your mother says that she wishes she could send them to you.

And me? Well, I am growing old, my Miracle Child. If you saw me you would be surprised to find me a little bent with knobs and bumps where once all was straight. But I do not worry. One day I will be happy to return to God's care. I've tried to live a good life so I pray that He will be pleased with me.

My Paolo has left and also gone to your country. He has gone to fish in West Australia, in the south near a town called Albany. He stayed for a long time after many of the others had left. But it became too difficult for him. He said that if he did not go he would disappear under a weight of cloud. He wrote to me that the islands are fading, slipping from his memory. God will perhaps help him. Anyway, he will now share your vast land.

How are our granddaughters? Angelina and I keep a calendar on our wall to remember their ages. Menica must be thirteen by now, and Stella twelve! How I long to touch their hair and feed them island food. Always remember to give them the love and the stories of their grandmother and grandfather.

And you, my beautiful one, when I think of you my heart is full but not with sadness. I always remember the day you were born too soon, and I went to the Madonna for help. We will never be truly apart for we are linked, you and I, to the stories of Salina.

The feast of the Madonna del Terzito is coming soon and your mother will cook her usual treats for our special day. I will pray for you as always.

All our love,

Papa and Mamma Coltelli

Delfina read the letter three times and then let her hand fall to her side. The air bit through her clothes and her gloves, and a series of rasping coughs hurt her lungs. Her eyes watered and she could feel the damp settle on her hair. From up the river a paddle steamer's throaty call was followed by a rhythmic chug-chug-chug. The steamer rounded the river bend and she watched a whistling kite hover and dip through the blue. Pale rushes bordered the banks, behind them a line of grey and russet winter willows. Bamboo sprouted in the shallows and little black hens floated amongst the stems. In the distance a fallen river red gum straddled the water that was dotted with white ibis. Pelicans swam past, their z-shaped bodies in single file as they glided though the wreckage of the gum.

She closed her eyes and saw the black-clad figure of Aurora who had given her comfort against the haranguing of Ludevina. She remembered how the frail woman became animated after scouring the slopes for the bones of yet another saint or the cloth of a martyr. To celebrate each birthday, she took the family through the dusty treasures in her room. So, Aurora had died and another cycle was completed. The image of the old woman moved across Delfina's closed eyelids.

And Papa, old? It was not possible. Would she ever see him again? And Paolo in Australia! Delfina felt slightly sick. Enough time had passed for her to separate what happened with Paolo from its consequences. In the early years guilt had kept her focused on their son's brief life. Now, she recalled Paolo's gentle hands, his protestations of love, and his respect for her wishes when she could not see him. She choked back a longing for the tenderness that Nino was too busy to give her. Had Paolo forgiven her for sending his son away? The answer was obvious. He had chosen the other side of the continent as his home.

Delfina turned towards the house. The kite, giddied by its swirling, swooped over her head and landed on a nearby tree. For a few seconds it looked startled by its own activity. Then it fluffed its wings, bent its head and settled to sleep.

The cough that had been bothering her for weeks again scratched at her lungs. She stood for a moment waiting for the pain to subside. Then she folded the letter, placed it in her apron pocket and set off over the frostbitten ground.

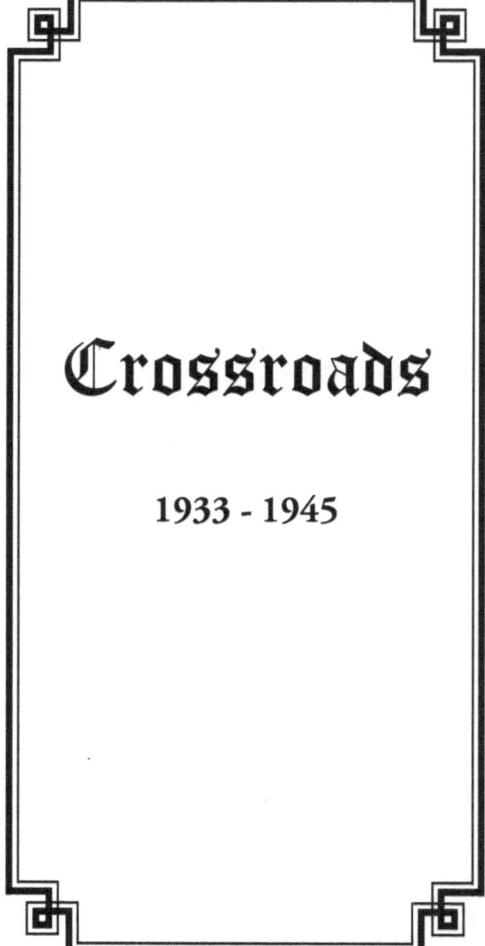

Crossroads

1933 - 1945

16

As she went about her chores Delfina tried to tell herself that it was just another letter, simply more news from a far away place. By late afternoon she was exhausted, swamped by memories, and a terrible heat that was spreading through her body. Her mind returned to her illness on the boat, close to seven years ago now. But no, it was just a mild influenza, the same one she had every year before being rescued by the onset of spring.

She sat in the kitchen, waiting for Nino and the girls to arrive home. Outside a feeble sun slid behind the cloud and the room darkened. In that split second the kitchen leached of colour. Delfina had the sensation that the floor was moving under her feet. A shiver ran through her, followed by a succession of quick, sharp pains, like the stabs she'd felt in her chest that morning near the river. She shifted in her chair, trying to dislodge the ache. She felt estranged from everything she usually felt close to. Delfina rubbed her forehead and saw that her hand glistened with sweat.

A car braked hard on the gravel. There were footsteps and the front door banged. With an effort of will Delfina walked unsteadily to the mirror on the far wall, wiped her forehead, and brushed her hair back into its ponytail. The room was dim; no one would notice.

Menica threw her bag against the wall. 'Hello, Mamma.'

'*Ciao*, Mamma,' said Stella. She hugged her mother and felt her clammy skin. 'Are you all right?'

'Yes, yes, I'm fine,' Delfina said. 'It's hot in here. That's all.'

Nino kissed Delfina and she smelled his peppermint-scented shaving cream and the aroma of his hair oil. He'd slicked back his hair, not a strand out of place, and wore his shirt unbuttoned to reveal a firm neck and dark curling chest hair.

Delfina sat down at the table again and began to string a pile of beans. She watched her husband hang his jacket on a peg near the door, stoke the fire and settle with his usual glass of grappa.

'I have a letter from Papa,' she said.

'So, what news is there of the old country?' said Nino. He elongated the word 'old', making it sound comical.

Menica looked up from her schoolbooks and giggled.

'Aurora has died,' Delfina said. 'Papa said it was last spring. I suppose about two or three months ago.'

Nino remembered Aurora as a woman in black who said little and took long walks. Ludevina had overshadowed his grandmother. Aurora would have been over seventy by now. 'She's lucky to have lived so long,' he said. 'Any other news?'

Delfina bit her lip. 'Papa said your mother is not well.'

'What's wrong with her?' Nino turned around to face Delfina.

'I think she's well in her body,' Delfina said, 'but uneasy in her mind. You must remember that she's getting older. Her thoughts are probably not clear any more and this makes her angry. Your mother was always a forceful woman. Papa says Aldo has help with her.' Delfina stopped. She did not want to talk about Ludevina.

'I suppose there's nothing we can do from here.' Nino prodded the fire with the poker. 'When you write back tell Fortunato that I'll send some money. Is there anything else in the letter?'

'Paolo has gone to Western Australia.' Delfina tried to keep her voice steady. 'So we probably won't see him.'

'Well, Paolo finally realised it was time to move on,' said Nino.

'And Papa and Mamma send the girls their love.'

Nino pulled his chair closer to the fire and sat with his eyes closed. Delfina folded the letter. If only he understood how much news from Salina meant to her. She was no longer his still point but had become an anchor that weighed Nino down. Perhaps now that she was nearly thirty-three and Nino thirty-six, it was foolish to expect him to need her as he had when they were young. She wished she had conceived another child, but her bleeding had been irregular or absent. She put this down to the trauma of the journey. And now there was her annual recurrence of influenza and Nino's increasing absences. It worried her that he only came home three or four nights a week, blaming work and distance. But she didn't argue. How could she?

Later that evening when the girls had gone to bed Delfina opened the small chest that had come with her from Salina. In it she kept the linen that had been stitched in the cool stone rooms of her childhood home. She could chart her girlhood in the embroidery: Angelina had stitched with the blue sea and purple vines, and Delfina's own stitching was of the island flowers.

She felt Stella's breath on her neck and held up a cloth threaded with shades of scarlet.

'It's very pretty,' Stella whispered. 'I wish I could make things like that.'

'I'll teach you when the time is right.'

'Mamma.' Stella sat on the floor near the linen chest and concentrated on flexing the fingers of her left hand. 'Why did Nonno call you a miracle child?'

'What do you mean? How do you know he called me that? Did you read the letter?'

'Menica read it and she told me,' said Stella, 'but she didn't know all the words and had to look some up in Papa's book. She thinks she's so clever because she's good at school.'

Here she was again, back in the clutches of her island, Papa Fortunato sucking on his pipe, telling his favourite story.

'Mamma, why did he call you that? Why?'

'Listen,' Delfina said, 'I will only tell you this once. When I was born, I couldn't breathe properly and the women believed I might die. Papa went up to the church of the Madonna del Terzito to pray for me and when he was there he saw a baby lying on the floor.'

'Who had left the baby on the floor?'

'No one had left the baby. It was a vision, a sign from God that I would become well.' Delfina hesitated. Amongst the corrugated iron, the concrete, the sand and the dry heat this revelation of a miracle seemed preposterous. 'Papa believes he carried the breath home to me, that he was brought from the mountaintop by a host of angels,' Delfina finished helplessly. 'So that is why I am his miracle child.'

Delfina rose and pulled Stella to her feet. 'Come on,' she said, 'you should be in bed. Menica's fast asleep. And Papa and I'll be going to bed soon.'

A loose sheet of iron rattled in the wind and they heard the back door slam as Nino went to secure it.

Stella lingered. 'Mamma,' she said. 'I wish I was a miracle child.'

'You are, my darling,' Delfina said, and she bent and kissed the top of her daughter's head.

The next morning Nino reached for his wife and twined his fingers through her hair. When his gentle game failed to stir her, Nino placed his hand on her neck. Still Delfina did not wake. He sat upright to look at her. Overnight her eyes had become sunken. Her skin looked sickly and was damp with sweat. Delfina opened her eyes and tried to rise, but fell back on the bed.

Shuja sat at Delfina's bedside, sponging her forehead. She searched her friend's face for signs of recovery. It had been two weeks now.

On the wall opposite the bed she had stuck pictures drawn by Enrico. In one a woman stood by the side of a road holding an orange in one hand and a lemon in the other. In another a group of children played against a desert backdrop. Behind them a wide river cut through the sand and sky.

As she leaned over to rinse her sponge in the bowl of water on the side table, Shuja picked up the letter that lay on the floor next to the bed. She sat back in the chair, dropped her sponge into the bowl, and straightened the pages. From among Papa Fortunato's uneven script she could only pick out a few words that were close to English words. Shuja clicked her tongue at her own curiosity and placed the letter on the table. 'You will be better soon,' she said to Delfina. 'You must fight against your demons. What are your thoughts, Delfina?'

The answer came from behind her. 'Her thoughts? It's impossible to know. I think they are a long way from here.' Nino came closer and picked up the letter from the table.

'This is from her papa. He still calls her by her childhood names, still believes in miracles and calls them up like ghosts. He reaches across the water and she cannot let go.'

Shuja continued to bathe Delfina's forehead. 'Sometimes the future disappears for a while. Illness is just one place it disappears into. In the end each person decides which road to take. Delfina lies at the crossroads.'

She returned to her task and took no notice when Nino walked from the room.

It was Salvatore who suggested that Nino send for the priest. Nino hesitated, but when Delfina again lapsed into a fever he called at the Mildura presbytery after his day's work with Alfredo. An elderly housekeeper disappeared down the musty hallway and returned with Pietro Silvi.

'It's unfortunate that Father O'Flaherty is in Melbourne this week. Maybe I can help?'

Nino had expected the irascible Irish priest and was relieved at the sight of Pietro Silvi. 'Yes, um…I'm Nino Palmerino. My wife, Delfina, is very ill,' he said, 'and I know she would like to be visited by a priest.'

Pietro Silvi's expression changed to concern and he reached a hand towards Nino. 'Yes, yes, of course I'll come,' he said. 'What's the matter with her?'

'It's pneumonia and it's been two weeks now. She gets it every year. But this year she hasn't recovered as quickly as usual.'

'Please come inside,' the priest said. 'My housekeeper will get you a drink and I'll write down directions to your house.' He gestured for Nino to hang his hat on the hallstand and they walked down the passage. 'You live to the west, don't you?' he said. 'I remember your name.' When Nino looked surprised, the priest explained, 'I see your children at Fay Price's school. You have two little girls, don't you? But I haven't met your wife.'

The sitting room was dim and stuffed with heavy furniture smelling of polish. The housekeeper brought in a tray with two glasses of lemon cordial. 'Sit down, sit down,' the priest said. He rummaged for pen and paper and talked as if he and Nino were old friends. 'You see, it's impossible for one man to visit every parishioner. I go to the south and east of Mildura and Father O'Flaherty tries to visit the rest. It's not easy though.' Pietro Silvi smiled at Nino. 'Ah! Finally! Things never seem to stay where I put them.' He held up a tattered notepad and a pencil. 'Now, how do I get to your place?'

When Pietro Silvi left Italy he was a young man, newly ordained with God by his side. In his Capuchin brown, with the crucifix close to his chest, he came to Australia to help his Italian brothers and sisters negotiate its unknown paths. He was a link to the country of their birth and they came to him when homesick. He told them to create a homeland of the heart.

In the heat of the desert he had shed his brown robes but still held the crucifix close to his chest. The bishop had given it to him before he left to become a missionary in Australia. Missionaries offered God's mercy to those as yet unaware of it, and buttressed the faith of others whose devotions had slipped. Pietro Silvi felt suited to this task of bringing his faith to a new land. Even so, on his journey across the seas, he envisaged pagan peoples worshipping foreign gods. When he arrived in Mildura and found the soft brown eyes and mellifluous voices of his fellow Italians, he knew that he had come home.

Pietro Silvi came by cart early the next morning and stood at Delfina's bedroom door. He took in the bare floors scrubbed to a dull sheen but now dusty, the threadbare furniture, and the thin lace curtains with their exuberant floral design. Shuja, shy of her friend's faith, ushered the priest forward. As Pietro Silvi neared the bed she reached forward to smooth the coverlet.

The priest stayed her hand. 'Please, there is no need to worry. I come for souls not for bedclothes.'

Shuja relaxed. Pietro Silvi's eyes were friendly and he placed his left hand on Delfina's forehead, his right raised in blessing.

There was a scuffle in the hallway, followed by the squeak of the door.

Stella tiptoed towards the bed, behind her a breathless Nino. Menica remained near the door, her arms behind her and her head bent.

The priest's singsong voice filled the room. When he finished, Pietro Silvi bent and picked up a dog-eared holy picture from the floor. '*Un santino*,' he said. 'You don't see many of these in Australia.' He smiled and placed it on the table.

'My wife still holds on to the old ways,' said Nino.

'When I have built my church at Werrimull,' said the priest, 'I will bring the old ways closer. I've found that some do not let go so easily and for them the road is difficult.'

Stella tugged at the priest's cassock. 'You are really going to build a church? Like the one you told us about at school?'

'Yes, Stella. I've planned it already. I have some money back in the old country. I will bring a little piece of Italy to Australia. It will have the shape of a real church and maybe some paintings.' He laid his hand on Delfina's forehead. 'And maybe for your mother it will be a true home of the soul and she need not be ill.'

'How's your mother? Has Father Silvi visited yet?' said Salvatore. 'I've been worried about you all.'

Menica looked up from the kitchen sink, her face red with heat and frustration. A pile of unwashed dishes was stacked on the bench beside her. She brushed back a strand of hair with her forearm. 'Mamma's just the same. Father Silvi stayed for tea. He's just left.'

Salvatore found himself wondering again how it was possible for Delfina and Menica to look so alike yet be so different? At thirteen Menica had switched from childhood to girlhood without fuss. She had physically softened yet lost none of the drive that kept her at the top of her class.

'Where's Stella?' Salvatore said.

'She'll turn up when she's ready. She's never around when there's work to do.' Menica had her back towards Salvatore and her arms were now elbow-deep in suds.

'I'll go and see if I can find her.' Salvatore closed the wire door behind him and stepped out into the weak July sunlight. In the distance he saw Stella seated on the ground near a clump of porcupine grass. To one side a Mallee eucalypt fanned outward, its papery branches forming a cup shape that ended in a tangle of leaves. He waited for her to move but she was staring at the eucalypt's branches.

He opened his mouth to call and closed it again. To yell into this space would be irreverent, like yelling in a cathedral. He set off across the scrub. As he neared the girl, curiosity replaced annoyance. Stella was crouched on her haunches, her head bent; she appeared to be talking to the tree. He couldn't make sense of the child's whispers. He walked closer but she didn't notice him. It wasn't until he stood directly above her that he saw what she was doing.

Salvatore could not move. It was years since he had been confronted with such a shrine. He felt as if he was choking, as if he was a small boy again, standing on a mountain slope in remote Calabria.

Stella looked up. 'Mamma doesn't know that I have found this.' She pointed towards the heart of the tree and then looked down as if she had done something forbidden. 'It's all right, isn't it? That I come here when Mamma can't?'

At the tree's heart stood the miniature statue of the Virgin Mary, her blue cloak faded and her halo of stars askew. She stood beneath a tepee made from pieces of bark and fastened at the top with string. Around her feet were vestiges of faded, dead flowers.

Salvatore reached down and ruffled Stella's hair. 'Of course it's all right.' He waited, smoked a cigarette and stubbed it in the dust.

'Come on, I reckon you've said enough prayers.'

'Mamma comes here a lot.' Stella looked up at him.

'Why, Stella? Why does she come here?'

'When Mamma was born she was very small and they didn't think she would live. Nonno went to the sanctuary of the Madonna del Terzito to pray. Mamma says that he saw a baby on the floor and knew that she would be all right. It was a miracle, you know. Nonno was carried home by angels.'

'So, your mother comes here to give thanks for this'—Salvatore hesitated—'for this miracle.'

Stella took his hand and patted it, pleased that he had understood. 'Yes. Mamma says it's a small thing to do.'

They set off towards the house over the stubby Mallee scrub.

Stella ran into the kitchen ahead of Salvatore. 'Is Mamma better?'

Menica looked at her quizzically. 'No, how could she be? You've only been gone a couple of hours. Actually you've been gone for ages.'

Stella looked crestfallen. 'Mamma's not better yet,' she reported to Salvatore who stood in the doorway.

'All things take time, Stella,' he said.

Menica handed her sister a knife. 'Here, you can cut up those vegetables. You can't expect me to do everything.' She locked glances with Salvatore who felt pinned under the gaze of this confident older girl.

That night a ferocious wind blew in from the desert. It whipped across the red sand, snapped the dry vegetation and bound it into a wiry tumbleweed.

Stella stood at the back door watching the tumbleweed bump towards the house. There were no stars and a sliver of moon had already disappeared into the black sky.

She stood with her back to her father and sister who were playing cards at the kitchen table.

The tumbleweed disappeared and she opened the door further to see where it had gone. A sharp gust scattered cards over the table and onto the floor.

'What are you doing?' Menica groaned. 'You've ruined our game.'

'Stella, shut the door,' Nino scolded. 'It's cold enough as it is and Menica's right, you've spoilt our game.'

Stella turned to them, her eyes watery and bright. 'It's the wind, you see.'

'Of course it's the wind,' Nino said. 'What on earth are you on about?'

'Maybe the wind will bring…It did before, you know… When Mamma was a child and Nonno…'

Nino froze. He dropped his left hand to the table top with a thud. In his right hand a perfect fan of cards stiffened. His voice was low and he didn't look at his daughter, but at the cards. 'What will the wind bring, Stella?'

'Nothing Papa, nothing at all.'

Menica looked from one to the other. 'What's all this about?'

Nino slapped two pairs on the table and laughed. 'It's nothing. Nothing but her imagination and anyway, Menica'— he looked first at the cards in front of him and then at his eldest daughter—'despite the wind it seems that I have won this round. Go and see if your mother is sleeping, Stella. Perhaps it's time for another drink.'

Stella ran to the hall door, pausing on her way to see if the tumbleweed was still pressed to the side of the house.

On the twenty-second of July, exactly three weeks after she had first been forced to bed, Delfina walked unsteadily to the kitchen. She took what she needed from the cupboards and began to weigh piles of dry ingredients on the kitchen table. She worked slowly. Tomorrow was the feast of her Madonna. They had not celebrated for four years. Nino was always busy and the girls were moving towards a life their mother only saw from a distance.

Shuja arrived and watched her friend from the door. Delfina lifted and poured, responding to the soft whoosh of the ingredients and the clink of the metal weights. She turned when sunlight flashed on the gold embroidery of Shuja's sari. 'Here you are again! You have been too good to me, you know. Look, I'm baking for the Madonna. Remember? Well, tomorrow is her feast day. Will you come and celebrate with us?'

'Why are you doing this, Delfina?' said Shuja. 'You'll get sick again.'

Delfina sat the kettle over the flame and took some cups from the dresser. Shuja sat down and the kettle's whistle faded as Delfina poured water into the coffeepot. 'I've been here for over seven years now,' she said. 'I've cooked and sewed and tended my garden and with your help I've made a success of my small venture. But I have never forgotten my island.' She drummed on the sides of her cup. 'Even as a young boy, Nino was filled with the need to move onwards. I've always liked to dream, and to dream you need to be still. I was happy in my life on Salina. I came here to do my duty and for a while I stopped dreaming. Nino and the children needed me to do this. But now I need time to return to my memories, to my Madonna.' She poured coffee into their cups.

Shuja picked up a weight and dropped it onto the scales. 'Then, we must get to work. Tomorrow you have a lot to celebrate.'

The following afternoon Menica carried a basket of fruit out to the stall. She usually helped Delfina before beginning her homework. She rubbed her hands where the basket had dug into her flesh.

'Mamma's not coming out today. She said she has a lot to do in the house and that we would see her later. What did she mean?'

Shuja looked up from the oranges she was piling into a pyramid. 'You'll see!'

'A surprise! It's good Mamma's better but she's so quiet,' Menica said.

'Your mother will get even better in time,' Shuja said. 'A bad illness eats at the body and the soul.' She smiled at Menica. 'And the soul heals slowly.'

Nino arrived home just before nightfall and saw his wife and Stella set off through the scrub, each carrying a bunch of early jonquils and daffodils. Stella stopped and performed a small pirouette. As she tried to keep her balance, she dropped her bunch of flowers. Nino watched Delfina help her daughter reassemble the scattered blooms. He rubbed his hand through his hair and walked into the house.

The kitchen was warm and filled with the aroma of baking. On the table, under a net throw to keep off insects, was a plate piled with glazed *panini di frutta*, a dish with different types of *biscotti* and an oval platter of uncut fruit. At one end stood a dozen unlit candles. A single lit candle flickered in front of a picture of the Virgin on the window ledge.

Nino's heart sank. He had wanted his wife to feel the same way he did about this exciting land. Delfina's new preparations for the feast of the Madonna del Terzito were final proof that this would never happen.

17

For an hour Nino had waited for Gaspare on a bench in the centre of Mildura. He dipped his head every so often to take a drag from a cigarette held loosely between his fingers. Maria Rossi walked out of a nearby shop in a satin skirt and high heels. She gave Nino a sideways glance and he shaded his eyes in order to follow her more closely.

Gaspare crept up behind him and pushed him in the back. Nino lost balance and dropped his cigarette. 'Why don't you, Nino?' he said. 'From what I've heard, she's not a bad sort. Pretty good time to be had all around I reckon.'

'What makes you think I need a whore?' Nino said.

Gaspare clasped Nino's shoulders and looked into his eyes with mock surprise. His breath reeked with the yeasty odour of last night's beer. 'My dear fellow, all men have need of a whore.'

Nino peered at Maria. It was two months since Delfina's illness. She had become more a ghost than a wife. Nino went home even less frequently, or very late at night. That way he could avoid the candles and the prayers, and the sight of his wife scurrying across the scrub bearing flowers.

Maria stopped at the bus stop. She waved at Nino and Gaspare, and ostentatiously smoothed her gloved hands over her slender hips. Nino looked her up and down.

'Come on,' said Gaspare, 'we have a good day ahead of us today.' Gaspare was a chameleon. He rubbed his fingers under Nino's nose and set off towards his car.

Alfredo di Nola ran his business on the principle that where there is need there is money. He had started with the poorer migrants who spoke little English. They had bills to pay and intolerant bureaucracies to negotiate. It was daunting and they welcomed his offers of translation and assistance. He, in turn, accepted payment for helping them. Next he targeted the wealthier migrants who used his services out of complacency and camaraderie. His influence established, he spread through the local business community and linked with like-minded countrymen in Melbourne. Once a month, Nino and Gaspare collected money from the outlying areas of Mildura. It was a profitable day for them. These smaller clients were no longer Alfredo's main interest and he let his men keep a high percentage of the takings.

As he got into the car, Nino glanced over to the Grand Hotel, but Maria Rossi had gone. Perhaps it wouldn't matter if he stayed in Mildura for the night again.

Amelia Calleo stood at her front door flanked by two children and a scrawny dog. The dog slunk close to her side, its tail drooping. A frayed rope tethered it to the verandah post. The house was built from galvanised iron and had three small rooms and no bathroom. In the soaring summer temperatures it heated like a pot on a stove. On the days when she was feeling strong, Amelia told her children that they need not fear hell because it was here in Mildura. When she had used the last of the bread and the flour, she prayed to the faded picture on the wall and received solace from the Saviour's red heart and rapt expression.

In the winter, rain streamed down the corrugations of the iron walls and chilled the house. The children grew even thinner.

Her husband, Luigi, worked for the Italian butcher, Bruno Massari, on Eleventh Street, hawking meat in a covered wagon. Every day he sliced chunks from the bloodied carcasses and dipped his hand inside to retrieve the precious slippery offal. His customers pointed to the sections they wanted. Luigi didn't speak English. He couldn't get his tongue around the slurring new language.

It was not the life Luigi and Amelia had imagined.

Amelia glanced up and down the street. Nino would be here soon and she didn't have all the money he had asked for. The last weeks had been hard. Bruno had closed for a few days when early spring rains flooded the back of his shop. The water banked up in the coolroom and washed over the slaughtered animals. When Luigi went in to load the wagon he was greeted by a swirl of water, streaked with blood and fat.

The children pulled at her hands and danced on the balls of their feet but still Amelia did not move. Would Nino let her pay the rest of the money next time? She did a quick calculation. It would be all right if she was given work in the new fruit shop in Langtree Avenue.

The car door opened even before the vehicle slammed to a halt. Nino leaped out. He strode towards the house, fuelled by the successes of the morning and tantalising thoughts of the evening. Amelia braced herself and paled.

'Amelia, my good woman!' said Nino. 'I hope you've had a good month?'

'Nino, it's good to see you. Come into the house and I'll make you some coffee.'

Nino followed her while Gaspare sat on the verandah, smoking and baiting the captive dog. 'Well, has it been a good month?' he pressed.

'Difficult,' said Amelia. She put the last of her coffee on the table in front of Nino. 'I don't have all the money. I've only got eight pounds. But I've got work in the new fruit shop next week so I'll be able to pay you the rest then.'

Nino tapped his fingers on the wooden tabletop. He wasn't interested in her excuses. 'So you have problems with your payment,' he said. 'Such a pity when we can give you so much.' He let his thoughts drift to Maria Rossi and he suddenly felt magnanimous. 'Well, Amelia. You're lucky I'm such a generous man. Next time it will be double with perhaps a little interest for our trouble?'

Nino drained his cup and walked out the front door, followed by Amelia. As they stood on the porch, Nino held out his hand and Amelia counted the notes into it. Nino tipped his hat to her and cuffed Gaspare as he passed. 'Come on Gaspare. Leave that animal alone. Haven't you got anything better to play with?'

The two men guffawed and headed to the car.

They did not see Amelia spit hard into the gravel or the uniformed man watching from a distance.

Nino and Gaspare drove back into the centre of town. At the corner of Eighth Street and Deakin Avenue they saw Maria Rossi strolling in the direction of the Grand Hotel.

Gaspare slowed the car and looked over at Nino. 'Well, what about it?' he said.

Nino's desire was fuelled by resentment, but his scruples made him feel awkward. In the meantime, Maria walked under the hotel verandah.

Gaspare crept forward and drew into the curb. When he was just behind her, Maria swivelled round to see who was following her.

Gaspare nudged Nino hard in the ribs. 'It'll do you good,' he said. 'A little rest, a bit of a good time. I'll finish today's lot.'

He winked, leaned across Nino and opened the passenger side door.

Maria Rossi read the signals. In a flash she was at Nino's door. She had always rather fancied him. She held out her hand.

Sergeant George Larson was a stout man whose homely appearance held him in good stead. It fooled the lawless and over the years helped him build up an impressive file. On this spring afternoon he settled into his office chair and at regular intervals he scratched his scalp with a sharp fingernail. His deputy, Vito Bosco, watched him from the outer office. The sun beat against the walls of the building and Vito's small office was stifling. He sat back in his chair and gave himself up to some routine paperwork and the ticking of the clock.

Midway through the afternoon he heard a chair scrape and the tinny sound of a filing cabinet being opened. Next thing Vito received a painful slap on the back and George flourished a sheaf of yellowing paper in front of him. 'Bloody bleeding heart, that's what he was!'

'What are you talking about?' said Vito.

'I knew something was going on,' George said. 'Couldn't quite get the time and the place but knew I'd been told something a long time ago.'

Vito waited.

'This is what I was looking for.' George waved the papers triumphantly and Vito recognised the margins of a formal report.

'Do you remember the fellow who was here before me?' George sat on the edge of the chair next to his deputy and sucked at his lips. 'Blackman I think his name was.'

'Big man, been here thirty odd years before we came,' said Vito. 'Not a bad boxer from what I've heard, but what use is that if you don't use it. He was the one who set this place up. Left to go live in the mountains or something.'

'Before he left he told me he had filed this report,' George said. He fanned the thin sheets of paper and then flicked them with his forefinger. 'He'd been watching some of those dagos. You know that fellow di Nola. The one always walking around with a smirk—as if he owns the place. And his mate, the one always dressed to kill, who lives on a block near the big bend in the river. The report says that money passed between them. That there was some evidence it was connected to standover practices. Bloody fool didn't give any details. As I said, too much of a bleeding heart. Can't always give a fellow the benefit of the doubt you know. Sometimes we have to take that doubt and shake it.'

George splayed the papers over the desk and hammered them with his fist. 'I think I've got them this time,' he said. 'I saw the bastards take money from that woman yesterday.'

This morning, to reduce the coming heat, Amelia had wedged a row of wet bags in the juncture between the floor and the walls. Now she was damping down the hessian lining of the walls. There was a knock at the door. Panic shot through her. Summer would be a nightmare; and was this more bad news at the door? Her husband's snores rumbled through the thin interior walls. He had not coped well with the news of Nino's visit yesterday, and was sleeping it off while the children whined in a corner of the house and the unhappy dog, still tethered to the verandah, licked at its mange. Amelia looked up at the Sacred Heart on the wall. 'Damn Luigi,' she muttered. She choked back her tears and went to answer the door.

George Larson squared his shoulders and adjusted his braces. 'Vito, this is our chance to nail those thieving bastards,' he muttered.

Vito stood beside him, one hand stroking the dog's head. The animal crept closer.

George knocked again.

Amelia was startled at the sight of the two policemen.

In a glance George took in the bare interior of the house and the resignation on the woman's face, and held out his hand. 'I'm Sergeant George Larson,' he said.

Amelia looked from one to the other. George pushed Vito forward and the deputy took Amelia's right hand in his own.

'My name is Vito Bosco,' he said in Italian. 'And this is Sergeant George Larson.' Vito flashed a badge and some papers.

'Can we come in? We'd like to talk to you.'

Amelia hesitated and then ushered both men through the door, down the hallway and into the kitchen. She indicated for them to sit down and looked awkwardly from one to the other.

'Why don't you sit down and join us?' Vito said. 'We're here to help you.'

George thrummed his fingers on the edge of the table. He loathed these conversations when linguistic barriers sidelined him while Vito enjoyed being the director and the interpreter.

'Do you think your husband could join us?' Vito said.

'He's not well,' said Amelia. 'If you want to speak with him you'll need to come back another day.'

Vito translated and George frowned. It would be better if the husband was present, but this was urgent. He wanted to catch the woman while she still felt angry. From his vantage point at the end of the street yesterday, he had seen her spit on the ground. He knew that it would not be long before she felt vulnerable again and then questioning would be a lost cause.

The tension in the room heightened. One of the children whimpered and Amelia snapped back in dialect.

Vito felt sorry for women like Amelia. They usually had feckless husbands, hungry children and no English to improve their lives. He leaned over the table towards her. 'Yesterday you were paid a visit by Nino Palmerino,' he said. 'We were nearby at the time. What did he want?'

Amelia was frightened; her eyes darted between Vito and the tabletop.

Vito raised his eyebrows in mock frustration. 'We know that he has been collecting money from families in the area as payment for, for—his assistance,' he said. 'Is this true?' He noticed the tears starting in Amelia's eyes. 'Is this true?' he repeated. 'Did he collect money from you, Amelia?'

When she nodded, he lowered his voice and reached towards her hands with his own. He stopped just short of making contact. 'Why did he take money from you, Amelia?'

Amelia looked from Vito to George. She had long ago decided that she could not trust anyone. She wasn't a fool. She was only trapped and she knew this made her weak. She looked at the wad of household bills and letters stuck on the nail above the kitchen sink. She couldn't read them. It was Nino who told her where to sign and who to pay.

Vito watched her. Amelia's face clouded.

She directed her answer to George. 'We owed him money for some vegetables and other things. His wife, you know, grows produce out on their block.'

Vito tried again. 'There is nothing else you want to tell us, Amelia?'

But it was too late. It was not often that Amelia had the upper hand. She would hold on to this moment of triumph for a day or two. She might wonder at herself some other time, but not now—there was too much to lose. 'No, there is nothing I need to tell you,' she said.

18

It was past midnight. The moon slid from behind the gum next to Delfina's house. Several branches had fallen during the previous summer and others, leafless and gnarled, still clung to the trunk. It was not surprising that the tree was dying, thought Delfina. How could it survive so far from the water? But it was too close to the house and might fall in the wind. She would have to ask Nino to chop it down. They would miss the shade it cast over the house.

Delfina walked around the yard, glancing at the rows of vegetables, her basket and tools, the crooked line of the house itself. When she finished she sat on the back step and watched the moon climb higher.

Still Nino did not come.

Delfina woke to a flash of orange light forcing its way through the slit between the window frame and the curtain. The sheets on Nino's side of the bed were still smooth and the blanket neatly turned down. She ran her hand over the empty space. During his early absences, Delfina went about her routine and tried not to blame herself. It was his erratic homecomings and her own anxiety that prevented her from conceiving a child. A son might have bound them together. Lately, she feared that her infertility was a punishment for the birth of her lost son. Perhaps

Ludevina had been right to taunt her about her inadequacies. Nino's absences hurt but she felt too guilty to question him. She kept her despair to herself and turned to her rituals.

Delfina slid from the bed, walked to the window and pulled back the curtains. Disturbed by the movement, a magpie ceased its carolling and turned sharp eyes in her direction.

In Mildura, spring was fleeting. There was no gentle period of growing but rather a frenzied burst. Did the plants sense they would not last long in this harsh summer? How much could she remember of spring in Salina? Crisp sunlight on white stone houses; red poppies unfurling from their pods; shopkeepers crying the first of the season's produce. Delfina heard voices in the kitchen and looked at the clock. She had slept later than usual.

'Mamma, Shuja will be here soon,' called Menica. 'She and Enrico are just on the other side of the road. Hurry up!'

Delfina pulled on her clothes, brushed at her hair and left the bedroom. She stopped at the kitchen door and looked at her daughters. Stella laboured over her schoolwork while Menica moved about the kitchen, doing her mother's chores.

Shuja entered the room. 'It is a beautiful day, is it not?' she said. She looked at Delfina. 'Something is wrong?'

'Papa didn't come home again last night,' Stella blurted out. 'He hasn't been home for a week now.'

'Why doesn't he come home, Mamma?' Menica demanded.

Shuja and Delfina glanced at each other across the room. Shuja hoisted a basket onto her left hip. 'I must begin,' she said brightly. 'The work will not do itself. As for those who sleep on while the day grows old…'

Delfina looked at her gratefully and began to stack vegetables into a carton.

Nino arrived home after lunch. The car ground to a halt and he sat for a few minutes before getting out. George Larson had bailed him up in Deakin Avenue that morning and asked questions about his relationship to Amelia Calleo. It was obvious that the policeman was only fishing, but he would have to visit the woman later and make sure she kept it that way. As long as each party held to the arrangement, the police could do nothing.

Delfina looked up from her work at the stall. It was not like Nino to stay in one place for long. Even then he walked rather than sat. At last he strolled over as she arranged the last of her lilies in a tall preserving jar, interspersing the upright flowers with fan-shaped leaves.

Shuja ran a finger the length of a fine stem. 'These are beautiful. Don't you think so, Nino?' She turned to Delfina. 'Where are you going to put them?'

Delfina stared at the lilies. She looked at Nino, and at Shuja. Then she looked into the middle distance and spoke, not to the red earth and the Mallee scrub, but to something only she could see. 'They are for my Madonna.'

Shuja looked from Delfina to Nino, gathered into her basket the few vegetables she needed to make lunch, and set off for the house.

Nino breathed deeply to stop the anger that welled inside him. He wanted to take the jar of flowers and throw it to the ground. How did Delfina expect them to live when all she did was reach backwards? He could only cope as long as she kept her rituals out of his way. Now she was flaunting them.

'What do you mean? What do you expect her to do for you?'

'They are for my Madonna,' Delfina repeated. 'An offering for her shrine.'

'Can't you leave that stuff alone?' Nino said. On the islands it was as if God had set the routines himself. In this new country, God had not set up anything for the workers. They had to do it themselves. So why should they invoke divine help?

'Why does this make you angry?' Delfina said.

'You make me feel trapped,' said Nino. 'You bring out letters and candles and flowers. I have work to do and a future to plan.' He jabbed at the flowers. 'These things have nothing to do with real life.'

Delfina picked up the jar of white lilies. 'But these things are my life,' she said.

'Then, you'll understand why I'll need to spend more time in Mildura,' Nino retaliated. There was more to his threat than malice. Delfina's kisses were like quicksand while Maria's came without complications and let him get on with business.

As Shuja picked her way through the spring growth the viscous gold thread at the base of her sari gathered a garland of grass seed. At the back door she turned to make sure the latch held; the little flies were out already, invading the air like winged ants. As she bent to pick the seeds from her gown, she glanced back at Nino and Delfina. Shuja knew there was an ocean between them.

Nino and Delfina did not discuss their differences again. Nino took Menica and Stella to school each morning; when he was in Mildura, they walked.

Delfina was quieter now, fixed on something Shuja couldn't fathom. In a cloud of colour and incense her gods laughed with her in the outback. Delfina's God and his pensive mother were confined to the shrines of candles and flowers. Shuja didn't understand why the Sacred Heart and the Virgin were imprisoned in the worn holy pictures stuck to Delfina's kitchen window.

Father Pietro Silvi was reassigned from Mildura to his new church in 1934, two years after the parish of Werrimull rose from the desert. He was glad to leave the cold English church in the town dedicated to that saddest of images, the bleeding heart of God. He knew his miniature house of God at Werrimull was a folly: it had a squat campanile, Corinthian capitals supporting the portico, and a rose window. But it brought back for him the Romanesque architecture of his boyhood in Lombardy. His heart leaped the first time he put his foot onto the portico, and as he turned to enter the main door, he expected to see a Renaissance fresco on the limestone walls behind the capitals.

The priest dedicated his church to Our Lady of Lourdes. He slept some nights in the belltower on a thin, flowered bedroll. Other nights, as he patrolled the Mallee, he set up camp in the back of his battered Pontiac. With the windows wound down, he played his mandolin with the full orchestra of a Mallee night.

It had not been difficult to find help with the building of the church. The Italians were thrilled at the chance to recreate something of their homeland. Day after day, loaded with provisions, they made their way from Mildura to nearby Red Cliffs and then took the new rail line to Werrimull.

One year after her illness, Delfina went with Stella to see the newly constructed Our Lady of Lourdes.

Delfina took in the church's ornate exterior and was transported back to Valdichiesa where her Madonna's sanctuary watched over the villages of Leni and Malfa. She looked about her but instead of the distant blue sea rolling outwards in a line as light as a whisper, she was surrounded by desert grit and a searing sun.

'Mamma, come on. Let's have a look inside,' said Stella.

Delfina let Stella lead her into the church. It was plain inside, more Protestant than Roman Catholic, despite the external flourishes. The walls were creamy, the pews a complementary varnished brown. Only the altar and pulpit, irregular and wrought from the local stone, brought the desert inside.

Delfina genuflected on both knees and looked at the single crucifix on the blank wall above the altar. Joy surged through her. This church was built for her. She would consecrate it with the mysteries of the Rosary.

She walked to the front pew and took out a booklet. She leafed through the pages and stopped at the Joyful Mysteries. It was Thursday, one of the traditional days for their recitation.

With Stella beside her, she worked her way along her rosary beads, beginning with a Hail Mary dedicated to the Virgin before the Archangel Gabriel announced the conception of Jesus, and ending with the child living a life of prayer with his parents.

When she finished, there were tears on her face.

For the next five years Delfina went to Mass each fortnight and on Holy Days, trailed by her two daughters. It was a one-hour walk from the fruit block to Our Lady of Lourdes and, on the alternate weeks, she reverted to her rosary in the front room. Although she was polite to her fellow parishioners, Delfina kept to herself.

Menica and Stella both left school at fifteen. They helped their mother increase the volume of produce for sale from the garden. Delfina refined her daughters' sewing skills and, using the contacts made through their mother's stall, they ran a small business making clothes for the wives of the wealthier farmers. All the while, Menica waited impatiently for Delfina to consider her old enough to apply for work in Mildura.

Between Delfina and Nino there grew an uneasy truce; she did not ask questions and he was relieved not to have to give answers.

19

Father Pietro Silvi plucked the highest string on his mandolin. A single note cut the night. He listened until only a vibration remained, then he plucked a tune, an idyll to calm his God and soothe the spirits of the desert. The priest leaned from the belltower window of his church at Werrimull, his home now for nearly five years, and fancied that he could touch the grace notes falling through the air like stars.

He raised his voice and recited to the accompaniment of his mandolin, to no one in particular. 'Hospital chaplain.' He played more loudly and recited with increasing gusto. 'Missionary. Employment officer. Social worker. Banker.' Then he played a diminishing chord and chanted, 'Loving brother to my community of migrants.'

Pietro Silvi did not fear for his Italian brothers and sisters. He trusted in the abiding values that ran in their blood, but he knew there were times when these were challenged. He had been called on to convince people that the struggle was worthwhile, that a letter to Mamma and Papa might keep open the channels between the past and the present. He had also lifted the rope from the necks of the newly dead and wished his compatriots had gone home to their family while there was still time. He cried with those who were left behind.

Some brothers were too lazy to work hard and had turned to ways that brought shame on the name of Italy. They preyed on their own, eating the flesh of the dying. Pietro Silvi put down his mandolin and left the window. It was a small belltower, with as yet no bell, but he sang to God with the aid of his mandolin. The bells would come later.

He climbed down the stone steps and opened the belltower door. The velvety night blew at him, on its breath the scent of the desert and the rustle of the night creatures. Small gums clustered at the point where the church grounds met the rutted municipal track. The leafy tops of two trees formed a natural grotto, and it was here that Cecilia Vivianti had seen the Blessed Virgin when she was a young girl. When the old woman heard of the Mildura priest's plans to build a church at Werrimull she promised him twenty-four rose bushes. Pietro Silvi rubbed the toe of his boot into the sand. Under the soft upper layer it was as hard as stone. He tried to tell Cecilia that the roses might not grow but she insisted. Tomorrow he would let the men plant them, and trust that his Blessed Lady would occasionally water them with her prayers. He peered at the trees and thought he saw a golden glow. But it was only a single star emerging into the fathomless sky.

Father Silvi retraced his steps to the tower room to practise his music. He sat at the window and looked down at his hands. These were God's gift to him, to play music that would comfort those in need.

He picked up the mandolin and strummed as he imagined the desert and the settlers squatting about the edges. He felt compassion for these whose safety nets of tradition and faith had helped them in their homelands, but not here. For Pietro Silvi, Australia was a great theatre of sacrifice with freedom as its reward. He was on a triumphal march. He baptised a child in the morning, found employment for its father in the afternoon, and listened to the sins of the parish in the evening.

It was near to one in the morning when Pietro Silvi placed his hand on his heart, leaned even further out the window, and pronounced that this was the Great Southern Land of the Holy Spirit. Tomorrow his fellow countrymen were returning to build a presbytery for Father Pietro Silvi, loving brother to his community of migrants.

Pietro Silvi slept until after nine o'clock. It was Sunday and he said Mass at eleven to make things easier for his scattered congregation. The service did not end until noon and he had to be at the station to meet the men by half past twelve. It was good of them to give up their weekends to build the presbytery.

There was a tap on the belltower door and he went to answer it. 'Ah, it's you, Delfina! And Stella, Menica, how are you?'

Delfina was holding a bunch of hydrangeas, their mop-heads in shades of blue and pink. She had wrapped them in damp newspaper to keep them moist.

'Flowers for Mass, when you have such a long walk to get here! We'd better put them in the church before they wilt,' he said.

'It's nothing. I love to do it,' Delfina said. Her spirits lifted. She was proud of the flowers she brought to decorate the altar.

She followed Father Silvi to the sacristy and waited while he searched through the cupboards for some vases. His chasuble hung on a nearby coat rack. It was emerald green with an orphrey of intricate gold embroidery. She walked over and ran her finger along its edge. 'It's beautiful,' she said. 'My mother taught me needlework when I was a small girl.'

Father Silvi turned around. 'Then you have many talents, Delfina. We should all do what we're good at. I think of the parable of the three servants. We mustn't be like the third servant who didn't use his gifts. You have your flowers and your embroidery. I have my music.' He rubbed his chin with the tips of his fingers. 'When I was a small boy, my grandmother told me that flowers, music and children would never let me down. And between us'—he looked at Stella and Menica who were walking down the centre aisle—'we have all three. Although your daughters are no longer children.'

Now that she was nineteen, Menica wore her blond hair in an elaborate coil. Her clear gaze and pursed mouth showed confidence in her own beauty. Although a year younger, Stella was still the taller of the two. Her unruly hair stood out like a black nimbus and she was striking rather than pretty, with deep-set eyes and an aquiline nose.

'Menica's going to begin work in the haberdashery shop in Mildura next week. Aren't you?' Delfina pulled playfully at her daughter's sleeve.

'I can't wait,' Menica said. 'I'll go into town with Papa and, when he has to stay a few days on business, I'll sleep at the boarding house.'

'And what about you, Stella?' the priest said.

'I work two days a week on the Lincolns' farm. Sometimes it's packing, or sorting. It depends on the season.' Stella was topping up Delfina's floral arrangements with water. 'The rest of the time, I help Mamma on the block.'

Pietro Silvi turned to Delfina. 'Is Nino coming today?'

'I'm not sure,' Delfina said. 'Nino had to stay in Mildura last night.' She rearranged the hydrangeas carefully. 'It's work, you see.'

Mildura was still an outpost and gossip circulated efficiently. The priest knew how Nino spent his days but not that he stayed away so often at night. 'Of course,' he said. 'I understand.'

Father Silvi was fond of Delfina and her two daughters. When he had given the girls religious instruction at Fay Price's school, he had sometimes smarted under Menica's quick intelligence, but Stella absorbed all he had to say without question. Delfina was a devoted mother and he wondered how she would cope now that the girls were growing up. He watched Delfina place a fat candle on each end of the altar and position her vases. There was a hiss as the match struck the flint. The candles flared and then steadied in the still air.

Enrico rubbed grit from the train window and pressed his nose to the glass. Not far from the track an immense Mallee root lay upended, like a giant tooth. He pulled a battered notebook from his pocket and made a sketch. He was just feathering the edges where fine roots like veins blended grey into white, when the train stopped. His pencil gouged a dark line across his work. 'Damn and blast. Bugger.'

He ducked as a light slap stung the side of his head. His father grinned at him.

'Who do you think you are? Swearing like that,' said Salvatore. 'You're still only fourteen.'

Enrico sat up straight. He was taller than his father. Salvatore ruffled his son's hair and put his arm around him.

At the other end of the carriage men sang a bawdy round, voices joining in until the song had no beginning and no end. Nino sang in a liquid tenor. Salvatore thought he could hear the rhythm of the harvest on Salina in the lower notes. Gaspare barked out his verse, the notes off-key but full of the man's satisfaction with himself. Other voices joined in, some refined and some husky from too many cigarettes and too much whisky.

Then Salvatore began to sing, his rich, restrained bass underpinning the efforts of the others. Enrico listened. Occasionally their various dialects meant they sang different words but Enrico understood that they sang of a communal heritage. In their singing, the men called up something from deep within this place he had never been and he felt his guts knot with longing.

When the men stopped singing, the train grew hotter and sweat ran down their faces. 'What's going on?' Nino said in English. 'Why have we stopped just outside the station? I hope there aren't problems with the construction already? God should be on our side with this project.'

The others laughed and Gaspare lit up a cigarette and blew smoke rings into the air. He was bored and irritable. 'And we do all this,' he said, as he wiped the sweat from his brow, 'to humour a *padre* with a fetish for architecture and the mandolin. I, for one, think there might be better things to do.'

'Then why are you here?' Salvatore stared at him.

He no longer worked for Alfredo di Nola. He had returned to the vineyards and the orchards where he did not have to do daily battle with his conscience.

Gaspare tapped ash on the window ledge and then ground the stub underfoot. 'I come'—he placed both hands on his breast and then extended them outwards—'to give you the benefit of my expertise and to get some credit for the afterlife.'

'I think it's too late for you,' Nino said.

Enrico was curious. He sat hugging his knees with his feet balanced on the edge of the seat.

There was no love lost between Salvatore and Gaspare. Enrico knew it was connected to Shuja's friend Delfina. He knew that Nino, mostly under the wing of the roughneck Gaspare, worked for Alfredo di Nola. He also knew that at some point his father had broken contact with the trio of Alfredo, Gaspare and Nino. It had happened when Delfina was ill with pneumonia. After that Salvatore announced he was going to prune the vines that winter. Francesca wept and said they would have no money.

With a grunt and belch of steam the train pulled into Werrimull station.

Pietro Silvi parked his Pontiac under a tree near the station. He shaded his eyes and peered down the road. A cloud of dust plumed skywards and he heard the uneven rumble of George's lorry. The train had just arrived and all was going to plan. Father Silvi linked his thumbs across his chest and leaned against his car.

The men spilled from the train: a dark-haired bunch, lean from hot days and hard work.

Pietro Silvi could hear Salvatore above the spluttering of the approaching lorry. 'Hey, father, there are enough of us, hey? Plenty to make it a good day's work.' He waved enthusiastically in the direction of the men.

The good father looked at his helpers. Salvatore, of course, he had known would come. Then there were the regular churchgoers, shy in their second-best clothes. Working for the *padre* meant it was different from their weekday work. Pietro Silvi was surprised to see Nino. But the sight of Gaspare answered his question. Pietro Silvi bit on his bottom lip. It was useful for both men to seem part of their crowd. Then the father noted Enrico behind the group, staring at a huge eucalypt. He was crouched on the ground, sketching rapidly.

Curious, Father Silvi left his car and stood behind him, watching the deft movements of Enrico's pencil and the grace of his long, thin fingers. 'Ah, my son, you are a true child of Italy,' he said. 'In your hands lies the legacy of Leonardo! Later, if you like, I will show you some books. I will show you some of the art of your motherland. I will show you…' He checked himself and chuckled. 'Ah, but come on, we must join the others. They have great things to create too.'

The lorry set off towards Our Lady of Lourdes. Enrico perched on a high seat at the back of the cabin. 'Why did the *padre* choose to build a church in such a place?' he asked. 'It would perhaps have been better near the water, a little closer to the river.'

Salvatore was sitting beside his son, knotting the corners of his handkerchief into a hat. 'There is no saying why the *padre* chose this place. Perhaps he wants to be like his God? To have his time in the desert.'

'Maybe it is a place of miracles?' a man in a blue shirt said. 'You know that Cecilia Vivianti said she saw the Blessed Virgin near the church, clothed in yellow with a halo of gold stars.'

Nino chortled. 'These women of ours. They see Madonnas in their dishwater and the will of God in the deeds of men.'

There was laughter followed by silence. No son of Italy could deride the visions of another for very long.

Taking no notice of Nino the man in the blue shirt pushed his way to the side of the truck and pointed to two arching eucalypts. 'It was under those trees. The ones that meet in the middle!'

Salvatore leaned back on his hands to steady himself. The lorry had turned sharp right and now stopped. He looked at the trees. There was nothing between their rangy limbs but the desert. He recalled Stella kneeling before Delfina's statue under its tepee, and grinned. It seemed he was destined to meet Madonnas beneath eucalypts.

nrico stepped from the portico into the church. The cool sandstone walls tempered the light as it flowed through the narrow windows. Enrico sucked in his breath and held it. He walked to the centre aisle and looked at the crucifix on the blank wall behind the altar. He stared hard. Christ's body drooped, alone and heavy with pain.

The men had gone straight to the building site of the new presbytery. He could hear their shouts.

He was pulled from his reverie by a mellow voice. 'I was wondering where you were.' Pietro Silvi stood beside him and followed his gaze. 'Ah! So you can see that's it's not quite right. I've come to the conclusion that something's missing.' The priest sat in the nearby pew and propped his chin in his hands.

The sun shifted and shadows leaped across the altar wall. Enrico turned to the priest. 'I will paint your wall with the story of God and his mother.'

Father Silvi opened his mouth and then closed it. There was something on the boy's face that made refusal difficult. He studied Enrico. What right had he to quench this ardour, especially when it was to the glory of God? After all, Pietro was an artist himself. He put both hands on Enrico's shoulders. 'So, you will bring the old country inside my beautiful church,' he said. He turned to the altar and made the sign of the cross. 'Holy Mother of God, it is a sign from above.'

Enrico did not back away. He was thinking about his pencils and his brushes and the art books he had looked at in the shop in Mildura, until the proprietor had told him to go away.

Father Silvi was excited; he tugged at Enrico's sleeve. He took off his glasses and put them on again just as quickly, twice in succession, as he always did when confronted with the unfathomable. 'Come now, my boy, come! I will give you some books to look at, some pictures. Together we will create a true home for our God.'

The boy and the priest climbed the steps to the belltower. There, Enrico curled up on the sill of Father Silvi's favourite window and learned about the land of his birth from the priest's thumbed volumes.

Enrico lifted his brush and drew the margins of a narrow frieze high on the nave wall. He balanced on a basic scaffold of timber and rope, anchored in sand-filled drums. While his father and the men worked on Father Silvi's presbytery, Enrico outlined a chorus of cherubim, plaited head to toe, and threaded through with bunches of grapes and stems of oranges. This first part was easy, this tangle of wings and flaxen ringlets plucking at abundance. Then, for a while, he found himself confronted by a blank wall.

He began with the Lady, high above the congregation. She floated amid a sea of clouds, her body subsumed in a swathe of blue and white, her bent knee nudging the fabric of her gown. Around her tumbled cherubim and seraphim, kicking with joy and whispering secrets. Pietro Silvi, his hand pressed to his heart, was reminded of Mantegna's angels caught like butterflies in a net, but Enrico's little ones inhabited a wider sky and looped the clouds with fine pink ribbons so that they looked like presents wrapped by the hand of a child.

When it was almost finished Enrico sat at the back of the church holding in his hand a creased and grubby holy picture. Then he lightly sketched a small bell in the right hand of his Virgin.

Pietro Silvi came in from inspecting his presbytery and noted the advent of the bell. He walked along the stone floor to the altar as Enrico washed his brush. He frowned. 'Why do you give the Virgin a bell?' he said. 'It's a symbol of a call. I can see that. But why here?'

'It was because of this.' Enrico held out his holy picture. 'My parents died when I was a baby. They drowned off the coast of Reggio di Calabria and this is the only thing I have that belonged to them.'

Enrico did not elaborate. His life with Francesca had taught him not to ask questions. He understood that she was still troubled by the death of her cousin long ago. She had been on her evening walk and was the first to find the wreckage of the small boat and the bodies spreadeagled on the sand. She became prone to long periods of silence that intensified after their arrival in Australia. The first time she forgot to cook their evening meal and tend to the house, Salvatore put her to bed and called on Shuja for help.

Once, when he was old enough to be curious, Enrico asked Francesca and Salvatore about the holy picture, but his mother shook her head and grew distressed. Salvatore waved aside his questions and sent him from the room. As he grew older, Enrico concluded that this Madonna had lived with them in their hills above Reggio di Calabria and that the holy picture rekindled Francesca's sad memories.

Pietro Silvi reached for the picture. He turned it over and squinted to read the faded message on the back. He had not envisaged a bell as part of his painting but he would accept it.

He read out loud the title of the incarnation. The Virgin made herself known in so many ways. He would never know them all.

'Madonna del Terzito. Where is this Madonna from, my son?'

Enrico shrugged again. 'I don't know. But perhaps it belongs to the home of my real parents.'

Enrico took the picture and put it in his pocket.

Father Silvi stood with his back to the congregation and his arms uplifted in praise. He was overjoyed. The painting was finished and so was the presbytery. His purgatory of nights in the Pontiac or the belltower was over. This Mass was a special celebration, a confirmation that he had listened and carried out the word.

Delfina heard nothing of the priest's prayers. She saw only the bell in the hand of the Lady and the spare form of Enrico. A tight band squeezed her head and pushed in at her temples. Her vision dimmed and she thought she might faint. She leaned on the pew in front for support. But her arms were weak and she sat down. This couldn't be her son? Delfina couldn't believe that in this very place she turned to for sanctuary, her past was laid out in front of her.

She stared at Enrico. The boy was taller than she was but had her fine bone structure and long neck. She gazed at his painting and saw her childhood Madonna. A shooting pain gripped her belly and took away her breath. This must be my punishment, she thought. All these years I have looked after and laughed with my son but I have not been allowed to know him. She lowered her head but she didn't pray. She watched Enrico and the beads from her rosary made indents in her palms.

When the service was over Delfina knelt with her head in her hands. Menica and Stella were used to their mother's devotions and left quietly. They began to walk home. If they were lucky someone would stop and offer them a lift in their car.

Enrico stood at the back of the church while the men and women embraced him and kissed his cheeks. Delfina did not leave her pew until the church was empty. Enrico felt a pull on his sleeve and turned. When he saw Delfina he shrugged. 'This is so embarrassing...'

Delfina tried to match the young man in front of her with the baby born on remote Filicudi. She saw his open mouth searching for her, tossing from side to side in his thick blanket. She heard his plaintive cry. And for a moment she felt island dew on her skin and she gasped. The only way I can be sure, she thought in desperation, is to touch him. But Enrico moved and her hand fell from his sleeve. He had been hoping for some lighthearted comment from Delfina, some relief from all the compliments and congratulations.

She pointed down the aisle to the painting on the wall. 'Why did you paint a bell in her hand?' she said.

'You, too?' Enrico was surprised. 'Father Silvi wanted to know about the bell. I don't think he liked it.'

Delfina faced Enrico. 'Why?'

Taken aback, Enrico repeated his story. 'So, you see, I painted the bell to honour the memory of my parents.'

'But where were your parents going when they drowned?' Delfina said. 'Who took care of you when they died?'

Enrico grimaced. These questions again.

'Salvatore said my parents were going to America,' he said. 'It was to be a new life. I was only a tiny baby. They boarded the ship off Reggio di Calabria. As it was there for one week, they went back to shore to visit family. A freak wave turned their boat over when they were returning to the ship and they drowned. Francesca adopted me even before she married Salvatore.'

'Where did your parents come from?' said Delfina.

Enrico rummaged in his pocket and pulled out the holy picture. He held it out to Delfina. 'I don't know where they came from,' he said. 'I only know that it is the home of this Madonna. My mother says that my life began in Reggio di Calabria when she took me in. I don't think even Salvatore knows any more than that. But I know my life began somewhere else. I just don't know where it is.'

The Madonna in the picture inclined her head towards the bell held between her thumb and forefinger. Her gown was shades of indigo, a thin drapery of white across her breast. Her head was swathed in the deepest blue. Her feet were bare and her left hand rested just below a long ivory neck. Her expression was kind and her garments swirled about her, disarranged by the wind perhaps or by the surrounding bevy of angels.

Enrico looked up at Delfina. 'Why do you want to know all this?'

Delfina fought the urge to tell Enrico the truth. She had harboured her secret all these years and lived with the memory of a child she had thought was dead. She wanted to embrace Enrico and never let him go. Instead she swallowed hard and pushed her arms into her sides. She knew that now he did not belong to her. If the truth were known, so many would suffer.

'You were destined to paint this church,' she said. She ran her forefinger across the face of the holy picture and then returned it to Enrico. Her fingertips brushed against his hand and a shiver ran through her body. 'In this painting you're discovering the story of your life. When the time is right you will find the rest of your story.'

Enrico studied the holy picture first, then the painting. He looked pleased.

Delfina watched him. He has none of Paolo's fisherman's strength, she thought, but his eyes are as deep as the sea. Her son had brought her the gift of her Madonna and the gift of his life. But she felt the Salina wind sharp between her shoulder blades and the bitter tang of sea salt on her lips.

21

Angelina's letter to Delfina arrived in early March. Nino collected it from their roadside mailbox on his way into Mildura. He tucked it between the sun visor and the roof of the car, and promptly forgot about it. On the other side of the continent, in Albany, Paolo also received a letter from Angelina. He sat and peered at it.

> *My dear Paolo,*
>
> *This time it is I who write to you instead of my beloved Fortunato.*
>
> *In all these years he has kept me abreast of your news. How he loved to receive your letters!*
>
> *But he has died, my Paolo, and I am bereft.*
>
> *In the last days he asked me to write to you, to ask you to go to Delfina. We both felt that it must be so...*
>
> *Do not worry about me for I will go on as I have always done. God looks after us all.*
>
> *With all my love and my prayers,*
>
> *Angelina Coltelli*

In the weeks after her conversation with Enrico, Delfina withdrew into herself. She prayed each day in front of her Madonna at the shrine in the eucalypt. On the days she went to Our Lady of Lourdes, she stayed after the Mass finished and stared at Enrico's painting. When she saw her son, straight and proud, she felt as if she could hardly breathe.

And at night she dreamed the same dream.

In this dream she, or at least some part of her, from some time long before she was born, was riding on a spread of angels' wings. Feathers sprouted from the sides of the thick tendon running the length of each wing, locking and interlocking so that they formed a bridge of feathers. Her father rode with her and the sweeping sinews easily carried them to the pale, shining baby lying on its mother's breast at the far end of her dream. Just as Fortunato bent to puff the air over the sleeping child, the wind rose and whipped between them and cackled as it swept off into the distance.

Then she was very small and stood at the bottom of a flight of multi-coloured stairs. A voice travelled up from the recesses of her dream and wound its way down the rocky hillside beside the steps. It hid amongst the gorse and the broom and teased her when it grew faint. And, just when she thought it had gone, the voice broke free. Relieved, she held out her hands and waited to feel its rush against her palms, to hold it in the cup of her ear. But the wind again whipped across the path in front of her and it was gone. There was nothing but the path leading nowhere and silence.

After that came firelight and stories spilling like jewels from the flames. She gathered them as they fell, filling her pockets. But they grew too heavy and she lay down amongst the grapevines, helpless as the stories tumbled down the mountainside and splashed into the sea.

Delfina woke in darkness and sat up in bed. After several minutes she made out some familiar shapes and was comforted.

But the dream had come again. This time the detail was sharper and the colour brighter. She lay down, watching the shapes shift in the night.

She woke the following morning to the moan of the wind and the flick of sand against her window. Her unease had turned into foreboding.

When Nino came home later in the day she was waiting.

He handed her the mail. There was one letter that was a little more creased and grubby than the rest. It bore a postmark from six weeks previous and it was bordered in black. 'You can't rely on the mail,' Nino said. 'Can you? Living in the desert as we do.'

Delfina slid her fingernail beneath the loose flap of the letter. The others fluttered to the ground. She pulled out a sheet of paper, bordered like the envelope, and turned her back to the sun to read it.

Nino heard a dry gasp, like a deep hiccup, and then nothing. The early evening warmth settled around them. The discarded letters skipped along the sand, driven by a rising breeze. The sheet of paper in Delfina's hand rustled.

'What is it?' Nino said.

Delfina turned towards him and he blanched.

Her voice was quiet and controlled. 'It's Papa.'

Nino stood helpless. Until this moment he had kept the past at a distance. Now it overwhelmed him. During their long days amongst the vines Nino and his father had exchanged banter about the fisherman with the silent wife and the beautiful daughter. They knew of Fortunato's absolute confidence in a divine plan, manifest in the simplicity of his life. Now Nino forgot the swaggering Alfredo and the seductive Maria Rossi, and remembered that he had taken the daughter of Fortunato Coltelli. And that he shared in her sorrow.

He moved towards Delfina and she leaned against his chest for support. She did not try to embrace him or even hold onto him. She kept her hands clasped against her chest. Between them stood Papa Fortunato with his stories, his laughter and his God, while behind them stretched years, oceans and continents.

Nino went to put his arms around his wife, but dropped them to his sides. He looked up hastily to regain his bearings: there was the block, his car and the two girls standing uneasily in the doorway. 'I'll get Stella to make tea,' he said.

Then he sat on a nearby log and watched as Delfina wept.

It was only a few days after this that Paolo saw the Murray River for the first time. The water was still, waiting for the change already written in the sky. Mildura was much larger than he had imagined and Paolo had made no clear plans. He needed to find work and a place to stay. He flexed the muscles of his back, sore from nights spent sleeping rough.

It had taken Paolo eight years to leave Western Australia. He had a steady job on a fishing trawler and the other fishermen appreciated his skills. He knew Delfina lived in Victoria and at times he desperately wanted to see her again. But he was kept away by his promise to respect her wishes. During that time he fished waters bordered by alabaster sands, the horizon curving into a milky distance. The sea had been some consolation for the loss of Salina, although he found its vastness disorienting. This new landscape of Mildura was a further surprise. The air was suffocating and even the water lay flaccid. Blues and sea greens had been replaced by yellows and olives and ochres. A palette faded by the sun and the constant rubbing of sand.

Paolo did not hear the footsteps until they were close. He was exhausted. He heard a rolling accent with upward inflections and soft endings.

'The river waits for winter, for sleep and then rain.' The speaker laughed at his own words. 'She's like a mighty beast, running with the seasons. They've built locks to control her flow of water but maybe she will be stronger than all their efforts.'

The man sat down beside him and held out a callused hand. 'My name is Salvatore di Maggio. And that is my wife, Francesca'—he pointed to a woman sitting a short distance away under the canopy of a pepper tree—'it's good to meet you. Francesca likes to rest by the river after she's finished her shopping. There's usually no one here at this time of day.'

Paolo could not remember his last proper human contact, apart from formal exchanges at ticket boxes or across shop counters.

'I don't think I've seen you around before. Have you just arrived?' Salvatore said.

Paolo didn't speak.

Salvatore tried again. 'Maybe I can help you? I've been here now for over ten years.'

Still the stranger said nothing.

Salvatore shrugged and made to get up. 'If there's anything I can do, ask for me at the Grand Hotel. We all end up there sooner or later.' As he stood up, he considered Paolo. There was something about the man, damn him!

'I've just arrived,' Paolo said suddenly. 'But I've been in the west for eight years, so I'm not new to this country.'

Salvatore noted the lines fanning from the corners of the stranger's eyes and his pinched smile.

'It's good of you to offer to help me,' the man said. 'My name's Paolo Paschini. I need to find work and then I need to find…'

'There might be work out at Werrimull with the *padre*,' Salvatore said. He put a hand on Paolo's shoulder. 'We've just built the new presbytery and there's still a lot of work to be done. I'll take Francesca home and then drive you there. Come and meet my wife.'

They walked over to where Francesca sat in the speckled shade of the tree. Paolo held out his hand. 'Your husband's been very kind,' he said.

Francesca looked up at him. Her face was angular and proud, her eyes deep set and ringed with dark shadows. She had the reserved air of a woman who had wrestled with demons. 'I'm pleased to meet you,' she said. 'I'm sure Salvatore will be able to help you.'

Salvatore looked from his wife to Paolo. He is an odd one, he thought, intense and sad. Through Francesca, he had learned to understand deep hurt. He shrugged. He was doing nothing more than his duty.

Around five o'clock in the evening Pietro Silvi felt the change in the weather. He licked his palm, held it skyward and rotated his wrist until he felt the saliva dry cold. In the Mallee true autumn came with this slight decrease in the temperature of the wind.

Pietro Silvi looked to the west. A purplish undertone softened the sky. The yellow sandstone of Our Lady of Lourdes had faded first to old gold, then to amber. Even Cecilia Vivianti's roses in their grave of sand looked more alive. Father Silvi picked up his bucket, filled it from the tap at the back of the church and proceeded to water each plant. He listened to the wind's thin whistle and the crackle of water on sand. Something made him look up. The desert was like that. Its clarity and quiet sharpened the senses. To Father Silvi it was no more than the voice of God reaching closer. The natural home of the Desert Fathers. He returned to his watering, oblivious to all but the dark watermarks in the sand. At first he was not sure whether it was the wind or a voice. The sounds were soft and could have been part of the evening *pastorale*.

'Hey, *padre*, it's me,' Salvatore called. 'I've brought Paolo Paschini to you. Maybe you can help him.'

Father Silvi broke off from his meditation. Already he heard the words of the Gospels, precise and unalterable. Which of you, if his son asks for bread, will give him a stone? He walked towards the two men and held out his hand to Paolo. 'Welcome, my son. How can I be of help?'

'He needs work,' Salvatore rushed in. 'Perhaps there's something he can do at the presbytery?'

'Yes, yes Salvatore,' said the priest. 'Give our good friend time.' He turned to Paolo and saw he had screwed his cap into a tight ball. 'Is work what you need?' he said.

Paolo nodded and cleared his throat.

Pietro Silvi put an arm around Paolo's shoulders and leaned closer to him. He winked at Salvatore. 'Come, I'll show you my new home,' he said. 'Did Salvatore tell you of my years in the belltower?'

The next day, Salvatore brought Paolo back to Our Lady of Lourdes to begin his work painting the presbytery. Before he left, he showed Paolo the church. They stood at the start of the centre aisle and Salvatore pointed to the painting above the altar.

'It's magnificent, isn't it?' he said. He doffed his cap and genuflected. 'You can thank my son for this.'

'Your son? Painted that?'

'Yes. He began to draw as a small child. Anything. Everything.'

Paolo hesitated. 'Are there a lot of Italians around here?'

Paolo's responses confounded Salvatore. You began to talk to him about one subject and you ended up somewhere entirely different. At least this time he was actually talking.

'Yes. There are a lot of us.' Salvatore sat down in a nearby pew. He slouched against the wooden bench with his legs splayed, batting his cap from one hand to the other. To his surprise, Paolo sat beside him.

'Tell me about them,' he said.

Salvatore thought for a moment. 'As I told you, I've been here for over ten years. My wife isn't well and because of her illness our son Enrico was often cared for by Shuja, a friend who lives out of town. All the migrants help each other. It doesn't matter which country you come from. It's hard, but when we share our winemaking, or even just our memories, it's that bit easier.

'There is a woman, Delfina, who set up a fruit and vegetable stall. Shuja and Enrico have been helping her for years. Enrico grew up alongside her two daughters.' Salvatore dropped his cap and bent to pick it up.

Paolo started at Delfina's name. He had been taken aback by Mildura's size. How would he ever find Delfina and her family? And now Salvatore was leading him to them. While Paolo was travelling, he had been preoccupied by memories. At times he still felt his fingers in Delfina's long hair and saw the rainbow that had arced above them. Now that they were close, he was confronted by more immediate realities. Would he recognise her? Thirteen years had passed and she would be thirty-eight. Her daughters would be not much younger than she had been when he last saw her. Paolo realised that his memories had become dreams and a longing for the past made a shiver run the length of his back. He knew all he could hope for was to touch his Delfina and share her sorrow. He nudged Salvatore who was staring at the painting. 'You were saying?'

'Yes, well. Most of the men work in the orchards or the vineyards, and some have joined the crews of travelling workers and moved on.' Salvatore paused. 'Of course,' he continued, 'we've those who set their own rules and make sure others obey. Alfredo di Nola has set up a lucrative racket, helped by others. There's Gaspare, Nino...'

'Then there is our *padre*,' continued Salvatore. 'We all praise God for the bit of *Italia* he's made for us here at Our Lady of Lourdes. Now it's your turn. Where have you come from?' Surely, he thought, there could be no more straightforward question.

Paolo stood up and walked the length of the aisle to the altar rails. Salvatore followed him. 'This Nino you mentioned,' Paolo said. 'He's married?'

The man had shifted the conversation again. 'Yes, of course. Delfina and Nino, for me, they've always lived different lives.' He laughed. 'But I could hardly have expected you to know who belonged to whom. You'll meet them soon. Delfina and the girls come to Mass at Werrimull every second Sunday. Nino's usually busy in Mildura.' He did a quick calculation in his head. 'Actually, they'll come here this week, if I'm right.'

Paolo turned his back on the altar and leaned against the rails, pressing his palms hard on the flat wooden surface. He stared at Salvatore. 'I know Nino and Delfina. I come from the island of Salina, too.'

Salvatore started. This man was all surprises. 'Then they'll be thrilled. You'll have a lot to talk about,' he said.

'I've known Nino and Delfina since childhood.' Paolo hesitated. 'And I've come here to share their sorrow. You would know of the death of Delfina's father, Fortunato Coltelli? He was also a father to me. He taught me the ways of the sea.' Paolo lowered his head. 'His wife, Angelina, wrote to me and asked me to come to Delfina, to the family.'

Salvatore crossed himself. The easy camaraderie evaporated and his voice came from far back in his throat. 'No, she hasn't said anything.'

Both men had the same thought. Was it possible that Delfina did not know of her father's death? Or perhaps she was not yet ready to share her sorrow?

'You must take me to her,' Paolo said.

Salvatore watched the muscles in Paolo's jaw tighten, and was taken aback when he strode down the aisle and out the church door. Paolo did not look back or cross himself.

Salvatore bent hastily on one knee, then followed Paolo from the church. Thin white strips of cloud streaked the sky, blown by a querulous wind. Salvatore looked about wildly, startled by the activity after the hush of the church. Then he settled his cap and hurried after Paolo. He had a few hours to spare and this was important. 'I'll go and tell Father Silvi we'll be back soon,' he called to Paolo. 'I'll meet you at the car.'

'Tell me more about Nino and Delfina,' said Paolo. He and Salvatore were driving along the bumpy road between Our Lady of Lourdes and Nino's fruit block.

'Nino works for Alfredo di Nola,' said Salvatore. 'Before that he worked amongst the fruit as we've all done. Wogs and fruit.' There was no bitterness in Salvatore's warm laugh. 'That's how they see us. They don't understand the importance of the crops to us. So they find it amusing. If the crops failed in the old country it was not so easy to move elsewhere or find some new occupation. Here, if things don't turn out as planned, people move on. It's different.'

Was his passenger listening? Salvatore decided to keep talking. 'Anyway, I also worked for Alfredo at the beginning. But in the end I returned to the fruit and now I have little money and a clear conscience.'

Paolo shifted in his seat.

Salvatore hesitated. Paolo's intense interest in Nino and Delfina surprised him. He guessed that he would never hear the full story. But Salvatore loved this family and sensed Paolo had played an important part in their lives. He decided to tell Paolo as much as might be helpful to him.

'I often collected Enrico from Delfina's place after work.'

A rabbit scooted onto the road and Salvatore swerved. It looked up, startled, before quivering the length of its body and scampering away.

'And Delfina's children? They must be grown up by now.'

'Menica, the oldest, is nineteen. A beauty like her mother, but fair-haired and not with her mother's temperament. The youngest daughter, Stella, has Delfina's quiet nature but doesn't look like her. She's just turned eighteen.'

'And there are no more children?'

'No, there were no more children.' Salvatore hesitated, reluctant to discredit his friend. 'Nino spends a lot of time in Mildura,' he finished lamely.

The two men fell silent. There had been little rain since the previous year and the paddocks around them lay cropped and yellowed. Skeletal sheep nosed amongst the blue bush. They followed the road around a bend in the river lined with white-grey gums, their trunks peeling bark in ribbons.

'That's the house, there, just near the river,' said Salvatore.

Paolo leaned forward.

Salvatore brought the car to a halt and let his hands fall into his lap.

'Delfina will be there. She rarely leaves, except to go to church. I haven't seen either of them for days.' He turned to Paolo. 'You've had the news for so long. Surely she must know, but I can't understand why she hasn't told us.'

Puzzled, he motioned to Paolo to open his door, and the two men set off towards the house.

The day was cool, one of those uncertain days marking the end of one season and the beginning of another. Delfina walked beside the narrow garden bed, occasionally plucking a last rotting fruit and throwing it into the basket she hauled behind her. She was dressed entirely in black.

Stella watched. The black clothes were proof that Delfina belonged to some other place. It had been all right when Stella simply shared her mother's beliefs. But these clothes singled Delfina out as different. Stella was not sure if she wanted to be that different. She was standing outside the back wire door and looked in at Menica, busy tying her hair at the mirror in the kitchen. Then she turned back to Delfina and shouted, 'Mamma, we're going.'

Delfina looked up and waved.

Menica poked her head around the door. 'Bye, Mamma. Papa will be waiting for us at the road. We're going shopping and then he's taking us to the pictures.' She didn't wait for a reply.

Stella eyed her sister, then called out again, tentatively. 'Bye, Mamma.'

The two girls hurried down the hallway and out the front door. 'Thank goodness,' Menica said. She grabbed Stella's hand and began to run. 'It's so good to get away from the house. And I love it when Papa takes me out to lunch. You know, when I stay at the boarding house, we go for a walk in the evening by the river. He's introduced me to lots of his friends.'

'I'm sure Mamma gets lonely when we're both not home.' Stella paused and looked for her mother around the side of the house.

'I don't think so,' said Menica. They had arrived at the letterbox and were waiting for Nino. 'You only work two days a week and you're here with Mamma for the rest of the time!'

Stella was pleased that Menica was happy. Menica had hated being confined to the block and her mother's prayers. Stella on the other hand enjoyed the peace of her mother's garden and was fond of the little Madonna now bleached white in the arms of the eucalypt. But even Stella was concerned at how Nonno's death had changed their mother. She craned her neck and glimpsed Delfina bending over the garden bed at the back of the house. For the first time, it seemed to Stella that her mother was a long way away.

Paolo thought he recognised the tune, a series of humming sounds. He was walking along the blind side of the house and, at the familiar reprise, he stopped short, waiting for what he guessed would follow. There was an interval, as if the singer had been distracted, and then the melodic minor notes of an old sea song. Fortunato's song.

Paolo moved a few steps forward to the corner and looked around. Delfina was sweeping the concrete outside the back door.

Her shoulders were stooped, as if she had begun to fold inwards on herself. It was the way of the women of Italy, Paolo thought. They gradually disappeared, first behind their husbands, then their children, and finally behind an accumulation of deaths. He swallowed hard as he took in Delfina's straight black skirt and black cardigan buttoned to the neck. Her sensible court shoes and seamed stockings were also black. She wore no jewellery. Her only ornament was a black lace mantilla tied around her head. Her hair was pinned into a tight bun. He thought of the young woman in the vibrant red dress, laughing as she brushed water droplets from her hair.

Paolo stepped into full view.

Delfina looked up. She was the first to speak. 'When did you hear the news?'

'Six weeks ago. And you?'

'Only last week. Nino brought the letter. Sometimes letters get lost.'

Both guessed at the truth but it could not be said. She is still beautiful, Paolo thought, still fine-boned with eyes too deep to read.

Delfina walked over to him and held his hands. She took a step back to see him clearly. Then she bent forward to kiss him and her lips were soft on his cheeks.

'Papa wrote to me…Oh, a long time ago. He told me that you had left Salina and come here.' She waited but he did not speak. 'I didn't expect to see you again.'

Paolo shuffled. 'When our child went away it was if he had never been. Then you left to come here and our time together seemed like a dream. I loved you but whatever had brought us together had gone.' Delfina shook her head but Paolo continued. 'I stayed for as long as I could and then I travelled. I was searching for something but I couldn't let it be you. I had to let you live the life you had chosen.'

The sun broke the cloud lining and a chorus of cicadas burst from the garden.

'Then I received Angelina's letter and she told me to come to you,' Paolo said.

Delfina led Paolo into the cool of the house. There they exchanged the litanies of memory, love and longing common to all deaths.

Suddenly, Delfina clutched at the edge of the table. The colour went from beneath her fingernails and the veins stood out on the backs of her hands. There were things to be said. She knew there would never be a right time, only now, a moment. 'There's a boy living here. He's been with me since he was a child. Salvatore's son. His name is Enrico.'

Paolo interrupted. 'Salvatore showed me his painting inside Our Lady of Lourdes. He's very talented for one so young.'

Delfina shook her head to silence him. 'Did you notice anything about the painting? Try to remember the detail.'

Paolo was perplexed but Delfina's intensity made him feel as if he were holding a delicate flower that might spoil. 'In the painting there's a Madonna,' he murmured, as if in a trance. 'Ah… The Madonna del Terzito. She's holding the little bell.'

Delfina's eyes were blazing. 'Yes, it's my Madonna.'

'You told Enrico about Salina?' Paolo asked.

'No, Enrico painted it from a holy picture he's carried since he was a child.'

'But Salvatore told me he came from Calabria.'

'Enrico is no blood son of Salvatore,' Delfina said. 'He lived with Salvatore's wife even before they married.'

Paolo made to interrupt but she raised her hand.

'He is not her child either, but the child of her cousin. He told me the cousin and her husband drowned near Reggio di Calabria. They were going to America.'

Paolo frowned, fitting the fragments together in his mind. 'So this boy is really...'

Delfina leant across the table and touched his hand. 'Yes, I only realised it when I saw the painting and then questioned Enrico. He is our son. The son of a woman who has been away for too long and a man who is still travelling.'

Paolo's elbows rested on the table top, his chin cupped in the tips of his fingers. He was watching Delfina intently. At her words his shoulders sagged and he dropped his head, rubbing his fingers back and forth across his forehead. He heard Fortunato's voice, that all would come full circle in the end. *It might not be as you would wish. But of what consequence are our wishes?*

Delfina had not finished. 'You must promise not to tell anyone. Especially Enrico.'

'But why haven't you told him?'

Delfina withdrew her hand. 'Enrico's life has been difficult enough. It's not that I don't want to tell him. When I first realised who he was I thought my heart would break. You must understand that this secret has torn me apart. I remember the night Mario rowed us from Filicudi. I knew what Ludevina had planned for my son. But could I ever tell Enrico that I gave him away?' Delfina stared at Paolo as her words came out fast and passionate. 'Enrico loves Salvatore and Francesca and is happy with them. He wouldn't want them hurt. And there's Nino, and my daughters. I don't want to hurt them. Maybe the time will come when Enrico can be told. But not now.'

Paolo looked at Delfina. She has become so strong, he thought. She has made difficult choices and given up many things: her parents, her island and her son. It had taken love and courage to do what she did. He had respected her wishes then and he would respect them again. 'No, it's not the time to tell him,' he agreed.

Salvatore knocked on the door. He somehow knew that Paolo and Delfina would have a lot to say to each other and had left them alone. 'I'm sorry to interrupt,' he said. 'But we'd better go, I promised to pick up Enrico from Mildura at five o'clock.'

Delfina walked with them to the car. As Salvatore started the engine, she leaned in the passenger side window and put her hand on Paolo's cheek. He pressed his hand over hers and their eyes met. As Salvatore drove away, Paolo watched Delfina shrink until he could no longer distinguish her from the landscape.

22

From where she sat by the window, Delfina watched the frost glitter in the morning sun. Over the last six weeks her pneumonia worsened. She ate little and with difficulty. When she closed her eyes to rest, she saw not only Nino and her daughters but also Paolo and Enrico.

Stella entered the room and walked over to her mother. 'Mamma, you're supposed to stay in bed until lunchtime. You should have waited for me to help.' She handed Delfina a cup of tea and sat beside her. 'It might be warm enough later for you to go outside.'

Delfina sipped her drink and looked out the window. 'You know, even after all these years, frost still makes me think of the sea,' she said.

'I don't think you could get two more different things than frost and sea,' said Stella.

'It's like sun on water,' Delfina explained. 'When the crests of the waves are so bright you have to close your eyes.'

Stella was worried. Since her mother had fallen ill in June, she'd left the household routine to her daughters, preferring to sit alone by the window.

Delfina turned to Stella. But before she could continue, a hacking cough made her double over in pain. She straightened slowly and took a shallow breath. 'If anything happens to me,' she wheezed, 'I want you and Menica to share the money I've saved from the stall.'

'Mamma, don't say things like that,' said Stella. 'Nothing will happen.' She took the empty cup and fussed with the cushions.

'There's enough money for you to visit Salina,' Delfina said. 'You need to see the place where you were born. I chose for you to come here but I would like you to make your own choice.'

Lately her mother's reminiscences had made Stella wonder about Angelina and her white house above the sea. She thought she might like to walk the favourite paths of Delfina's childhood.

Menica came into the room with a bundle of washing. 'There's so much to do,' she said, shaking her head at Stella. 'We need to finish the housework and box up the oranges. Mr Lincoln still wants them, doesn't he?' She picked up the blanket that had fallen from Delfina's knees. 'You should go for a walk, Mamma. And then have a sleep.'

Menica and Stella helped her walk to the stall. She sat on a low seat outside and leaned against the warm timber walls. The girls began stacking the boxes they needed for the oranges. The frost had melted and the Murray River lay still and yellow. In the distance Delfina made out her eucalyptus shrine and imagined the Madonna snug in its branches. Poor little Madonna, she thought, I wonder how you've enjoyed your sanctuary so far from home? She closed her eyes and saw the sanctuary in Salina, safe in Valdichiesa. When she opened them she saw papery eucalypts and grassland razed to dust by cattle and sheep and the foraging of native animals.

August came and Delfina's health did not improve. An icy wind blew across the Mallee for three weeks. There was no rain, just a chill that seeped through the cracks in the walls and even through the warmest clothing.

By the end of August, she was too ill to leave her bed. Her dark hair lay across the pillow and hung over the sides of the bed. She has the look of the dying, Pietro Silvi thought. Her eyelids were hooded and bruised. He watched as she stirred.

'We both know, don't we?' she whispered.

Pietro Silvi traced a cross on her forehead. 'We know nothing. With God's help you will get well. But you must believe this to be so.'

'I want to tell you,' said Delfina. But the priest shook his head. Experience had taught him not to encourage an ill person to accept death. His role was to minister to the sick but not to reinforce their fears.

'Are you sure you want to tell me these things, Delfina?' he said. 'It's too easy when you are ill to say things better left unsaid. You lead a good and quiet life alongside your God. You do not need me to come between you. If you want to mention some general sadness I will bless it and consign it to our God's mercy.'

'I have let my family down,' she said. There was desperation in her voice. Pietro Silvi was puzzled. Here was a woman who had travelled across the world for husband and children, who had left the culture she understood to battle with a strange land. Why would she feel she had let people down? But he knew one did not exist without the other, that she must also feel let down. He took her hand.

'We will say the rosary,' he said. 'The Glorious Mysteries.' He walked to the door and called Menica and Stella to join them.

'*Padre nostro che sei nei cieli…*' intoned Pietro Silvi. Delfina closed her eyes at the familiar words. The priest led, her daughters responded and Delfina thought of her family. She had left Salina for them. She had hoped that rejoining Nino in a place far from Paolo and the memory of her son would be a new start. She did not take into account that those three years of separation from her husband could seem like a lifetime. She had thought to protect her daughters from Ludevina's influence, to keep them immersed in the traditions that shored up her own life. Instead, she watched Menica assimilate into a new culture and drift from her, while Stella hovered between the old and the new. She had been the cause of Nino's frustrations and her daughters' displacement.

Of the extended family she hoped to assuage by leaving Salina, Papa was dead and Angelina reliant on their cousins and relatives. Ludevina was no longer in control of her mind and Aldo would be distraught.

And then there was Paolo. She had sacrificed both him and their son for the good of them all. She had loved Paolo but believed that real love was lived out in selflessness. She had been naïve to think she could provide answers by running away. Her past ghosts returned when least expected and collided with the life she had created. When she thought of Enrico, however, she felt kinship with her Madonna; she had held pain in the palm of her hand.

When he reached the first Hail Mary of the last decade of the glorious mysteries, Pietro Silvi bent over Delfina, '*Ave Maria, piena di grazia…*' he began. Then he paused and listened. Delfina's breath was quiet but came from deep in her belly and Pietro Silvi heard the rattle of death, and then all was silent.

The next morning, Stella visited her mother's eucalyptus shrine for the last time. When she returned she sat on the back step.

The wind was bitter and she pulled her coat around her. Her face was blotched and her eyes were swollen from crying. She felt a hand on her shoulder. 'My poor girl,' said Shuja. Shuja sat down and drew Stella close to her. Her silk sari was cool against Stella's face.

Menica's voice came from inside the house. 'Stella, where are you? We still have a lot to do.'

'Coming,' Stella called. She turned to Shuja. 'Thank you for your help. Mamma was too young to die.'

'I know,' Shuja said. 'I loved your mother. She was my friend. We shared things: laughter, our troubles, and the success of our stall.'

They rose and went into the house where Delfina's body lay in the front room on a plain white linen cloth on a makeshift table. The blinds were lowered and the room was dim and cold. Menica had crossed her mother's arms over her chest. The girls had not wanted their mother to be buried in her black day clothes and had dressed her in a grey satin dress with a long full skirt.

Stella walked over to her mother. She reached into her pocket and pulled out a grimy figurine. It was Delfina's Madonna. Time and weather had worn the Madonna's cream gown to white, its girdle reduced to golden speckles. The turquoise cloak was now the light blue of an outback sky. The corona had snapped and six stars stuck out from each of the Madonna's shoulders. Stella tried to rejoin the wire but it had rusted and one side broke off in her fingers. She laid the statue and the broken piece beside Delfina. 'Mamma would not want to be separated from her now,' she said. Menica put her arms around her sister.

Shuja bent over Delfina. 'Goodbye, Delfina,' she whispered. 'May the gods and your Madonna go with you.'

The three spent the morning cleaning and tidying until the slip covers were unruffled, the antimacassars lay straight over the arms and backs of the chairs, and large vases of greenery interspersed with winter camellias stood on either side of the door. The kitchen benches were spread with cakes and plates of sandwiches covered with damp tea towels.

When the funeral directors came to take Delfina to Our Lady of Lourdes, they were surprised to be given an old, broken figurine to bury with her.

Father Pietro Silvi watched Nino, Paolo, Salvatore and Enrico carry the coffin down the aisle of the church. The men set the coffin on the bier at the front of the altar and there was an expectant silence. Pietro Silvi cleared his throat and began. 'We have come here today to celebrate the life of Delfina Terzito Palmerino,' he said. 'Her family told me that Delfina's parents prayed to the Madonna del Terzito when their baby daughter's life was in danger. It is fitting that we should ask Delfina's Madonna to intercede for her at the hour of her death.'

Paolo stared at the mural on the wall. Pietro Silvi bowed his head and began to pray the Mass.

The mourners processed from the church to the adjoining cemetery. The air was heavy with the scent of freshly dug earth. The men placed the coffin beside the grave and Pietro Silvi walked slowly around it swinging his censer. The incense wafted across the heaped dirt and onto the black-clad mourners. They were all from the Italian community with the exception of Shuja who stood to the back dressed in her white mourning sari. Pietro Silvi crooked his finger and gathered them all to him. 'Now, we will consign Delfina to the earth and her God,' he said. There was a soft thud as a clod of dirt hit the lid of the coffin. Menica and Stella wept silently. Nino, pale and stiff, walked forward and placed some early white lilies at the foot of his wife's grave. He put one arm around each of his daughters and drew them to him. Paolo fumbled with his hat; his shoulders slumped and the veins stood out in his neck. Salvatore and Enrico held each other. Their faces were ashen. Then the mourners linked arms and walked from the gravesite.

When the burial was over, Pietro Silvi folded his vestments onto the back seat of his car and slammed the door. He flicked his fingers to ward off the cold, rubbed them hard against each other and glanced in the direction of the grave. Only Paolo remained standing by the heaped mounds of earth.

The revving of car engines interrupted the quiet of the burial. The mourners were heading for Nino's fruit block. Pietro Silvi did not immediately follow the convoy. He liked to be alone in the space between the burial and the wake. It was unusual for anyone other than himself to stay behind. He bunched up the skirts of his cassock and set off towards the grave.

The Werrimull cemetery was arid, its compressed, yellow surface broken by intermittent graves with concrete edges and sandy centres, guarded by angels or crosses. Other graves were unadorned. As he weeded and tidied the graveyard, Father Silvi made up lives for the names etched into the memorials. He liked to talk to their spirits, to feel that they were all his family under this vast sky.

He reached the gravesite and bent to replace a bunch of scarlet camellias knocked away from the nearby floral guard-of-honour. He blew on their petals to remove the dust and looked sideways at Paolo. 'She was a good woman, a good mother. She was devout,' he said. He was frustrated by the inadequacy of his words.

'Is that enough?' Paolo said.

'It's not enough for you?'

'Loyalty and duty can be mistaken,' Paolo said. He paused, deciding whether to finish his sentence. 'For love.'

'Is this what you believe happened to Delfina?'

Paolo looked at the priest. 'A long time ago Delfina's father told me that things often work out differently from what we hope. He believed that was how it should be. Delfina believed this.' There was sorrow in his face and pride in his voice. 'When we discovered...' Paolo checked himself. 'When we met again she told me she had been away for too long. Do you think this was how the end should have been for her?'

Paolo clutched at the priest's sleeve and Pietro Silvi placed his hand over Paolo's. 'It doesn't matter what I think. Do you think this was how it should have been?'

Paolo didn't answer. He looked down at the wooden coffin, already coated with a fine layer of dirt, and wept.

There was a full moon the night of the wake. Salvatore took a long drag of his cigarette and exhaled. He looked over towards the house. The back door slammed and Stella, her frizzy hair framed in the light, looked around before walking towards him. Her face was like a mask, stiff from the effort of the day. Salvatore paced up and down the rows of vegetable and flower beds, now overgrown with weeds. Delfina had been too ill in the late autumn and early winter to tend to the rampant growth. He ran his fingers through the feathery heads of seeded parsley. Stella arrived at his side as seeds began their slow fall and she reached out a hand to catch them.

'Mamma would have hated to see the garden like this,' she said.

Salvatore placed his arm around her shoulders and Stella wept. At first a few silent tears, then sobs hurled from her. He let her cry, while the moon rose higher and his own sadness stuck in his throat.

'Delfina died when the news came about Fortunato,' he said.

Stella looked at him with relief. 'So you do understand. I thought you might. When Papa Fortunato died Mamma put on black clothes.' She stopped and thought hard. 'Mamma was suddenly a long way from all of us. Menica didn't notice. No, it's not fair of me to say such things. Menica and Mamma are... were...different. Menica didn't want to know about Mamma's old life, Mamma's island.' Stella looked anxiously at Salvatore. 'Does this seem unfair?'

Salvatore shook his head.

'It was too hard for Mamma,' Stella said.

In the distance they heard car doors slam, and walked back to the house. Salvatore did not take his arm from Stella's shoulders. Just before they reached the back door, he halted, forcing her to check her steps. 'What will you do?' he asked.

At first Stella looked puzzled. 'What do you mean? Oh, I see. Of course. When I'm older I'll go back to Mamma's island. To see if I belong...Before she died, Mamma told me there was money for me to do this. She saved and hid the money she earned from her stall.' Stella hesitated. 'Where do you belong, Salvatore?'

Salvatore was saved by Nino's drunken shouting. He wanted to give Stella an answer but he didn't know what to say.

'Salvatore. Hey, Salvatore! SALVATORE!' Nino did not move from his chair. Each time he called out, he raised his voice. He slurped some more red wine, sat back and closed his eyes. Nausea washed through his body leaving him weakened and, for a moment, blessedly unaware.

Salvatore crouched on his haunches in front of Nino, lit another cigarette and studied it. 'What can I do for you?' he said.

'Is it my fault?' Nino's voice slurred.

For a second Salvatore wondered if Nino felt some remorse. It seemed more probable that the occasion had loosened in him the peculiar alchemy of sorrow and alcohol. Observing Nino's half-closed eyes and dejected slouch, Salvatore thought how impossible it often was to tell the difference between self-pity and sympathy for others. 'What do you mean?' he asked.

Nino bent forward and grasped at his wrist. 'I brought her here didn't I? Look at how hard I worked. When I was a boy I followed my father around the hills like a puppy. Even then I knew that if I stayed I would never do anything different. I would go around and around those hills and eventually die.' Nino made spiralling gestures with his forefinger. 'Yoked to my father, and his father, and his father before him. But it's good, what I've done here. I've done well.'

Nino had answered his own question.

Salvatore pressed his hands on his knees for leverage, and stood up. 'You have, Nino, you've done a great deal.'

Nino grinned up at him. 'Every day I help people to find their way in this country.'

Salvatore flicked ash and let him talk on.

'I tried to help Delfina but'—Nino's mood changed with lightning speed—'there was always Fortunato and God.'

Nino is one of the lucky ones, Salvatore thought. Lucky enough to lose his thoughts if he hurls them far enough away.

Menica came and stood close to Nino, holding her plate of food. Salvatore sometimes believed he could see her analysing, looking for the straight line that would lead to her desired conclusion. Maybe she was one of the lucky ones, too.

Menica put down her plate and pulled at her father's arm. 'Come on, Papa! Nearly everyone has gone now. It's time to go to bed.'

When Nino did not move she tugged at him again. 'Come on! You can't sleep here all night.'

Obediently Nino got to his feet. He squinted at Menica. 'You sound just like Mamma,' he said. 'Just like Mamma calling from the villa when I was a child. Nino! Come here! Nino! There's work to do! Nino!'

Menica pulled at him but he shrugged away her arm.

'Nino! Nino!' he repeated, and he fell back in the chair.

Menica waited but, when her father didn't move, she pulled the rug from the back of the chair, threw it over him, and left the room.

A week after Delfina's funeral Francesca di Maggio sat at the front of her house with her back to the street. To passers-by she was a familiar sight, lean and straight on her hard wooden chair.

Each day after the chores were done, before she returned to the kitchen, she sat outside and knitted. She wore a black wooden rosary around her neck, its beads strung together with a tarnished silver chain. She timed each row with one Hail Mary, and at the end of ten Hail Marys she stopped knitting and recited, '*Gloria al Padre e al Figlio e allo Spirito Santo.*'

It was a ritual that calmed her. She had knitted her way through a multitude of jumpers for the poor, driven by religious zeal and the need to stave off the vision of her cousins' bloated bodies washed up near Reggio di Calabria.

At around two o'clock in the afternoon, she wound her wool and pushed the pointed ends of the needles deep into the skein. She returned to the kitchen and sang as she shelled peas, or baked capsicum and tomatoes for dinner. She didn't bother to carry in her chair. Salvatore would do that when he returned from work.

Francesca had never spoken to Delfina but knew of her through Salvatore. She knew Delfina had seldom left the fruit block and understood her need for boundaries. This new world was best taken in small amounts. Eventually you reached the point where you could take in no more and there you stayed, on your block or with your back to the street. It was no good trying to make others understand.

She looked up at the sound of a key in the front door lock.

'Francesca?' Salvatore called. 'Francesca?'

The hesitancy in her husband's voice, and his companion's heavy footfall, told her that Enrico was not with him.

Salvatore entered the kitchen, accompanied by Paolo. 'I thought Paolo could have dinner with us,' Salvatore said. 'Paolo is from Salina. You know, like Nino and Delfina.'

Francesca nodded. 'And Enrico?'

'Enrico is staying for dinner with Stella and Menica. I'll get a drink for Paolo.'

Salvatore had taken a liking to Paolo. He had been unsure whether to bring him back to his house, but saw how deeply Delfina's death had affected him and knew he spent all his time alone. He also knew Francesca's dislike of being disturbed.

'Delfina's death must have been very hard for you. A friend from the same island,' Francesca said. 'God rest her soul. Sit down and Salvatore will get you some of our wine.' She turned back to the pot of thick meat sauce.

Salvatore touched his wife on the arm. His poor Francesca. He glanced around for some way to thank her. The woodpile near the stove was low. Tomorrow he would bring in a stack so that Francesca would have plenty for the rest of the week. In the meantime, he would bring in enough for the night.

Paolo waited until Salvatore left the room and the back door slammed shut.

'I need you to answer a question, if you will,' he pleaded. 'Salvatore told me the tragic story of your cousins and how Enrico came to live with you.'

Francesca stopped stirring and she stared at the wall above the combustion stove. It had been a cold night with a cruel moon and the bodies were roped with seaweed.

'What were their names?' Paolo said. 'I think I might have known them.'

'Does it matter now?' Francesca turned back to the pot and smoothed the simmering sauce with the back of her spoon.

'It matters to me,' Paolo said.

They heard Salvatore's footsteps and the thump of logs on the woodpile outside the door.

Francesca looked anxiously from Paolo to Salvatore. 'Their name was Gullo, Gisella and Franco Gullo. Does this tell you what you need?'

Paolo had believed Delfina; the evidence had fitted with jigsaw precision. But now he knew without doubt. Enrico was their son.

He pulled Francesca towards him so that she could not avoid looking at his face. 'Yes,' he said.

Pietro Silvi pushed his pitchfork hard into the ground. A spray of pebbles and small balls of clumped sand flew back at him.

He rolled his eyes. 'Madonna! Why do I do this?' But his words contained no hint of frustration; he knew why he persevered with his desert garden.

'You won't have any success there, *padre*!'

A boy's voice called across the morning stillness. Pietro Silvi straightened and saw Enrico. What did he want at this hour of the day?

Enrico swung a satchel from his back, dumped it on the ground and answered the priest's thoughts. 'I'd like to paint a line of angels around the whole of the church. Make them into a sort of garland,' he said.

'A garland of angels,' Pietro Silvi repeated. 'Why do you want to do this now? The mural has been finished for months.'

Enrico cast about for the right words. 'It all feels empty. I mean, after the funeral.'

'So you feel the need to fill the space.' Pietro Silvi put his arm around Enrico's shoulders and hugged him. 'You are a true artist, my son. Of course you must paint your angels. But what will happen when there are no more spaces in our little church?'

Enrico spent the afternoon sketching a chain of figures on the wall; chubby buttocks nudged one against the other and plump arms and hands clasped at stars and ribbons.

It was the playfulness of Enrico's vision that caught Pietro Silvi's eye as he watched the boy. He signalled to Paolo who was painting the outside of the nearby presbytery. Paolo put his brush in a murky tin of turpentine and rubbed his spattered hands on the sides of his pants. He had been working for the *padre* for four months and the two men went about the grounds of Our Lady of Lourdes in comfortable silence.

'What is it, *padre?*' he said as he walked over.

Pietro Silvi pointed to Enrico, who was lying on the floor, flat on his stomach, in order to reach a tight corner beside the door. Behind him a train of pencilled figures laced the walls. Paolo baulked and stared.

Father Silvi looked at his watch. 'There is someone I promised to see. I sometimes get so sidetracked.' He shook his head at his own negligence. 'I will let you inspect the work of our artist for a while. It's good for the soul.' He slipped from the church, leaving Paolo alone with the boy.

Enrico was unaware of the man watching him from the porch. He rose and walked to the altar to view his work at the back of the church. A cherub too low or too high? A ribbon or a limb breaking the continuum?

He stretched his neck, moving it from side to side. It was his mother's neck, thrown back to see a Salina sunset explode, shimmer above the curve of the island, and then fall.

Paolo shivered. He had become fatalistic, convinced that people are given grand passions just to see them extinguished. They were like the sunset, lighting a dark place and then disappearing. Enrico was lucky, his passion had form and substance and gave him a medium in which to exorcise his demons. Paolo stepped forward. 'I hear this is all your work,' he said.

In Enrico's face there was no mistaking Delfina's eyes and his own indented cheekbones. The boy nodded and bent to search for something in his satchel.

'The Madonna is the Madonna del Terzito. Isn't she?' Paolo walked quickly forward, pointing at the altarpiece. 'See, the little bell. The stars. The colours.'

Enrico looked at Paolo.

'I'm from Salina, you know,' Paolo said. 'The same island as this Madonna. The island of Nino and Delfina…' His words trailed away and Paolo was frightened that this was where it might all end. A declaration of facts to a silent boy.

'I painted this Madonna from a holy picture,' Enrico said. 'My real parents gave it to me when I was born. I never knew them. They drowned.' Enrico took the holy picture from his pocket. 'Now you tell me that the Madonna is from Delfina's island. If this is true then I'm from that island too. Why didn't Delfina tell me? She might have known my parents.' Enrico turned to Paolo, his eyes bright. 'Do you know who my parents were?'

Paolo leaned back and inhaled deeply. There was no going back. It was just as Fortunato Coltelli had said.

'My mother and father died when I was a child and I was taken to live on Salina with my aunt and uncle,' Paolo said. 'There I met Delfina and Nino and we spent our childhoods on the beach or in the vineyards.'

'Does this have anything to do with my parents?' said Enrico. He was confused.

'Please, just listen,' Paolo replied. 'Delfina and Nino married and then Nino came to Australia. Delfina was to follow him a few years later. She lived with her mother-in-law, a bitter woman who made life difficult.' Paolo hesitated. 'It was a beautiful evening with a brilliant sunset and a rainbow.' Paolo's voice quavered at the memory. 'Delfina and I…we were both lonely and…'

Paolo searched for the right words but Enrico sat down in a nearby pew and said it for him. 'You,' he said, 'you are my father and Delfina was my mother.'

Paolo nodded and sat beside his son.

'Why didn't Delfina tell me?' Enrico said. There was resentment in his voice.

'She didn't know until she saw your painting in the church. And I didn't know until I came to visit her after her father's death,' Paolo said. 'She made me promise not to tell you. The decision broke her heart but she said too many people would suffer if they knew: Nino, Menica and Stella and, of course, you.'

'Why have you told me?'

'It would have been easier not to tell you,' Paolo said ruefully. 'But I've lived with buried dreams all my life. I lost my parents and my home as a child. I lost Delfina. And I lost you. I don't think I'll ever find the end of my story but you need to know the beginning of yours.' Paolo touched his son's face lightly and let his hand drop. 'How else are you to reach the end?'

Two hours later Paolo reeled though the church door like a drunken man. Enrico stayed behind. None of what he had been told seemed real. His Delfina belonged to the dry Mallee block, not to Italy. He had watched her grow fruit and vegetables in the harsh sun. In his mind's eye he saw her brush strands of hair from her hot face, look up and hand him a piece of fruit. A lump came into his throat. He had loved Delfina but not as a mother. It was too late for that. He picked up a paintbrush. When he eventually emerged from the church he was soft-eyed and distant.

'It's good, isn't it, that I am a man who does not need to know secrets?' Pietro Silvi posed his question to himself out loud. It was late in the day and he was on his way to shut the church doors for the evening. There was no need to lock them, only to keep the animals from bedding in the church's quiet corners. Paolo had returned to the tin shack near the railway siding. After work on the lines finished, no one objected to the itinerant workers sheltering in the lean-to.

The priest looked around with satisfaction at the sandstone walls of Our Lady of Lourdes. It was still until a rat-like marsupial sprung from under a nearby bush, looked at Pietro Silvi, and scurried into a pile of leaf litter.

Father Silvi sat on a large boulder, ran his fingers absently through a tuft of grass and flinched as it pricked his forefinger. He sucked at the oozing drop of blood and knew this was God's message to his servant, Pietro Silvi. He looked skyward and nodded. 'Yes, yes, I hear. It's not my role to know secrets. Merely to minister to their results.'

He rose and continued on his way, startling the animal snuffling nearby. Just as he was about to swing the doors closed Pietro Silvi hesitated and re-entered the church to pray. He reached the altar and squinted up at the painting on the wall. Something was different. He traced over the familiar images and then stopped. It was not immediately obvious. It was small and low down, on the far right of the altar wall.

Enrico had painted another Madonna below the munificent lady gracing the wall in front of him. This Madonna wore a white gown and a white veil. Coils of black hair trailed down to her waist. She rested her hand against the blotched trunk of a gum tree and bowed her head beneath a fall of eucalypt leaves. Around her feet were scattered the fruits of the Mildura sun: the warm glow of oranges, clusters of grapes, sunburst tomatoes.

Pietro Silvi absorbed the confusion of images and symbols. He bowed and prayed to this new Madonna from the desert, a Madonna for Delfina.

Houses and shops flanked the waterfront and lined the sloping streets, their facades a patchwork of cement, render and stone. The town was built below the ramparts of a Norman castle and above it soared a green mountain. To Enrico's right the walls of the old fortress ran the upper seaward reaches of the town, the stonework softened by sproutings of prickly pear. Seagulls danced above the ferry, cawing into the wind. Enrico shivered and plunged his gloved hands into his pockets. He wiped at the window and peered outside. He was not sure if they had docked. The ferry still rocked wildly and Lipari bobbed up and down outside his window, occasionally disappearing from view.

He felt a nudge in his ribs and a voice, hot with garlic and fish, shouted through the clamour. 'You can get off now. The ferry has docked. Hurry up! We've got a lot to do to keep her safe until the morning.' The man worked his way through the ferry, repeating his announcement.

Enrico gathered up his bag and his bedroll and crossed the gangplank. A stretch of asphalt linked the terminal to the island. Between sprays of sea foam, he dashed for higher ground. He looked back at the capering ferry and then at the line of small shops running up the hill. He had enough money for coffee but not for accommodation. He would have to find a doorway or some place out of the wind.

Enrico went into a *trattoria* on the waterfront opposite the docked ferry. It smelled of smoke, coffee and leavened dough. The shopkeeper eyed him curiously when he heard the medley of accents in Enrico's Italian. He took his coffee and bag outside to one of the empty tables.

It was six years since Delfina's death. Paolo had stayed in Mildura to help Enrico come to terms with the revelations about his birth. But the discoveries had eventually brought him on this journey to Salina, the home of his mother and father. He thought of Delfina and her sand-swept grave in the Werrimull cemetery. He accepted that he would never fully link Delfina with Paolo. He had too many other mothers and fathers: the unknown Franco and Gisella Gullo; Francesca, the troubled wife of his beloved Salvatore; his exotic Shuja. But Paolo's story had given Enrico a past and he had to return to the islands where, from among the layers of stone buildings, he might find the sources of his paintings.

He drained the last of his coffee and peered along the steep alleyway. The Norman walls had almost disappeared under an early mist and he felt like he was in a fairytale.

Enrico spent the night sheltered beneath a rocky overhang in the grounds of the archaeological museum. Around him were identical tombs, each a rectangle of unadorned grey stone. He fell asleep listening to the rush of the sea while birds plumped and settled into crevices amongst the stone.

In the morning light the sea had calmed and there was a distant murmur of voices. Enrico picked up his bag and made his way between the tombs to the path in front of the cathedral of Saint Bartholomew. Steep stairs ran from the front of the church to a narrow alley below, and a succession of women and black-eyed children climbed their way to Sunday Mass. The men smoked in clusters near the outside walls of the church. Enrico stood apart. They were looking at him and talking about him but he was reluctant to walk against the tide to the alley below.

An old man with gold front teeth broke away from a group. 'You're from here. From the islands. Aren't you?' he said to Enrico. He drew close and studied his face. 'Yes, you're from here. I see it in your features. Have you been travelling? I travelled when I was young. I went to Australia and made some money.' The man tapped at his teeth and grinned. 'But now I've come back. A man needs to die in the place where he was born.'

The old man stopped talking. He had told his story. It was the stranger's turn.

'I've just arrived from Australia,' Enrico said. 'But I was only a baby when I was taken from here. I've not been back before.'

'We call Australia the eighth Aeolian Island,' the man said. 'So many left during those days, first of hunger, then of war. Not all return but some do, and their home is still waiting here.'

The bells rang and the crowd began to file through the doors of the cathedral. The old man went to join them but turned back to Enrico. 'Welcome and good luck, my boy,' he said.

Enrico walked down the stairs, aware of nothing but the soft thud of his boots on the stone steps. He turned left at the bottom and continued on down the alley. Narrow houses towered on each side. Occasionally he heard the flap of rugs or laundry being strung out on the upper balconies, or the plaintive cries of cats winding their way home after the long night.

At Marina Corta he checked the departure time of his ferry to Salina and then returned to the *trattoria* of the previous evening. The waiting ferry rocked on a slight swell. In the shallows the fishermen were busy sorting and gutting their day's catch, dishevelled from the sea and with yesterday's shadows dark on their chins. The shops were opening one by one with a rip of roller shutters, the blue haze of cigarette smoke and the staccato of bargaining voices. His painter's eye saw the night mist still drifting, a milky gauze over the lowest of the buildings. For a moment he was filled with longing. He did not know what he was longing for, only that something insatiable had risen from within him. He shook his head, like a dog after a swim in the sea, but the feeling remained.

Angelina sat alone on the terrace. Below her Fortunato's stone stairs veered seaward, their clear pastels bleached by sun and wind. Time had cracked the weaker sections of the concrete, and chipped at the edges of the steps. Angelina was looking for something no longer there but often quite visible to her. She was old and her thoughts dwelt on familiar subjects, like pigeons let loose from their cage to circle overhead before roosting at nightfall.

She felt hands on her shoulders and smelt newly baked bread. 'What are you thinking about, Nonna?'

'The same thoughts I always have when I sit here looking over the sea,' Angelina said.

Stella sat down and wiped her hands on her apron. A puff of wind plucked at some geraniums, mingled the smell of the bread with sea salt, and disappeared around the corner of the terrace. All around them was silence. In the Australian silence people scurried like ants, in search of their fortunes. The island silence was different, saturated with history, religion and myth. The islanders seemed content with what was there. Here Stella felt complete. She had been able to forget her mother's plastic Madonna and the feeling that home was in some place far away. On Salina she stood still and felt her empty spaces fill up. She turned back to her grandmother. 'And what thoughts are they?'

Angelina patted her playfully. 'I've told you so many times,' she said. 'Today I looked at my beloved Fortunato's stairs. When Delfina, your mother, was a child she used to hop up and down the steps on one leg. She would see how long she could go before she put down the other foot. Then, she would try to jump from colour to colour.'

Angelina leaned forward and pointed a finger at the steps. The back of her hand bore a tracery of veins as dark as the indigo sea.

'But she never jumped too far. Only enough to give her a little excitement and then she would sit and watch the sea and eat tomatoes, even though I told her not to because I needed them for bottling.'

Angelina stopped and pulled herself back to the present. Stella pushed both feet against the low wall in front of her. 'Mamma was the same in Australia. She stayed close to the house, growing fruit and vegetables. She hardly ever went to Mildura. She said she didn't like the wide streets and all the shops.' Stella looked pointedly at Angelina. 'For someone who didn't like excitement it's difficult to understand why she went to Australia. Now, that was a really big jump.'

'As I've told you, there seemed no choice. Australia was far away. A good place to leave the past behind and begin again. Ludevina made it clear to Delfina that Nino was not to be told about her baby. Enrico went, we thought, to America...'

Angelina smiled as she said her grandson's name. She had not been allowed to see her daughter's son when Ludevina whisked him away. Now, thanks to Stella, she would know him. She reached into the pocket of her apron, pulled out Enrico's photograph and held it between them. Enrico looked back, fine-boned and un-smiling. The photograph, in profile, high-lighted both the crease that ran the width of his forehead and his thin aristocratic nose.

'And now Enrico is coming to Salina,' she said.

Enrico pushed through the throng of fish, people and bicycles at the exit to the ferry. He craned his neck to see above the crowd and caught sight of Stella with her frizzy halo of hair. She was standing apart from the others, waving to him and pointing behind her at the same time. Enrico saw Angelina. He saw the clear outline of Delfina's cheekbones and her wide eyes which, while looking straight at you, had also looked into you. Angelina realised that he had seen her and held out her arms.

'Why did you tell Stella your story and not the others?' Angelina said.

'Stella and I belong to the old country.' Enrico corrected himself. 'To these islands. To Salina. After Delfina died, Stella told me she wanted to come back here.'

He looked at his half-sister. She was leaning against the wall of the house, her serious grey eyes lit up by her smile. She smiled more frequently now.

'Stella needed to know the truth. Paolo told me that some people need to know about the past.' It was complicated. Enrico rubbed his forehead. 'But for others it's not so important. Nino will never return here.'

Stella interrupted. 'And I remember the night we travelled from Melbourne to Mildura. Menica was so excited. I was so scared. When I look back, the patterns were set even then.'

'Yes, yes, that's it!' Enrico said. 'Paolo said everything goes in cycles, that he was meant to return to Delfina in order to find me. He said not everyone *completes* a cycle. That sometimes it takes several generations. And that for some people like Nino and Menica it even becomes irrelevant. He said it was my painting that gave him the permission to tell me.'

'And what about Paolo?' Angelina said. 'He was a true son of my beloved Fortunato. Will he return to us?'

Enrico shook his head. 'He told me he'll stay in Mildura for a while and then move on.'

'And you? Do you think you'll stay here? Is this where you are meant to be?' Angelina picked up her needlework and knotted the end of a thread.

Enrico glanced at Stella but she was looking out to sea. Irritation welled inside him. He didn't want to think about the future. He knew it was impossible for him to sidestep his past and slip back into the life of the island. He had travelled oceans and deserts. But he was not ready to tackle whatever came next.

'I'm here, aren't I?' he said.

The old woman patted his shoulder. 'Yes, you're here.'

Behind Paolo's words, behind Enrico's words, Angelina heard Fortunato's voice. It was as clear as the sea on a summer evening when shoals of fish swooped far below the surface. Life was like the seasons; there were no endings, only renewals. Delfina's son was meant to return to Salina. He would go away and he would return again. His soul was caught in the cycle of migration. It was easy to shift the body to a new land, but not so easy to satisfy the longings of the soul.

Angelina smiled at the two young people pipping olives into a blue ceramic bowl.

Salina was flooded with the light of a clear winter's morning. Enrico and Stella had set out three hours earlier to walk to the Church of the Madonna del Terzito. A gravel road zigzagged up the slope in a series of hairpin bends. Below them the town of Malfa spread out from the curve of the bay, its houses bold in the sun and its outskirts fringed by dormant grapevines. Ahead of them Valdichiesa rested between the Monte dei Porri and the Monte Fossa della Felci, and the road flattened as it neared the centre of the island.

It was close to lunchtime when they saw the two domes of the church at the end of a short tree-lined road, set against a backdrop of almost vertical rock. The Madonna of Enrico's holy picture was carved in high relief above the door between the domes.

Stella looked sideways at Enrico. It was warm and he had rolled up his shirtsleeves; his arms were brown from his recent Australian summer. He was twenty-one but seemed vulnerable, at odds with his youth and health. He dumped his haversack on the ground and fumbled with the buckles. Stella saw that his fingers shook.

He pulled out a sheaf of papers and shuffled through them, finally pulling out his holy picture of the Madonna. He held it high, in line with the carving between the domes, the swathed paper vision of his childhood silhouetted against the real lines of the church's sculpted Madonna. He slid the picture into his pocket, took Stella's arm, and they hurried the short distance to the open doors of the Church of the Madonna del Terzito.

Enrico moved to the centre of the church and pivoted on one foot. The many stops he'd made to reach the islands had prepared him for what he now saw. During those hours waiting for trains and buses, he had idled through dozens of Italian churches and monuments.

Although he and Stella were alone he lowered his voice to a whisper. 'Pietro Silvi would love this!'

Stella nodded. 'It explains why he let a boy paint Our Lady of Lourdes.'

Enrico grinned and turned back to contemplate the interior. Next to him, at right angles to one of the marble side altars, a bleeding, life-size figure of Christ lay in a glass casket.

In front of him six cherubs with oversize wings gleamed like giant bakelite dolls. The ceiling was studded with ornate white and gold rosettes, supported by pillars of beige, pink and grey striated marble. And then there were the statues of the Madonna herself: wearing the gold crown of majesty above the main altar, mirrored in white and gold in front of the pulpit, clothed in subdued blues and browns on her own side altar.

Enrico didn't hear the creak of the main doors or the shuffle of footsteps into one of the back pews. A man cleared his throat. 'There have been miracles in this church, you know.'

Enrico and Stella turned. Mario continued. 'A long time ago a man came here to pray for the life of his child who had been born before her time, and his prayer was answered. He was visited…'

Mario stopped for breath and Enrico took up the tale. '…by angels and carried life back to his baby daughter.'

Mario looked first at Stella and then at Enrico. 'Who are you?' He tapped his stick on the floor and waved it in the air. 'How do you know these things?'

Enrico sat beside him and Mario took his face in his hands and turned it from side to side. 'Paolo!' he said. Then he turned to Stella. 'And who are you?'

'I'm Delfina's daughter,' Stella said.

Mario closed his eyes. For a moment he seemed to forget them. He was concentrating, dredging the past for something he knew he must ask. Stella and Enrico exchanged glances.

'Before your mother,' Mario said, 'before Delfina went to Australia, she told me she had to go to find her fate. I told her that if she found it she should bring it back to our islands and it would belong to all of us. Tell me, did she find it?'

DISCUSSION NOTES

- In what ways do the descriptions of landscape reflect Delfina's inner state?

- 'The local children believed that the souls of drowned fishermen slept there [in the cave on the beach] at night and went out with the morning's flotilla to guide the day's catch.' The island of Salina is steeped in traditions and spirituality is a way of life. Is Salina special in this respect?

- Fortunato worships at the church of the Madonna del Terzito, and the baby Delfina survives. Henceforth she is for him, and for the islanders, a miracle child. Is this a blessing or a curse?

- How important is class in the novel? What impact does it have on the lives of the characters?

- The island of Salina is described as heavenly by many of its inhabitants. Yet in the 1920s its population is almost halved, as the young leave to seek better lives abroad. Fortunato says in his letter to Delfina, 'Sometimes I think it was not only the people who left our islands but also the vines…So many of the young have gone and we cannot afford to lose our elders.' Are migration and the decline in local industry interlinked? Which is the cause, which the effect?

- Is Delfina's religious ardour a result of her upbringing, or was she born devout?

- Shuja's gods had 'shifted their mythologies to foreign soil in a cloud of colour and incense and laughed with her in the Australian outback. Delfina's God and his pensive mother were confined to the shrines of candles and flowers.' In Australia there was 'nowhere to feel that God was in heaven.' What happened to God in the new world?

- Nino, Delfina and Paolo are constant childhood companions. Are Nino and Delfina destined to be together?

- After Nino departs for Australia, Delfina is 'shocked at how the distance between them highlighted that their relationship was founded on need.' What does this mean? How does their relationship change once they are both in Australia?

- Delfina receives the brunt of Ludevina's pent-up anger. Delfina fears Ludevina and is baffled by her behaviour. Yet both Ludevina and Delfina share similar fates. Both experience crushed hopes, unhappy marriages, and sexual liaisons. Why does neither woman recognise that they are in fact kindred spirits? Is it simply due to their relationship as mother/daughter-in-law, or is it something more?

- Fortunato says to Paolo, 'You know, all will come full circle in the end. It might not be as we wish. But of what consequences are our wishes?'

- When Stella asks, 'Where will I go when I die?' Delfina answers, 'You will go to God and the circle will be complete.' Mortality and fate are key themes in the novel. Are the characters on a pre-ordained trajectory or do they have some choice in their lives?

- 'In Sicily honour was bound into a complex system of debt and debtor. This network of brotherhood had travelled the oceans and grown with Mildura's flourishing vineyards. It was as intricate as the tendrils of the vine itself.' Why was Nino drawn into this lifestyle only after leaving the place of its origin?

- Delfina is determined to keep the father of her son a secret, to protect the memory of their time together. On the sea voyage to Australia she asks, 'What have I done? Will my girls forget the land where they were born, or will it return to them only in dreams and snatches of memory?' Why does Delfina leave Salina?

- Sparnon describes the wives of Nino's workmates in Mildura: 'their faces etched with stories they could only exchange in halting English…were too shy to share their memories, as if to tell them would be to commit a sin or misdemeanour.' The preciousness of memories is a constant theme in *Madonna of the Eucalypts*. In protecting her memories, how does Delfina change the course of her life and that of many others?

- 'Sometimes I think Stella is lucky. She's like I was as a child. It's as if she has never changed countries,' says Delfina. Shuja replies, 'Yes, she is different from Menica. I can see that. The one always reaching out for the new and the other reaching inward for, I don't know what? Enrico too is a thoughtful one. He has his future already deep inside him. It doesn't matter what we do. We can't alter this fact.' Which approach do you think is better, or easier to live with?

- On arrival in Australia, Delfina 'felt as if every step she took was into the unknown, and almost every word she heard was incomprehensible.' Do you think this is how all new arrivals felt at the time? Is this how immigrants feel today?

- When Delfina arrives in Mildura, the local policeman predicts that she, like so many migrant women before her, will 'disappear inside one of the tin shanties on the newly created fruit blocks and never be seen or heard of again.' This coupled with her hesitation to learn the new language make it surprising that, for a time at least, she manages to pave her own way. She becomes known not as Nino's wife, but as 'the pretty, dark-haired woman who lived out of town and sold produce every day from the roadside.' How does Delfina accomplish what she does? And, having done so, what changes?

- Salvatore comments to Delfina and Shuja, 'This is a young country. It's like a new actor in a play, just learning the lines. It gets things wrong and casts light or shade where they are not meant to be.' What does he mean?

- Nino embraces the new country and its wealth of possibilities. But Salvatore comments, 'We are not the same as we were in our old countries. Some find the new difficult. For many it is a Garden of Eden and there are snakes in every corner.' Is Salvatore merely sympathising with those who find it hard to adjust, or is it a pointed comment? Is he talking about sin and temptation? Has Nino succumbed or is he just doing his best to support his family?

- When Delfina's daughters ask her to tell of her miracle birth, she responds, 'stories like mine are not meant for countries like this.' Why is there no room for such beliefs in the new country?

- Delfina is bound to the islands, the mountains and the Madonnas. Nino, by her sick-bed, with a letter from Fortunato says, 'This is from her papa. He still calls her by her childhood names, still believes in miracles and calls them up like ghosts. He reaches across the water and she cannot let go.' Is this a universal theme of immigration? Do you think women were more affected at the time?

- Father Silvi builds the church at Werrimull to bring 'the old ways a little closer.' Did it help Delfina in the end? From what did she die?

- Delfina is a woman with a secret. In what way does this affect her physically and mentally?

- 'You were destined to paint this church,' Delfina says to Enrico. Why does she not enlighten him about the mystery of his past?

- Referring to Delfina, Paolo asks Father Silvi, 'Do you think this is how the end should have been for her?' What does Paolo think?

- Why did Paolo keep away, and respect Delfina's wishes for so many years?

- Delfina 'had loved Paolo but believed that real love was lived out in selflessness.' Did she regret sacrificing Paolo and her son for the love of her family? Delfina said she had to go to Australia to find her fate. Did she find it? And what do you think becomes of Paolo after Delfina's death?

- Menica clearly takes after her father, embracing life in Australia and looking to the future there with outstretched arms. Where does Stella belong?

- 'Nino chortled. 'These women of ours. They see Madonnas in their dishwater and the will of God in the deeds of men.' There was laughter followed by silence. No son of Italy could deride the visions of another for very long.' Is *Madonna of the Eucalypts* successful in its portrait of a religious life?

- Delfina sheltered her past in rituals, to avoid circumstances where questions might be asked and she would be confronted by memories. Is it possible to avoid one's past?

ACKNOWLEDGMENTS

Much love to my husband Ken and daughters, Rachael and Laura, who make space in their lives for my writing. My gratitude goes to everyone at Text Publishing for believing in my vision. I owe much to Dr Don Ferrell who told me that I must one day write a novel; to Alex Miller whose wise words and encouragement came at the right time; and to Judith Rodriguez who was at the birth of this novel.

Madonna of the Eucalypts is dedicated to Jean Sparnon but a special mention must be made of her sisters, Zita Carew and Marion Chivers. Thank you to my dear friends Patricia and Maurice Dunne who always believed. To Joan Scott, Cheryl Simpson and Glenda Dickinson who gave support and encouragement. And to Polly, Oscar and Sam.

I am indebted to Flora and Neil Noyce, the Modica family, and the many wonderful people who helped me during my research in Mildura and on Salina. Many thanks to Linda Salpietro for her generous reading of my work, and to Laura Mecca from CO.AS.IT for her assistance early in my writing.

Karen Sparnon's first novel, *Madonna of the Eucalypts*, was published by Text Publishing in 2006, and in 2007 won the Victorian Premier's Literary Award for writing about Italians in Australia (The Grollo Ruzzene Foundation Prize). She has a PhD in Professional Writing and Editing, and over twenty-five years teaching experience across all educational sectors - university, TAFE and secondary schools. She now works as a freelance writer and editor and teaches creative writing classes. She lives in Ballarat, Victoria.